DEADLY
IMPROVISATION

Gallagher lobbed the stone like a grenade. It described a beautiful parabola as it arched through the trees to slam against a distant trunk. The sound it made was so sudden and exaggeratedly loud that the waiting man could not have helped himself. He was up with rifle pointing almost in one motion; but Gallagher had also moved, on the instant of having lobbed the stone.

He had already covered the distance before the man suddenly became aware of his immediate danger. Gallagher heard the sharp hiss of surprise just before he slipped the noose over and pulled, moving away and around the trunk as it tightened.

The man dropped his rifle to claw at the strap at his throat. Gallagher sensed him panic momentarily before training took over. Instead of trying to get away and thus tighten the noose further, he tried to back around the trunk towards Gallagher and gain some slack. But Gallagher was ready for that move. . . .

WIND SHEAR

JULIAN JAY SAVARIN

HarperPaperbacks
A Division of HarperCollins*Publishers*

This is a work of fiction. The characters, incidents, and
dialogues are products of the author's imagination and
are not to be construed as real. Any resemblance to
actual events or persons, living or dead, is entirely
coincidental.

HarperPaperbacks   *A Division of* HarperCollins*Publishers*
                    10 East 53rd Street, New York, N.Y. 10022

This book is published by arrangement with the author.

Cover photography by Herman Estevez

First HarperPaperbacks printing: November 1992

Printed in the United States of America

HarperPaperbacks and colophon are trademarks of
HarperCollins*Publishers*

10 9 8 7 6 5 4 3 2 1

For Elizabeth

Prologue

i

The man shivered in the cold air of the Nottinghamshire evening. It was late October. He remained in his hiding place and watched the two men climb out of the police car. They stood briefly together, their solid figures silhouetted in the failing light.

It was already five o'clock, he told himself impatiently. He had to get moving. He hoped the men would give up, climb into their car and disappear. He wanted them to leave so he could continue his journey.

They didn't. As if they'd listened to his thoughts, they turned as one to face his temporary shelter. They couldn't see him, he knew.

Behind him, the soft murmur of the stream that fed itself into the river Trent only yards away on the other side of the road seemed to rise to a crescendo in the waiting silence. No cars came down the road from Rolleston, the village just over a mile away, from which he'd just walked. He was trying to make it to Bleasby, where he knew someone; two miles or so in the opposite direction, and here were these bastards putting the stopper on the bottle.

He wondered if they'd stopped all traffic too.

"We know you're in there!" one of them shouted suddenly, voice echoing in the coming night. "You haven't got a chance!"

The stream gurgled, the Trent murmured deeply. The man kept his silence.

"Give up now!" the voice reasoned. "It's the end of the line."

Silence.

"All right!" Impatience now. "It's your funeral."

The figures moved away from each other and began to advance. All things considered, they were taking a suicidal chance; but they seemed supremely confident, as if he presented no danger to them.

His refuge was within a copse of low trees and sparse bushes on the bank of the stream. He remained quite still, hoping he would not slide down the short, steep incline into the shallow water, and thus warn them. He heard faint scurryings in the undergrowth, but paid them scant attention. All his senses were tuned on the approaching men.

He hid behind a low mound that was covered with the casual rubbish thrown there by motorists who, over the years, had pulled off the road for a picnic or a hasty call of nature. This part of the Trent was a favorite spot for anglers too, and the detritus of the careless ones mingled with that of the motorists, leaving a carpet of debris that formed a perfect warning system; which was why he had picked this spot. The approaching men could not know how beautifully silhouetted they were, nor that every crunch their cautious feet made pinpointed them accurately. They came on, still with no sign of caution.

They paused.

The man waited. Then he saw their right arms move slowly, and knew with resignation they had drawn weapons. He was philosophical about it. It was going to be *their* funeral.

He chose his moment well, rose suddenly before them, an avenging spirit from an unknown grave. Their momentary shock gave him all the time he needed.

His silenced automatic made a sneezing sound at them; four times. They fell like sawn logs to the ground, their weapons unfired.

He did not waste time. He hauled them back to the police car one at a time, feeling himself grow hot with the effort. He shoved the bodies into the back, piling them in like laden sacks; then he climbed into the front and drove the car away.

No one took notice of him during his eighteen-mile journey. Most people preferred not to see police cars, treating them with studious blindness. Police were invisible beings. The man's gamble had paid off.

He drove the car off the road and got out leaving the bodies in it. Throughout, he had worn thin cotton gloves. He left these on as he headed back across country towards Bleasby.

The straight-line distance was only ten miles. None of those hunting him would know of his destination. He'd long made sure of that. He reckoned he would make it to Bleasby long before the person he intended to see decided to go to bed.

He kept his gun.

ii

On a specially re-activated forward base of the 46th Air Army of the Soviet Union, three men strapped themselves into their aircraft. The base, which owed its genesis to the Second World War, was not on the standard aviation rosters and, despite satellite surveillance, it appeared to have escaped Western intelligence snooping.

It was an arctic base, well into the northern extremities of the vast country. Had Western intelligence known of the existence of the aircraft, they would have dubbed it the Tupolev Tu-22M *Backfire* D, a potent variation on the latest Soviet long-range bomber in current service. They would have been only partially correct.

The bomber was a variant of the huge swing-wing Tupolev, but it was unlike its earlier stablemates in a number of vitally important ways. Its performance and size were greater than that of the other variants, but its crew had been reduced by one to three; two pilots, and a weapons systems officer. They knew their aircraft as the Tu-22P.

Colonel Yevgeny Kakunin settled himself in his seat and felt the straps secure him. As commander of the aircraft, failure or success of the mission depended entirely upon him. He glanced at his co-pilot. The younger man's eyes looked back expressionlessly at him from beneath the raised visor of the fully-enclosed helmet. They stared from the aperture, animals with no life of their own.

A man whose soul belonged to the Party, Kakunin thought without rancor. The merits or demerits of being a staunch Party member were of little interest to him. His indifference to the Party was well known. It had not stopped him making it to Colonel. Everyone appreciated his skill as a superb aviator, and no one could ever accuse him of a lack of patriotism. He loved his country. The Party was another thing altogether. So while those of fainter hearts worried about his sometimes cutting remarks, spoken in private, he got on with the job which he performed with such consummate skill. Kakunin was thirty, young for his rank.

He was sure the KGB had sniffed round him more than once; but even they wouldn't touch him. He was too good. An aircraft such as this would not have been placed in the hands of someone who was patriotically suspect. The prize at the end of this mission was command of the first twelve of the new aircraft to come off the production line, with command of a full regiment of forty-eight aircraft as a very real future prospect. No, he thought. They would not have allowed it, had he not been trusted. They also knew he was their best chance.

He stared into the darkness of the arctic night. "Commence starting sequence." There was a storm brewing, but it would be all right.

"Sequence commencing," came the voice of his co-pilot through his helmet phones.

They went through their routine as the powerful, twin Koliesov turbojets spooled up to pre-take-off thrust; then Kakunin brought the throttles back. He eased off the brakes. They began to taxi.

He liked the feel of the aircraft. The different engines gave it an immense power margin over the Tu-22M. It had a Mach speed of 2.85 over target, and a ceiling of nearly 30,000 meters. No Western fighters would catch it, and certainly no surface-to-air missiles.

They reached the end of the runway. Kakunin smiled within his helmet as he lowered his visor. Was the West in for a surprise! He sensed rather than saw his co-pilot lower his own visor.

"Time to go, Velensky."

The visored head turned briefly. "Yes, Comrade Colonel."

Kakunin grimaced in his mask. Comrade Colonel. Velensky was a parrot. But he was a good pilot too.

Kakunin said, "Are we all right, Narenko?"

"Weapons and countermeasures systems are all warmed up, Colonel," the weapons systems officer answered. "They'll be on-line for you when you need them."

"Good."

The tower came through, warning them of windshear at the other end of the runway, right in their path during take-off. Did they wish to abort?

Kakunin knew all about windshear, the sudden and erratic changes of wind speed and direction that could terminate the career of anyone unlucky enough to be caught in one. They produced microbursts, powerful low-level downdrafts that could slam an unwary aircraft into the ground. Because a microburst flowed outwards radially after striking the earth, the aircraft would encounter a headwind, then a downdraft, then a tailwind, all within a fleeting second or two of its brief flight. It was a lot to ask of any airplane. The uncanny thing about it was that another aircraft following in the same spot soon after would encounter air as still as a frozen sea.

Kakunin told the tower he would not abort, asked for the windshear information to be fed into the Tu-22P's computer. Soon the display unit was telling him the power mode to select for a trouble-free take-off.

He smiled. Windshear did not worry this aircraft.

"Let's go," he said to his crew, and opened the throttles.

Halfway down the runway, he hit the after-burners. Flames from the neat fuel injected into the exhausts seared the cold darkness as the Tu-22P leapt into the air, a huge, barely visible bat whose spread wings were automatically being swept back as the speed built in answer to the awesome power of its engines.

Kakunin knew Velensky had selected gear-up even as he hauled the bomber into a steep climb. As a team, they worked perfectly; which was as it should be. Velensky held the rank of Major. Apart from being a Party fanatic, he was ambitious. Kakunin knew he could depend on Velensky. His subordinate's ambition would see to that. The mission would be a success.

Much lighter than its stablemates, the Tu-22P gained height swiftly.

Some time later, Narenko said, "We're off their screens now."

"Is that absolute?" Kakunin asked.

"Absolute," Narenko answered. He sounded peeved.

Kakunin said lightly, "I was not questioning your capabilities, Alexei, just the wizardry of our new equipment."

Narenko's voice was relaxed once more as he said, "You can be assured that no one can see us on their radar screens. We can go anywhere in the world. We're invisible."

Kakunin glanced in Velensky's direction. "Tempting. It would be so easy to defect to the West."

There was laughter in Narenko's voice. "Very tempting."

Velensky sat stiffly.

Kakunin smiled in his mask as he swung the aircraft on to a new course, heading for the northern fringes of British airspace. Two hours later, the Tu-22P penetrated deep. It hurtled across Scotland, swung across the north of Ireland, and then headed south before retracing its course. It passed over Holy Loch, headed east to Leuchars then out to sea. It photographed everything beneath its track.

It made it safely back to base.

The air-defense net of the U.K. had been breached, and no one knew it had occurred.

Monday

"No!"

Kingston-Wyatt got up from behind his huge inlaid desk, went over to his favorite window and stared down at the sleepy London square. It was a habit of his. He remained there for long moments.

Watching him, Fowler could not rid himself of the feeling that the stocky form made a good target for an enterprising assassin. Fowler hated windows. They made him feel strangely naked. Kingston-Wyatt, on the other hand, didn't seem to mind. The office, five stories up, was practically surrounded by panes of glass. Despite this sop to modernity, its furnishings none the less gave it the well-upholstered air of an inner sanctum reserved strictly for the privileged members of an exclusive private club; which, in a way, was precisely what it was.

Kingston-Wyatt turned from the window at last, conscious of Fowler's waiting silence. An expatriate Australian, he had been Head of the Department for over seven years, and

Fowler had been with him for all of that time. He was not worried about Fowler.

"No," he repeated.

"Why not?" Fowler spoke mildly. Tall, almost gangly, he wore glasses which gave him a benign air that was totally false. He was every bit as devious as Kingston-Wyatt. Approaching his fifty-sixth year, Fowler looked years younger whereas Kingston-Wyatt, in his early fifties, seemed careworn by comparison. They were very good friends; normally. They also respected each other.

"Why not?" Fowler said again.

"I am not deaf, Adrian." Kingston-Wyatt returned to his seat.

"Well?"

"No."

"Three times. Going for a record, are you?"

Kingston-Wyatt glared. "If you're going to keep this up, you can take your wit somewhere else."

"Oh, we are in a pleasant mood today." Fowler did not move.

"Gallagher no longer works for us," Kingston-Wyatt said, as if reluctant to mention the very name, "and has not done so for some time. That singular fact, I trust, has not escaped you."

Fowler ignored the sarcasm. "I seem to remember you once passing a remark to the effect that one never left the Department."

Fowler could well understand Kingston-Wyatt's objections. Gallagher had little cause to love them, Kingston-Wyatt in particular.

"He used to be your blue-eyed boy, after

all," Fowler went on, "if you'll pardon the expression."

"Your humor is quite off its usual form, Adrian."

Fowler smiled imperturbably, allowing this fresh crop of sarcasm to find stony ground. "You know he's the only one capable of getting close to Dalgleish; if we want Dalgleish brought in without open warfare in the countryside. Gallagher can make him see sense."

"Why should Gallagher lift a finger to pull our chestnuts out of the fire?"

"We can still ask him. He's due back on Friday, landing at Heathrow at eleven hundred."

Kingston-Wyatt passed a hand over his thinning hair. Fowler gave a slight frown. He had never seen his superior do that, even under pressure. Kingston-Wyatt was nervous: an unheard-of condition.

Fowler said, "I'll make contact with him."

"No."

Fowler stared. "Four times," he said, and went out.

Kingston-Wyatt waited some moments after the door had shut before pulling at a desk drawer. Slowly, with the caution of someone handling a bomb, he lifted a large brown envelope out of it. He shut the drawer equally slowly, laid the envelope on the desk. He stared at the envelope with morbid fascination before lifting the flap. He took out a set of enlarged black and white photographs. There were five. He laid them side by side across the desk, as if playing solitaire with a giant pack of cards. He stared at them expressionlessly for a good five minutes before his features took on a look of deep despair. He sighed, gathered the photographs and turned them over. There was a brief message, written in pencil, on the back of the bottom of the pack.

Kingston-Wyatt's mouth tightened as he read it, then he replaced the photographs. For some seconds he held the envelope, remaining quite still; then he reached for the intercom on his desk.

He pressed a button. "Mrs. Arundel."

Delphine Arundel, widow of a Marine colonel who had been blown to bits in Northern Ireland. "Sir?"

"I am not to be disturbed for the next . . . let's see . . . fifteen minutes."

"Not even for Mr. Fowler?"

"Especially not for Mr. Fowler."

"Yes, sir." She sounded puzzled and was about to continue.

Kingston-Wyatt terminated the conversation before she could say more. He stood up, picked up the envelope and left the room by a different door from the one Fowler had used. He walked along a carpeted corridor, ignored the elevators and took the stairs at the end of it. He went up to another floor. Here the corridor was polished lino.

There was a wariness about him as he walked, as if he did not wish to be seen. He hurried without seeming to. He came to a pale blue unmarked door, took a bunch of keys from his pocket and opened it with two from the bunch. He entered, shut and bolted the door behind him. It was a small room, and the sole item within it was a shredding-machine. He turned it on, took the photographs from the envelope and fed them in sideways, dissecting the images into wispy slivers. He fed in the envelope too, then turned off the shredder.

He studied his handiwork for a brief moment before reaching with both hands into the collector to mix his recent addition with what was already there. No one would ever know what had gone in. Satisfied, he straightened, let himself out. The corridor was still empty. He locked the room with its two keys and returned to his office the way he had come. He made it back without being seen.

At his desk once more, he pressed the intercom switch. "You can cancel my last instruction now, Mrs. Arundel."

"Yes, sir." She would still be puzzled at the end of the day, when he wished her goodnight.

On the Hebridean island of Skye, Dalgleish stood just outside his cave in the haunting landscape of the Quiraing and looked about him. He had been here for nearly three weeks now, and no one had come looking for him; but he could not relax. He could not afford to.

He had chosen the Quiraing deliberately. It was a place of myth and legend on an island full of such things. No one, the story went, could spend a night in the Quiraing deliberately and retain his senses. It was a place to treat with respect; to fear. He was quite certain no one would disturb him. He stared down at the old road to Uig. Three weeks. The Quiraing had not yet taken his senses.

A light wind came across from the outer island of Lewis, freshening the bright, cold day; but he was well protected against it. He had prepared himself with care. The cave was dry, and he had plenty of food; enough to last another three weeks if need be. His beard, shorter than it should be after three weeks, none the less kept the chill of the wind off his cheeks. He never could grow a beard quickly, he thought wryly.

He pulled his commando balaclava further down on his head and wondered whether Gallagher had got his message.

Kingston-Wyatt rose slowly out of bed that night and stared at his sleeping wife. She did not move. Long accustomed to his nocturnal comings and goings, she had learned to sleep through them; yet she would have known instantly of an intruder. So she slept on, secure within the knowledge of a deep-rooted instinct that told her only her husband moved about in the still of the house.

Reaching cautiously into a bedside drawer Kingston-Wyatt took out a massive U.S. Army Colt .45. Still she did not move. The weapon was one he had exchanged against regulations for his service revolver when a young pilot on Meteors, during the Korean War.

He moved quietly out of the bedroom and went into the bathroom. There was a shower compartment. He stepped into that, slid the frosted-glass panel shut and turned on the spray. He made it hot.

In the steam of the spray, he put the .45 into his mouth and blew the back of his head off.

The Tu-22P streaked high across Europe until it reached Spain. It released into Spanish airspace a small cylinder that fell swiftly until its tumbling was halted by its barometrically operated parachute. For an hour, all military radars and communications systems in the general area of Manises suffered continuous jamming as the cylinder drifted to earth.

The Tu-22P was never detected.

In open country near Villamarchante, about twenty kilometers from Manises itself, a man lay on the ground watching through night glasses as the cylinder came to the end of its long descent. It landed about five hundred meters from him.

He got up and hurried to where he'd seen it fall. After a minute or so he traced it with an extreme-short-range seeker no bigger than a matchbox. He picked up the cylinder, still attached to its chute, wrapped the cylinder in it and raced back to where he'd left his car. He got in and drove unhurriedly away.

No one saw him.

Friday

It was a strange dream.

The silver wolf went up the steep slope, his mate at his side. Suddenly, she was no longer there. The wolf turned. Far below, his mate tumbled in the whiteness. He saw people with guns. He fell upon them, revenge in his heart. But they were insubstantial. He saw other people. They had not pulled the triggers, but he knew they were responsible.

He saw them, but they were too far away.

He trudged up the white slope alone, the pain of his loss weighing upon him. Heavy-footed, he at last made it to the top. He surveyed the cold whiteness of his domain, spread beneath him. She should have been there with him to share it. The loneliness gnawed at him. He felt a rage against those who had caused it; the others he had seen, far away.

He raised his snout into the cold sky, and howled.

It was a challenge.

* * *

Gallagher came awake with the change in the cadence of the engines. The descent had begun. No matter how deeply asleep, he would have instinctively reacted to the spooling back of the jets. As instinctively, he had fastened his seat-belt even before his eyes had been fully open. A passing stewardess, checking, gave him a brief smile of approval. For a fleeting second, a bond lived between them. It was as if she knew he had once lived with airplanes. Mentally, he began flying the aircraft down.

Another part of his mind recalled the dream. Nearly eleven months had gone by, and still it came to him. The memory, the pain of Lauren's death was still with him.

He had stayed away as long as possible, working abroad, dreading the thought of re-turning without her. Then he could put the in-evitable off no longer. He had had to stop running.

He'd found the killers, of course, and they had paid with their own lives; but it had not brought her back. There were others too; those who had known, and had done nothing to pre-vent it. He would find a way to make them pay.

The 747 banked into the final leg of its ap-proach, seeming to float upwards as the in-crease of flaps gave it more lift, lowering the mammoth airplane towards the runway. Touchdown was feather-smooth. Gallagher felt appreciation for the skills of the flightdeck crew.

He stared out at the bleak November day. Rain was drenching Heathrow. He looked away, closed his eyes as the 747 taxied to its slot. He was finally back in London. It was not cause for celebration. The day looked as bleak as he felt.

The aircraft stopped. People began to leave their seats. He remained where he was until they'd all gone; then he stood up and got his bag from the overhead rack.

The stewardess was at the door as he left. "Didn't you want to leave us?" Her smile was friendly, quite pretty.

It made him smile back at her, despite his mood. "You spoilt me."

This pleased her. "Thank you for flying with us."

It lifted his spirits a little.

After he'd collected his luggage, he went to a public phone and dialed his home number. He put his bleeper to the receiver, listening as his answering machine played back the latest messages. He'd called it several times from abroad, allowing him to take up the photo assignments that had kept him working away from home for so long. It had helped to put off the dread day of return.

The messages contained more offers and quite a few cancellations from those too impatient to wait for him to contact them. He was not worried. He'd decided to ease up on the work anyway, for the time being. The tape ended with two calls of interest. One pleased him enormously. His garage, whom he had contacted a week before, told him that his resprayed, modified *quattro* was ready for collection. Driving it back from Surrey was something to look forward to.

The last message brought the bleakness of his mood back with a vengeance. The Department wanted him to call.

Fuck you, he said in his mind. He had no intention of calling. They could whistle till the cows came home.

As he broke the connection, he frowned briefly. Several times, calls had been made to the machine, but the caller or callers had hung up. He shrugged. He knew many people who hated talking to answering machines. It was not important.

He made another call, this time to Central Garage, to tell them he'd be down to collect the car. He hung up and picked up his bags. Something in him rebelled against the idea of taking a taxi all the way to Cobham. He decided to use the subway to Waterloo, then take a train from there.

As he made his way down the escalator to the Underground, he failed to notice the man who had been taking an avid interest in him ever since he'd got off the plane.

The man made a quick telephone call before following at a discreet distance.

The rain had fled from Cobham by the time Gallagher arrived at his destination, leaving in its wake a wintry freshness that was brightened by a strong sun that hung in the now cloudless sky. The road outside the garage glistened.

Gallagher waited expectantly.

The sudden low bark of a powerful motor starting up came from within, then the aggressive black snout of his Audi *quattro* nosed its way into the open. It gleamed menacingly in its new coat of paint as its wedge-shaped body, easing itself slowly out like a prowling cat scenting prey, came fully into view. It seemed a little lower and meaner than when he'd last seen it.

Oh, yes, he said in his mind, in sheer admiration.

The familiar bulging-wheel arches were still there, but that was just about all. The silver car he remembered no longer existed. No brightwork, save for the special wheels, remained. After Lauren's death he had decided to have it painted this way. But the garage had done much more than that. The paintwork itself had been so exceptionally done it gleamed with almost three-dimensional translucence; and the single-piece rear spoiler on the trunklid had grown two extra pieces that reached to the rear quarterlights. But it was the engine note that sent the adrenalin pumping through him. It sounded as if it wanted to take a bite of something.

The *quattro* stopped directly in front of him. The sales director of the company climbed out, grinning at him.

"Like it?"

"My God!" Gallagher said, and began to walk around the car, inspecting it minutely. "Do I like it, the man says."

"You are now the proud owner of a Treser *quattro.* We've given you an extra fifty on top of what you'd had done."

Two hundred and seventy-five bhp. Gallagher could scarcely believe it. The pleasure this was giving him had removed the nasty taste of the Department from his mouth.

"Don't get caught," the garage man was saying with some amusement. "Take a look down there."

Gallagher glanced briefly in the direction indicated. A police car was just pulling into the curb about fifty yards away. His stomach tightened. Had the Department set them on his tail? He felt the anger building behind his eyes.

"Something wrong?" The garage man was looking at him curiously.

"What? Oh, no. No." He decided to make light of it. "Funny how they're always there when you don't want them, never when you do."

"I know the feeling," the other said sympathetically.

Gallagher returned his attention to the car. "Well . . . I'd better see how she handles." He stroked the roof once. "You're looking great, Lauren."

The man stared at him. " 'Lauren'?"

He smiled sheepishly. "It's a long story."

"Oh. Yes. Well. . . ."

Gallagher reached for the sliding catch in the jamb of the driver's door and tripped it. The trunk sprang open. He put his bags in and shut it. The garage man had come round to watch.

"You've done a fantastic job," Gallagher said to him. "Time to tell me what it's going to cost."

"We'll send you the bill. Try her out. See how you like it first. She's been nicely run in, so you can wind her up if the law will let you."

Gallagher stuck out his hand. "All right. Thanks again."

"Pleasure."

They shook hands, and Gallagher took his place behind the wheel and shut the door. He clipped on his seatbelt, savoring the smell of the car. He felt at home in it. As if remembering, it had already begun to absorb him, welcoming him back. They were becoming one.

The garage man leaned down to say, "You look at home. How does it feel?" He seemed anxious.

"Great. It feels just right."

"If you have any trouble. . . ."

"I know I won't." Gallagher blipped the throttle, once. The engine growled. It was beautiful.

The man straightened. Giving him a wave Gallagher nosed the *quattro* into the street. The police car was still there. He drove sedately past. Both heads turned to watch his progress.

If they were from the Department. . . .

Gallagher curbed the anger he could feel beginning to rise within him. Ignore the bastards. Enjoy the car.

He kept to his leisurely pace, allowing the car to continue its absorption of him. The police car did not follow. He began to feel better. Perhaps they were just bored with driving around.

He stayed on the Portsmouth road, heading for Esher and towards London. He did not increase speed. The car felt like a powerhouse waiting to be unleashed. He resisted the temptation to do just that. His mirrors showed him no police car lurking in them. He relaxed.

Just before Esher, he saw the white Mercedes; a big squat coupé. Something pinged a warning within him, but he told himself he was being paranoid. It was barely three hours since his return. Who could possibly be following him? Had the Department traced him down here after all? Since when had they switched to Mercs? The Department pool normally used Rovers, being patriotic and all that.

Gallagher drove apparently aimlessly through Esher, pretending to be lost, taking innumerable side turnings and getting caught in the one-way traffic system. The Mercedes apparently lost its way too. It followed.

They weren't doing their job very well, he thought disparagingly; unless they deliberately wanted him to know they were there. He decided only the Department would be so arrogant about it, telling him they could pull him in at any time.

"Bastards!" he said tightly. "Give me some air, will you!"

He towed the Mercedes on an invisible thread out of Esher and turned right at Littleworth Common on to the Kingston by-pass. As soon as the traffic allowed, he gave the *quattro* its head. As if it had been waiting on the edge of its patience for the opportunity, the car raised its snout and, with a sudden roar, hurled itself along the road. The acceleration pinned him to his seat. It seemed to go on and on as he shifted gears. The white Mercedes seemed to streak backwards in the mirror, receding in seconds to a mere dot. It was not unlike an afterburner take-off in his old Phantom, he thought with pleasure.

He approached a traffic circle at speed, negotiated it with barely a drop in power, took the *quattro* into a wide curve towards the Kingston district of Tolworth before another roundabout claimed his attention. Here he slowed right down, turned left at the roundabout and headed into Kingston itself. The Mercedes was nowhere to be seen. Up the hill past Richmond Park and still no Mercedes. He relaxed once more and patted the steering-wheel.

"Good for you, Lauren. Good for you."

He slowed down. The urge of the car had been exhilarating. He had almost enjoyed the chase; but full pleasure had been spoilt by the knowledge that the white Mercedes had not been after him for fun. This brought a tightness to his lips. He had one call to make before going home.

Delphine Arundel said, "Hello, Gordon. It's nice to see you."

"Oh, yes?" He studied her face. She seemed most unhappy. "Is that why you're so excited?"

"Mr. Fowler will explain."

"That's not all he's got to explain. I want to see Kingston-Wyatt."

"He's . . . he's not here. See Mr. Fowler. He'll. . . ."

But Gallagher was already moving towards Kingston-Wyatt's office. Delphine Arundel, in the act of leaving her seat, settled down again resignedly as he pushed the door open and strode in.

The man Gallagher saw in Kingston-Wyatt's chair had neatly cut hair streaked with gray that curled a little behind his ears, a round smooth face with just a tinge of red on the cheeks, and he was dressed in City uniform: dark pinstriped suit, with a tie that Gallagher assumed was either old school, regimental or club. It certainly wasn't Air Force. For some reason, this annoyed him. The strange man had a mouth that managed to look petulant and carry a smirk at the same time.

"You must be Gallagher," the petulant cherub said, looking up. The eyes were like a bad day on Brighton seafront: a dirty gray. They did not look friendly. "I'm Winterbourne. I've heard a lot about you."

Bully for you, Gallagher thought. He stopped near the huge desk. What, he wondered, was going on? Inter-departmental investigation? Despite his own hostility towards Kingston-Wyatt, it annoyed him to see this smug creature in his ex-boss's chair. What he felt was not unlike the reaction of someone in a family quarrel to an outsider poking his nose into it. If anyone's going to kick my brother's head in, I'll be the one to do it.

Winterbourne said, "You were, of course, expecting to see Kingston-Wyatt."

"Yes. Where is he?"

"Ah. Well. . . ."

"Perhaps I can have a word with Mr. Gallagher, Sir John."

Gallagher looked round, recognizing the voice. Fowler.

Fowler said, "Good to see you, Gordon."

"I can't say I feel good to be here. Where's the boss?"

Fowler cleared his throat. "Sir John *is* the boss."

Gallagher turned to Winterbourne. "You?" he said disbelievingly.

The petulant mouth pursed itself. "Me." It looked pleased too.

"Jesus." The mouth was beginning to tighten with outrage when Gallagher turned back to Fowler. "So where's Kingston-Wyatt?"

Fowler spoke to Winterbourne. "If you'll allow me to handle this, Sir John."

"Please do, Fowler. I will not have this rank insubordination."

Gallagher stared at him. "I don't believe I've just heard this. It may come as a shock to you, Winterbourne, but as I don't work for you, I can't be insubordinate."

"Let's go to my office, Gordon," Fowler put in quickly.

Gallagher allowed Fowler to lead him out. "Where the bloody hell did your lot find him?" he said loudly as they left Winterbourne.

Fowler did not speak until they had entered his own office, which was half the size of the one they'd just come from; nor was it as grand. Fowler's office was almost spartan by comparison. Every item within it spoke of functionality. There was not a filing cabinet in sight. The desk was so bare, it looked as if it had been swept clean only seconds before. A multi-mode telephone stood upon it.

Gallagher had always marveled at the way Fowler could operate with the barest of essentials. Winterbourne would be no match for him.

Gallagher said, "What in God's name is Winterbourne when he's in, and where is Kingston-Wyatt? I have a score to settle with the bastard, but even I wouldn't wish Winterbourne on the Department. Speaking of which, why are you having me followed?"

Fowler said mildly, "Which question do you want answered first?"

"Start with Kingston-Wyatt."

"Why don't you sit down?" Fowler moved to his desk, took his own advice. "You'll feel you need to."

Gallagher studied him warily, before taking the only other chair in the room. It was a comfortable armchair, incongruous in such a place.

"Kingston-Wyatt's dead," Fowler said without warning. "Shot himself."

Gallagher was shocked. At the same time he felt cheated. "Why?"

Fowler did not answer directly. "You don't know how to react. I can sense regret, but you wanted your own revenge. Am I correct?"

Gallagher said nothing.

"Coffee?" Fowler suggested with all seriousness. "I can ask Mrs. Arundel to have some brought. Or would you prefer a stronger liquid?"

"I'll have the coffee, thanks."

Fowler nodded as if with approval, reached for the phone and made the request.

"I'll repeat," he said as he replaced the receiver. "You wanted your own revenge. You believe we were responsible for your young lady's death."

"You may not have pulled the trigger. You knew about it."

Fowler sighed. "There you sit, so firm in your accusation . . . with all the answers, of course."

Gallagher stared at him balefully. "You're not talking to some idiot from the street, Fowler. I know how this Department works. Don't expect me to bleed for Kingston-Wyatt because he had the good sense to do a wet number on himself."

"Would it make any difference if I told you he was very upset by what happened? I had a shouting match with him over it. It was only then I realized how badly he'd taken it."

Gallagher was unmoved. "Come on, Fowler. Don't try that on me."

"He cared about you."

"Fowler, Kingston-Wyatt *used* me. I woke up just in time, or some corner of a foreign field would have been my home by now."

"You know that's not fair."

Suddenly, the eleven months of Gallagher's self-imposed exile, and the reasons for it, rushed bitterly to the surface. He rose out of the armchair, went over to the desk and placed his hands firmly upon it, leaning close to Fowler.

"Fair? What the hell do you know about fairness?" he shouted. "I escaped by bloody accident! I. . . ."

The door opened. Gallagher straightened, turned to look, the anger still in his eyes.

Delphine Arundel had chosen to bring the coffee in herself; a china service on a silver tray. She had obviously heard. Her eyes were wounded, but not accusing. She set the tray down on a small side table.

Gallagher, remembering the sad face that had first greeted him, said quietly, "I didn't know when I came in."

"It's all right, Gordon," she said. "I understand how you feel." She went out after a neutral glance at Fowler.

Fowler said, "Help yourself. I don't want one."

Gallagher went over to pour himself a cup, conscious that the initiative had been neatly taken from him. He decided to keep a tighter rein on his feelings. He poured with a steady hand, he was pleased to note. He went back to the armchair and sat down once more.

"Forget Kingston-Wyatt," he said. "Forget Winterbourne, who can't be Air Force. Tell me why you're having me followed, within hours of my return."

"Navy."

"What?"

"Winterbourne's Navy."

"Christ."

Fowler actually smiled. "Nice to see you feel so proprietary, even though you're no longer with us."

"Just keep remembering that, and you'll make me very happy."

"We weren't having you followed. We aren't."

"Say that again?" Gallagher drank some coffee. It was very good.

"Don't look so sceptical. I'm telling you the truth."

Gallagher liked that even less. He still did not trust Fowler, but he was beginning to give credence to the other's words. If not the Department, then who?

"You're not looking very happy," Fowler said. "You might find you need us, after all." Fowler looked happy.

"Some hope."

Fowler reached into his desk and pulled out some newspapers which he dropped on to its polished surface. They made the desk look grossly untidy.

"Take a look at these," Fowler said.

Gallagher looked at the papers, looked at Fowler, took another drink of his coffee. Finally, he stood up and walked over to the small table. He put the cup down and turned to face Fowler.

"Why? I can't imagine there's anything in those papers that I'd be particularly interested in, if it has anything to do with this place. Especially so."

"I think you will find something of interest," Fowler insisted. "It may have links with the people you say were following you."

"A white Mercedes. They used a white Merc."

Fowler gave a fleeting smile. "Our funds do not allow us to purchase fancy cars. We can't all afford Mercs and *quattros.*"

"Don't plead poverty to me, Fowler. I worked for my car."

Fowler said nothing. Instead, he tapped at the newspapers like an imperious schoolmaster.

Gallagher went slowly towards him, stopped by the desk and studied each of the newspapers in turn. Each was open at the page Fowler wanted read, and on each page, an article had been bordered in red with a broad felt-tipped pen. The articles were about the same subject matter.

Gallagher looked up. "A madman killed two policemen near Nottingham. If the Department's interested, I assume they may have been Special Branch, working with you on something; which is odd in itself. I still don't see what all this has to do with my being here, with the message you left on my answering machine, or with my being followed."

"Take another look. Something missing in each article."

Gallagher did not take his eyes from Fowler's. "Not interested."

"No photographs."

"Perhaps he's shy."

Fowler ignored the acid comment. "There is always a photograph. Mother, girlfriend, cousin, wife; someone always supplies a photograph. If the person has a record, the police do. Paul Emerson does not appear to have a photograph."

"As I've said, he's shy."

Fowler said, "Paul Emerson, gunman, does

not have a photograph of his desperate face in the papers because we do not want him to."

Gallagher waited for Fowler to continue.

"Further," Fowler went on, "his name is not Paul Emerson. We fed that to the papers. The policemen were not real police but imposters."

"Department personnel?"

"Worse. GRU."

"Jesus! Russian military intelligence hunting a man in Nottinghamshire? You've got to be joking."

"The two bodies we . . . or rather the Branch carted off for us were certainly real."

"Never thought you'd work with that lot."

"We didn't really work *with* them. They were used to fend off the straight boys. Can't have your average bobby getting too pally, can we?" Fowler's eyes seemed to gleam behind his spectacles. "Would you like to hear more?"

"Don't let me stop you."

"You won't."

Gallagher went over to the single narrow window in Fowler's room. He could never understand Fowler's passion for a lack of windows, especially as Fowler had a nice little mansion in the Cotswolds that sported vast areas of glass. Perhaps it was only in the office. Did he think someone would one day take a shot at him here?

Gallagher stared at a tall crane he could see beyond the buildings in the immediate vicinity. A good man with a good rifle in that high cabin, and *pow*. Perhaps it was just the office, he decided. But Fowler had never struck him as being windy. Perhaps it was just a thing with him. People had all kinds of. . . .

"Paul Emerson," Fowler was saying, "is one of ours."

Gallagher turned from the window. *"What?"*

"Paul Emerson is Andrew Uffa Dalgleish."

Gallagher went slowly back to his chair and sat heavily into it, disbelief plain on his face.

"I thought you'd be needing that," Fowler said drily. "Eventually."

"Dalgleish is dead!" Gallagher exclaimed. "He died in the Middle East over two years ago! The grapevine had it that someone blew him away in Sharjah. You yourself confirmed it."

"Yes," Fowler admitted, unrepentant.

"Then. . . ."

"It was a cover."

"And who was the poor sod who caught it?"

"A Russian."

"KGB? GRU?"

Fowler shook his head. "Neither."

"Not an innocent bystander."

"Since when is a Russian in the Middle East an innocent bystander? In the event, he was shot by his own side. He was an independent, working, he said at the time, for his country."

"I don't understand."

"You've been out of the business for a while. . . ."

"And I'm staying out."

Fowler said nothing to that. "There is," he continued, "a dissident intelligence service at work within the Soviet Union." He noted the scepticism on Gallagher's face. "What's so strange about that? Do you really think the Russians wish to be obliterated any more than we do? The vast majority of the populace know nothing of what goes on outside the borders of their towns and villages, let alone outside the borders of the nation, or rather group of nations. But within the power bloc, the unholy triad of Party, KGB and Army, as I like to call it, there are those who have looked closely at the accepted line and have begun to seriously question it.

"I don't propose to give you a potted history of the Soviet Union. You know well enough that one of the most direct ways of giving yourself an unhealthy life is to dissent. To do so from within the Party, the KGB or the Army—hence GRU—is the surest form of suicide, if you get caught. The man in Sharjah was there to meet Dalgleish. Luckily for us, the meeting had already taken place when they got to him. We put it about that one of our own men had died in the ensuing gun battle. That man, of course, was Dalgleish."

Gallagher was still full of disbelief. "You're trying to tell me there's an intelligence group inside Soviet Russia that is not only entirely independent of the KGB and the GRU but is also working *against* them?"

"I'm going further. These people, whoever they are, belong to the KGB and the GRU; on the surface."

"Jesus Christ. You believe this?"

"At first we didn't. We suspected, as you

are doing right now, a multi-layered bluff; something we all know they're very good at. But we had to find out. This group, we had been told, seriously opposed what they saw as a path that would lead inevitably to the destruction of their country. Make no mistake, they are not working against the Motherland. They see themselves as trying to preserve it."

"So you decided to send Dalgleish in."

"He was a natural for the job. As you know, he is exceptionally gifted linguistically, particularly in the Soviet languages and dialects." Fowler made a sound that could have been a chuckle. "Perhaps it's the Gaelic in him. But to continue. We first heard of the group when you were still with us. We were sceptical. We could find no substance to back the wispy rumours that came our way; but we sat tight even on those. We told no one, not even the Americans." There was a definite chuckle now, with a rich dryness to it. "All things considered these days, it was just as well.

"We were naturally anxious not to compromise this group, if it really did exist. So we waited, took no action. Eventually, news filtered through that they would be prepared to warn us of any new developments in weaponry they felt might destabilize the East-West balance. While they grew, and consolidated their position, they did not want the country blasted out from under their feet. At the same time, discovery would not only create an equally destabilizing purge within Russia itself, but would destroy their organization before it had time to influence policy, as well as raising international tension to a very dangerous level. We all know that the old chestnut of creating a war to stabilize the home front works just as well today as it did in Caesar's time.

"So, as I said, we waited. Then news came of a new weapon that would put the opposition so far ahead, they could be tempted to try something. The group did not identify the weapon. At the time, we felt they were as much in the dark as we were. Whatever it was, it was being kept very secret, even from the levels of the KGB and GRU where these people operated. Once and for all, we had to find out just how genuine they were. We decided to feed Dalgleish in. He knew the risks. He accepted the mission. The rendezvous was kept, and the group fed him in."

Gallagher did not speak for a while, finding that, despite himself, Fowler had got him hooked on the tale.

At last he said, "What about the man who was killed? Didn't that alert the KGB?"

Fowler smiled. "He was an engineer. Bona fide documents. He was simply trying to make a little capitalist cash on the side. It happens all the time, more often than the Russians would ever admit. There's a lovely little blackmarket operation in Afghanistan that is not unreminiscent of Berlin during my airlift days."

Gallagher should not have been appalled but he was. "You set the poor bugger up?"

"He set himself up. It was the only way, he said, to keep the identity of his group totally secret. He was, of course, KGB as well, as are so many of the 'engineers', 'advisers' and 'attachés'. He died a greedy KGB man. It was what he expected, if things went wrong for him. His group is still safe.

"We . . . er . . . gave the group a name. We all need identification tags. It's the nature of things. Oh, do help yourself to more coffee if you feel like it."

"No, thanks."

Fowler shrugged. "As you wish. You are, of course, familiar with the term 'windshear'. As a trained fast-jet pilot, you understand its meaning, and its effect. We decided to call the . . . er . . . 'invisible' intelligence unit the Windshear Group, or more simply, Windshear. We thought the effect it would have on Russian intelligence when its activities are fully appreciated would be as devastating, and therefore considered our name for it quite appropriate."

"Something went wrong though, didn't it? Badly wrong, or Dalgleish would not be over here, on the run from the GRU, and making a name for himself as a killer of policemen. If you're entertaining the idea of asking me to plant both feet into this mess, forget it. I've listened politely to your tale. I think it's about time I left."

Gallagher stood up.

Fowler held up a hand. "At least allow me to finish. You might yet change your mind."

"I doubt it." But he didn't leave.

Fowler said, "Won't you sit down?"

"No. I'll hear the rest, then I'll leave."

"As you wish." Fowler seemed unperturbed. "Dalgleish went in through Turkey, found himself in Tbilisi, headquarters of the Trans-Caucasus military district. He survived, moved to Baku, still in Trans-Caucasia. He moved again; through North Caucasus, into Volga, and finally the Urals. The military headquarters there is Sverdlovsk, but he kept away from it. Windshear found him a safe house in Kopeysk. They had also furnished him with all authorizations for his movements. By all accounts, he was safe for a whole year. Then he was blown, or we think he was blown."

"You *think?* Sweet Christ." Gallagher wanted to sigh. "So Windshear is compromised."

"It would appear not."

"It would appear. . . ." Gallagher found it hard to believe the Department could be so incompetent. "No wonder Dalgleish is on the warpath." The more Fowler spoke, the more Gallagher became suspicious. He was certain Fowler was not telling him the half of it.

"After a year," Fowler said, "news started filtering out that Dalgleish was dead. The name was not mentioned, but the way the information came out made us quite certain it was Dalgleish. Imagine our surprise when we heard from him, a year after he was supposed to have died."

"I'll bet."

"He wanted us to help get him out. He had important information. He was in grave danger. Of course, we suspected a KGB operation."

"Naturally."

"You're getting cynical in your old age,

Gordon. Not an old man at thirty-four, are you?"

"I had good teachers."

"Touché. But we had to be sure, after all," Fowler continued mildly, "if Windshear really existed, it could easily have been a KGB ruse to find out. If Windshear did not exist, nothing was lost."

"Except the poor bastard who went in."

"Dalgleish knew the risks."

"So you said."

"But now we know he is alive, and well."

"You call being hunted by the GRU alive and well?"

"We need you to get to Dalgleish. We have tried. He does not trust us. That is quite obvious."

"My heart bleeds for you, Fowler."

"He'll trust you," Fowler went on as if Gallagher had not spoken. "You were good friends once, weren't you? Cambridge days."

"We never worked together."

"He respects you. He'll listen to you. All we require is that you contact him. . . ."

"How? I don't bloody know where he is. Unless you think he's stupid enough to be anywhere near Nottingham."

"Of course he isn't. Try his family."

"In his place, with the GRU after me, and a total lack of trust in the Department, I wouldn't go near them. Besides, I'm quite sure you've got all his old haunts, and every living relative, under surveillance. You don't need me."

Fowler maintained his equanimity, which made Gallagher even more suspicious.

Gallagher said, "It still does not explain the fat white Mercedes."

"The Americans?" Fowler suggested.

"What would they want with me?"

Fowler smiled. "Who knows?"

"Goodbye, Fowler. Thanks for the little tale."

When Gallagher had reached the door, Fowler, who had remained seated, said in his mild voice, "The boss's funeral is tomorrow. Can we expect to see you?"

Gallagher just looked at him and left the room without speaking. In the corridor, he nearly bumped into Winterbourne.

"Well, Gallagher," Winterbourne began with faked heartiness, "are you with us?" The dirty gray eyes danced with a life Gallagher hated.

"No."

Winterbourne entered Fowler's office, face stained pink. "The man's rude, insolent, insubordinate. . . ."

Fowler closed his eyes wearily. "Sir John," he began quietly when he'd opened them again, "Gallagher is still under a great emotional stress. He has good reason not to love the Department. . . ."

"But dammit, Fowler—"

"Sir John, I believe you agreed to allow me to handle this in my own way."

"Yes. Of course. But—"

"I shall do just that."

"I want results, Fowler. Results."

Winterbourne stalked out, still fuming.

Fowler stared at the closing door expressionlessly. Soon after, Delphine Arundel came in.

"Gallagher refused, I take it?" she said.

"It was to be expected. We're not his favorite people at the moment."

"Can't say I blame him."

Fowler sighed. "Not you as well."

Gallagher stared at the yellow monstrosity clamped to the left front wheel of the *quattro* and wanted to kick it. As if by magic, a policeman appeared, speaking into his radio.

"We'll have that off in a minute, sir," he said to Gallagher, who gave him a look of disbelief. "The Landrover's coming."

Within a minute, the promised Landrover arrived, with two members of the traffic police who promptly freed the car. They got back into their Landrover and went prowling after more satisfying game.

Gallagher did not look up at the building he had just left. He knew Fowler had somehow seen the clamp and had swiftly had it removed. The Department showing what it could do.

Gallagher climbed in. "Thank you," he said to the still watching beat policeman.

The policeman nodded and walked slowly away.

"Stuff the lot of you," Gallagher said as he drove off, the *quattro* roaring its defiance.

The policeman, turning to look, did not hear.

As he drove home, Gallagher kept a wary eye on his mirrors. No Mercedes. No shadowing Rover either. That meant nothing. They knew where he lived.

He drove unhurriedly, enjoying the feel of the car, thinking about what Fowler had said. Knowing the ways of the Department as he did, he decided that Fowler had told him about ten per cent of the whole story. If Windshear truly existed, there was nothing to prove it was not itself a KGB Trojan horse to root out possible dissidents within its midst, as well as giving the West the spurious hope of dissension deep inside the Soviet power base. Windshear could well be the brainchild of the KGB, the GRU— hoping to eclipse its lifelong rival—or a joint operation by those two notorious enemies. If that were indeed the case, then whatever was going on would need to be of monumental importance to prevent the two organizations from indulging in their usual game of trying to outdo each other.

The black *quattro* sliced its way through the traffic at Hyde Park Corner and roared gently up Park Lane as Gallagher restrained the urge to floor the accelerator. Plenty of time for that later.

He shook his head slowly as he turned left at Marble Arch for Holland Park. The whole thing stank. He wanted no part of it. The thought of going home merely to collect a change of clothing and head for Dover began to appeal to him. The continent was a good place to try the car out in its new guise. Besides, he wanted to keep well away from Dalgleish, and the Department. There were lots of bolt-holes in Europe. Being out of the business did not necessarily mean losing all contact.

By the time he had made it to his maisonette in the quiet street off the main road, Gallagher had convinced himself it was a good idea.

There were no cars waiting for him. Again, that did not mean anything. He unloaded the *quattro* and made for the side entrance which gave him private access to the big Regency building. His ground-floor neighbor, on her way out through the front, saw him. He was not looking forward to the inevitable.

"Oh, Mr. Gallagher!" she trilled, adding, as if she'd just worked it out, "You're back."

"Yes," he said, sighing inwardly.

She was a middle-aged actress who had appeared in television operas and was rapidly losing what must have been a quite spectacular bloom of youth. The desperate eyes which showed full knowledge of this always saddened him. The trials of her life were deeply etched across her features like faults which blighted a landscape.

"New car," she said. "Lovely."

"Same one, changed a little."

"Still lovely. A change is always as good as a rest, isn't it?"

"It certainly is."

"You really must come for that coffee I promised you, you naughty boy."

"I will. I will. But you know how it is with work."

"I know how it is with photographers." She

smiled. "It's all those young things. No time for an old hag like me."

With sudden insight, Gallagher saw in the desperate eyes a brief glimpse of the beauty that had been, and felt ashamed. Without realizing it, he had leaned forward to kiss her cheek.

"You're not a hag," he said. "I promise to come for that coffee." He meant it.

She understood. "Thank you," she said quietly. "Coffee then."

But events would decree otherwise.

Gallagher opened all the windows in the maisonette, allowing the November cold to scythe through it, giving it a good airing. He had inspected the place minutely but discovered nothing untoward. In the eleven months of his absence, no one had forced an entry. Once a month, the cleaning lady had come. That was all. He suspected his neighbor had kept a vigilant eye on it.

He smiled. The least he could do was have coffee with her.

The smile disappeared as he thought of Lauren. She, of all people, had never been given the chance to see his home. He fought at the continuing pain of the loss. When would it fade?

Come off it, Gallagher, he chided himself irritably. *You can't bring her back.* This made him think of Kingston-Wyatt's suicide, which Fowler had been carefully vague about. Why had a hard nut like the former boss of the Department taken his own life?

Gallagher did not think it was because

Kingston-Wyatt had been particularly upset about what had happened to Lauren on the ski slopes of Courchevel. The hit had been meant for both of them, but one of the killers had missed. No, Kingston-Wyatt had killed himself for another reason.

"Well, I don't want to know," Gallagher said aloud, and went to do his unpacking. He would have a busy night developing his films.

The phone rang. He stopped and let it ring five times before taking it in the darkroom, to which he'd been carrying his cameras.

He gave his number, waited.

"Gordon!" a totally strange female voice said in his ear. "Where have you *been?* I've been calling you all day. Thanks for the historical dedication to Vespasian. Can't talk long. Busy. Call me at the office." The line went dead.

He held the receiver, staring at it for some moments, before slowly replacing it. She had spoken very quickly; too quickly, he thought, for anyone to have had time to trace. It was as if she expected his phone to be tapped. As the house was itself clean, he felt quite certain the Department had attached its clandestine ear to his line.

The message could only have come from Dalgleish. He was sure of it. Whoever the woman was, she obviously had Dalgleish's complete trust. The Department, however, would now have her brief message on tape, and were probably even now trying to make sense of it.

Gallagher proceeded to shut every window he'd opened, making sure each was secure; then he went to one of his bookshelves and took out

a copy of Tacitus—The Histories. Mention of
Vespasian had told him precisely what Dalgleish's message had meant. Most of the
woman's words could be disregarded. Only "historical", "Vespasian" and "Call me" mattered.

He opened the specially bound book. Its
deep-wine leather cover looked as new as it did
the day Dalgleish had given it to him as a birth-
day gift, during their Cambridge years. The
dedication was on the very first page, which
contained a potted history of the life of the
Roman historian.

Dalgleish's scrawl went from Tacitus's career during the time of Vespasian to cross the
year of his birth in AD 55. From the Vespasianic
period, he got AD 69–79. Gallagher took that as
the phone number. All he needed now was the
code to go with it. He assumed it to be 55, with
any digit from 0 to 9. A quick check of the phone
codes showed him an area encompassing East
Ham, Barking, Ilford, Stratford and Leyton-
stone. What was Dalgleish doing within the
Greater London area when he was supposed to
be at large in the countryside? Gallagher hoped
Fowler did not have a copy of Tacitus to hand.
It would be easy, too easy. Perhaps that was
what Dalgleish had hoped. Its very simplicity
would be its best disguise.

Gallagher decided he would have to act
quickly none the less. He would make the call.
Working for the Department was one thing.
Helping an old university friend and former
colleague in trouble was entirely different, especially when the call had come more or less
directly from him. It could be a trick of

Fowler's, but Gallagher doubted it. Even the Department could not have known of the book, unless they had inspected every one on the shelves. Dust lines showed they had not been disturbed in his absence. So much for the cleaning lady.

He left the house and climbed into the car. He would make the call from a public phone. No point in making life easier for Fowler. He checked his mirrors as he sped away: no Mercedes, no Rover. It didn't mean anything. The day was now gloomy and raining heavily, which pleased him.

He drove a meandering route for a while before parking in a side street. He left the car and found himself a café, not too far from it, where he ordered coffee. There was a payphone. He took his time, watching the street from his chosen secluded corner. The phone was downstairs, near the toilets. He waited. No suspicious-looking cars pulled up outside. He left his half-drunk coffee and went downstairs. He tried the codes at random, getting the correct number after the fourth attempt.

"Gallagher," he said.

"Where is the dedication?" It was the same woman.

"On the first page, running from left to right, upwards."

She gave him an address, and directions. "Be there tomorrow," she went on. "No one will answer if you should ring again." She hung up.

She had a pleasant voice. Gallagher reflected as he went back up the stairs. Her accent was that of someone who had been given a privi-

leged education. There had been nothing re-
gional upon which to pin her background; but
the voice, despite its urgency, had still managed
to carry the warmth of a generous person. She'd
sounded nervous too.

As he took his seat to finish his coffee, Gallagher wondered why he was going to see Dalgleish, knowing the dodginess of the whole
affair. He sighed as he admitted to himself it
was because he knew Dalgleish would have
done the same for him.

The address the woman had given him was
near Nottingham.

Fowler's brow furrowed briefly as he re-read
the transcript of the tap on Gallagher's phone.

Winterbourne said, "Well? Do you think
it's a message?"

Fowler took his time before replying. He
was beginning to feel strongly irritated by Winterbourne's constant invasion of his office.
Kingston-Wyatt had had the knack of knowing
when to stay away.

"Who knows?" Fowler at last replied
unhelpfully.

"Shouldn't we?" Winterbourne was getting
testy. "If something isn't done soon to appre-
hend Dalgleish before our soldier friends catch
up with him. . . ." Winterbourne allowed his
words to die, the upspoken fate awaiting Dalgleish hanging like a threat between them.

Winterbourne had gone, against Fowler's
wishes, for ministerial approval to turn the
SAS loose. They had not yet been put in the
field, but Winterbourne had no compunction

about using them to force Fowler's hand. Winterbourne held the leash and wanted Fowler to be well aware of it. Winterbourne had already insisted on the continuing use of the Branch.

Kingston-Wyatt would never have set another service upon one of his own. Nevertheless, Fowler smiled to himself. Dalgleish could be much nastier than the SAS, if pushed. He wondered why Winterbourne had not asked for the SBS, the Navy's equivalent. Perhaps Winterbourne wanted to take a sideways swipe at the Army too.

Fowler found himself smiling openly.

"Do you find me amusing, Fowler?"

Fowler was tempted to say yes. "I am thinking, Sir John, more about what could happen if Dalgleish and the SAS ever clash. Are you prepared to accept the responsibility for any deaths among the Army? It is on record that I am against bringing them in."

Winterbourne's dirty gray eyes surveyed Fowler without warmth. "Is that a threat?"

"I would call it protecting the Department. I consider it a tactical error to call in the SAS at this juncture. That does not mean they could not be brought in later, if things do get out of hand."

"Generous of you."

Fowler ignored the sarcasm. "I am thinking of us all, Sir John," he said reasonably. Stupid bastard, he thought.

"I do hope the reasons for Kingston-Wyatt's suicide are being thoroughly investigated," Winterbourne said with calculated nastiness. He turned away from Fowler abruptly and walked briskly out.

"God help us," Fowler muttered despairingly. "Dammit, Greg," he continued to the absent and dead Kingston-Wyatt, "couldn't you have waited for all this to sort itself out before blowing your head off?"

The phone on his desk warbled. He picked it up. "Fowler." A pause, then, "How could you possibly have lost him? His car is quite unmistakable and the car you're using is not one of ours. He'll be expecting a Rover. Yet despite these points in your favor, Inspector, you managed to lose him for a vital half-hour. He could have seen anybody, made any number of telephone calls." Fowler paused again. "Not to worry," he said wearily. "Now that he's home again, you can keep watch without fear of losing him, unless he knows how to disappear down a plug hole." He hung up. "God!"

He studied the transcript once more. Whatever its message, he was certain Gallagher had already acted upon it. He pushed it to one side. Like Vespasian, it was now ancient history.

The woman intrigued him. Was she a longstanding contact that Dalgleish had somehow managed to keep secret from the Department? Or a recent one, made upon his return?

He pursed his lips thoughtfully. Educated voice; so not a barmaid or a club hostess. His thoughts halted briefly. He was getting out of touch. These days, even graduates were glad to work in a bar if they could find the job.

He thought about the woman for a long time. It was a fruitless exercise. He even asked

Delphine Arundel to listen to the tape, in an attempt to see if she could identify the voice as belonging to someone she might have met, however briefly, with Dalgleish; but she had never met any of Dalgleish's women, so that was a no-go.

It had been a very long shot. Department operatives always kept their private lives to themselves. The files were a different matter; but they did not put voices to names. Perhaps one day soon they would. The technology was certainly available.

Fowler did his thinking unhurriedly, taking refuge in Micawber: something, he was sure, would soon turn up.

Saturday

It was 0010 hours at the arctic air base as the Tu-22P lowered its wheels for its landing on the unlighted runway. Kakunin swept his eyes over the three cathode-ray-tube displays—repeated identically at the co-pilot's station—that gave all the information he required for the task in hand. The advanced standard of the digital and CRT displays made nonsense of the Western belief that the Soviet Union lagged behind in up-to-date technology. The Tu-22P itself would have given many a strategic planner nightmares, had he but known of its existence.

The aircraft banked into its final turn, swooping down on spread wings to the pitch-black of the icy, wind-blasted earth below.

Kakunin watched as the right-hand display showed him the attitude of his ship to the approaching runway, the readouts updating his position continuously, giving him speed, heading, height, time-to-touch-down, glideslope and many other bits of information vital to a safe landing. There was little need to look out into the night. Nothing would be seen. It was all there on the CRTs.

He was not worried about the low infra-red radiation from his shielded engines being picked up by a satellite or a high-flying recon ship from the West. As with all his flights, a zero-recce window had been selected. As usual, the West would know nothing.

He smiled within his helmet as he brought the wings level. It had been another successful mission. All the way to Greece and back, refueling without lights over Siberia on a long circuitous flight that had taken them into the airspace of eight Soviet military districts, some being traversed twice, with none of them any the wiser, despite a directive putting them on the alert. As for the Greeks, the first they would have known of a transgression of their own airspace would have been the sudden disruption of their communications systems when the jammer released by the Tu-22P had begun operating.

Kakunin's smile widened a little as he brought the aircraft down to a smooth touchdown. Imagine the West having a bird like this! The poor devils were so far behind.

"This is becoming a habit, Colonel," Narenko's voice said in his ear.

"Do I detect relief?" Kakunin queried lightly.

"I have complete faith in the Comrade Colonel's skills."

"And you, Velensky? Do you also have faith in my ability to bring this ship down time after time?"

Velensky had himself done one landing. "It is what I would expect of the Comrade Colonel," he answered formally.

The brief levity expired abruptly and they taxied to their hardened shelter, speaking only to communicate with the control tower.

As they walked away from the aircraft towards the special crew carrier—designed to accommodate them and their personal equipment—Kakunin said, "Tell me, Velensky, does it ever worry you that one day you may be ordered to obliterate millions of human beings?"

In the subdued light of the huge shelter, Velensky stared at his commander. "Why should it, Comrade? They are preparing to obliterate millions of us. If we are able to hit them first, so much the better. The homeland comes first. Always."

Velensky walked on ahead, his small form hurrying, as if to get away.

Narenko said, "Sometimes, I think that little shrimp is a KGB snoop. He sees himself in the Kremlin one day."

Kakunin said thoughtfully as he watched Velensky stride towards the waiting vehicle, "You really should not talk about a superior officer in such a disrespectful manner in my presence, Alexei." The words were without censure. "Our Yuri is merely ambitious. Come, then. Let us go and talk to the destroyers of worlds."

As he accompanied his colleague, Narenko wished Kakunin would be a little more careful about what he said. Narenko did not put it past the KGB to secrete a recording machine aboard the aircraft, patched directly into their communication links, to be analyzed after each flight. The Comrade Colonel was sometimes .in the habit of making jokes that could, with the right amount of twisting, be considered seditious.

Kakunin was an excellent pilot, perhaps the best there was, in Narenko's opinion. He did not want to see his Colonel suddenly disappear, irrespective of skills.

As he climbed into the vehicle, Narenko hoped the Tu-22P would never be used in anger.

Outside the shelter, the arctic wind howled. The crew carrier nosed its way into the hostile night.

Gallagher came slowly awake. He did not switch on a light. Instead, he glanced at the glowing dial of the small traveling alarm clock on the bedside table: two a.m. He had set the alarm for 2:30. He got up and began to dress in the dark.

He had prepared everything before going to bed; the bag he was taking was already packed. He put on soft, calf-length boots of black leather with low cleated soles that were secured with long laces, rather like jungle boots. He pulled the bottoms of his black jeans over them. Next, he put on a black, wool-lined blouson and zipped it almost to the neck. He picked up his gloves and his bag. He was ready.

He went down from the bedroom to the lounge on the next floor and, flattening himself against a window, peered out. The dark-colored Ford Escort XR3 he had seen parked at the far end of the short street was still there. No one appeared to be in it. It had been there since eight o'clock that evening. He could see no Mercedes, no Rover.

He went down another flight of stairs to the door and let himself quietly out. He double-locked the door. Earlier, he had called the cleaning lady from a public phone to say he was back and that she need not come for a week. Best to keep her away.

The *quattro* was parked in a carport right next to the door. He unlocked it, dumped his bag in the back and climbed in. The powerful engine started instantly. He had reversed into the carport. Now, driving slowly out, he put his foot down as soon as the car's wheels hit the street. The *quattro* raised its nose and roared away. Gallagher switched on his lights as he swung into Holland Park Avenue, heading for Notting Hill. He was baulked by traffic lights, but decided against jumping them. There was always a patrol car somewhere waiting to pounce, especially at dead of night, when the streets were empty. He had no wish to waste time arguing with bored policemen before he'd even started his journey.

A glance in his mirror showed him a car creeping up behind him. It was the XR3. Now he knew.

The lights changed before the other car had got close, Gallagher booted the *quattro* off the line, swinging left into Pembridge Road. He was heading for the M1 and intended to lose the Ford long before he got there. He led the XR3 through the back streets of Notting Hill. On one occasion he had the jump on the lights, but the

Escort came through the red. By the time he'd made it to Kilburn, however, he'd lost it.

The *quattro* roared up the Edgware Road, heading for the motorway access. Gallagher kept a wary eye on his mirrors for eager patrol cars; but something else was occupying their attention for the night. He got to the M1, with still no sign of the Escort, and opened up. The Treser engine sang its joy and the *quattro* hurled itself along the glistening ribbon towards Nottingham. Gallagher held the wheel lightly as the dark shape flitted northwards in the gloom of the night.

He left the M1 at Loughborough, cut across to the A46 and continued northwards along the virtually straight, deserted road. Still no one appeared to be following him. He felt pleased with himself. Whoever his followers were, for the moment he was ahead of the game. He was not sure how long this would last. If Dalgleish did not want the Department to know of his whereabouts, the reasons must be very important, as important as only Dalgleish himself could know. Gallagher wondered what Dalgleish could possibly want of him; but uneasy as he felt, he had at least to hear what his former colleague and friend of his student days had to say. It was the least he could do.

The *quattro* tore along the A46 at 130 miles an hour. It sat solidly on the road, unfussed by its speed. Every so often, Gallagher's eyes flicked towards his mirrors. No sense in getting caught when so close to his destination. He came off the A46 near Newton, to head left on the A6097. At Lowdham he turned right, keeping to the directions the strange woman on the phone had given him. This took him on to the A612. By now he had dropped his speed to seventy. His mirrors were still clear of followers. The sparse traffic he had met on his journey had mainly been heavy trucks. Now and then, the odd car had excited his momentary interest; but he had passed them all, or they had been going the other way.

At Thurgarton he branched off to the right till he reached Goverton, where he took another road to the right. Soon he'd reached Bleasby. He drove through slowly, lights dimmed. From what he could see of the place, it appeared too big to be a village yet was far too small to be called a town. In moments, it seemed, he had reached its outskirts.

On a curve in the road to his left was a wooden, arched gateway. He turned into it. A gently sloping, unpaved drive led to a vast darkened shape a short distance ahead. He turned off the motor, allowing the *quattro* to roll quietly towards the building. The drive leveled out. The car slowed imperceptibly. Gallagher began putting gradual but firm pressure upon the now unpowered brakes. The car stopped quietly and without drama. He turned off the lights and waited.

His hand was on the key, ready for a fast start, should anything suspicious require it. Here he was in the Nottinghamshire night, waiting for a friend he had thought dead, having been directed to this place by a strange woman. The only reason he had not even now decided to start the car and get the hell out was the fact that no one but Dalgleish could have known about Tacitus; unless the KGB had somehow wrung such an inconsequential piece of information out of him, and Gallagher could not imagine any possible reason why they should have wanted to.

Nevertheless, he remained where he was, senses alert to every sound about him. The house was still in darkness. Before he had turned off the lights, the digital timer on the instrument panel had told him he'd arrived at four o'clock precisely.

A fine spray of rain began to fall, hissing gently on the car, Gallagher still did not move. He was quite certain no one had followed him; but that was no reason to suppose others were not already waiting for him; others who already knew of Dalgleish's whereabouts.

He glanced in the mirrors. No pinpoints of light starred their surfaces. Still he waited.

After a good fifteen minutes, he calculated, a light came on in the house. It was high up. Bedroom, perhaps. Some moments later a second light came on, this time at ground level. A door opened and, as Gallagher looked, a figure stood within the light that spilled out into the fine mist of the rainy night. A woman.

She came out into the rain. Walking towards the car her figure was distorted by the watery patterns on the car window. She rapped her knuckles on the glass. He turned the ignition key just far enough to get electrical power to lower the window.

She said, "Are you going to sit there all night?" It was the voice from the phone.

Now that she was more properly visible, Gallagher saw that she was hugging a raincoat about her. She did not wait for reply but turned and began walking back to the house. Once, she paused just long enough to look back at him.

With her back to the light when she had lowered her head to speak to him, he had seen the vague outlines of an interesting face with a head of abundant hair done up in a loose bun. She was a tall woman who walked with a fine dignity, despite the way she was dressed. The hem of a long dressing-gown played about her ankles as she hurried to get out of the rain.

So he had woken her up.

He raised the window, turned off the ignition, reached into the back for his bag, then climbed out of the *quattro*. He locked it and walked over, head bent against the rain, to where the woman was waiting for him in the doorway. The car chattered its locks home as the central locking system went to work.

She stood aside for him to enter, then shut and bolted the door.

She was, he guessed, about five-foot-nine, just four inches shorter than his own six-one. The plentiful hair was a rich fiery red. Her eyes, in the light, seemed a vivid blue; a blue-eyed redhead. She had a generous mouth with deeply-etched corners and a lower lip that seemed just slightly off-center. Her nose was sharp but the merest flare of the nostrils prevented it from being too finely pointed. High cheekbones, but it was a square sort of face, softened by the rounding off of the jawline. A beautiful face rather than a pretty one. She was about twenty-six, he guessed.

The blue eyes stared at him. "I'm Lucinda MacAusland. It was I who called you." She kept the coat wrapped about her.

"I know. I recognized your voice. I could have been anybody. You took a chance coming out like that."

She smiled, deepening the corners of her mouth even further. "I knew it would be you. No one else would have come at this time. Uffa said you tend to be unorthodox. He predicted you would get here at dead of night. I saw you arrive."

"You were waiting for me? Then why did you take so long to come down?"

"Why did you sit so long in the car?"

It was his turn to smile. "No answer to that. And where's Uffa?" he added.

"He's not here."

Gallagher stared at her. "Then why . . . ?"

"Surely you didn't think he'd remain in this area? I'm to send you on to where he is. We could hardly have risked telling you on the phone."

"We?"

"Uffa and I."

"And who else?"

"No one else."

Gallagher looked about him. They were in a wide hall. "You're alone in this place?"

"Oh, I'm quite safe. Usually my father and the staff are here but they're up at our other home at the moment. I live here because my work is in Nottingham. I only use part of the house, so it's quite easy, really."

Gallagher wondered about such a woman living in this great building alone, then admonished himself. It was no business of his. In the meantime, he remained alert.

"How do you know Uffa?"

The corner-deepening smile came on again. "We're cousins."

"Odd that Uffa never mentioned your existence in all the time I've known him."

"I didn't expect you to believe me. Uffa said I might have to convince you. Let's go into my study. We can sit and talk in comfort." She walked past him, expecting him to follow.

A gentle whiff of bed came from her as she passed. Obediently, he went after her, carrying his bag. She led him from the hall and into a short, narrow corridor. The study was at the end of it.

She opened the door for him to enter, smiled at his hesitation. "I'm not in your kind of business, you know. There are no people hidden in there waiting for you with guns."

"I'm a photographer," Gallagher said, almost sheepishly. "I do wish others would remember that."

"Once a Scout . . ." she said. Her eyes showed mischief.

Gallagher entered, making no comment.

She said, "I'll just get this coat off. Can I get you something? Coffee? Tea? I can make a swift sandwich if you're hungry."

Why not? he told himself silently. He was hungry. "Tea and toast?" he suggested.

"Done. Anything with the toast?"

"Just that, thanks."

She gave him another smile and left him to his devices. He watched her walk away. It was only then that he saw what the long dressing-gown had managed to hide. She was barefoot.

The study was smaller than he'd expected in such a large house, but there was a cosiness to it. It appeared to have more furniture than it needed, and in one corner was a splendid roll-top desk which had been kept in loving condition. It gleamed.

A private place, it was said, was a good indication of the workings of the person who used it. If such lightweight psychology could be given any credence, then Lucinda MacAusland was a neat, solitary person who liked her own private cosiness. Gallagher did not believe that for a second. People were far more complex. Arbitrary parameters within which they were supposed to operate were invariably unreliable. Armchair psychology was great for those who sat behind desks and dispensed it. In the field, it could get you killed.

The barefoot Lucinda did not fit the atmosphere in her study; and behind the somewhat spinsterish bun in her hair and the façade of neatness in the study, Gallagher decided, there was a woman of vibrant power and sexuality. Dalgleish, he reasoned, had found himself a woman he'd somehow managed to keep from the prying eyes of the Department; someone whom he would one day be able to use in a time of desperate need, in complete secrecy. A prudent move, long planned.

Lucinda was a lover even Kingston-Wyatt had not known about.

A vast chesterfield took up almost one entire side of the room. Gallagher sat down to wait. She was not long in returning, carrying with her a tray with the tea and toast. There was also a glass of hot milk. Removal of the raincoat had revealed a pale blue dressing-gown of indifferent style, done up to the neck. It was made of thick material and worn for warmth rather than show.

She pushed the door shut with a foot. "Do you mind if I put this on the floor? Easier than getting a table."

She didn't wait for his reply but placed the tray in front of the chesterfield, sat down next to him and began to pour. He watched the curve of her neck as she concentrated on the tea. The smell of bed came faintly to him once more. Her feet were still bare. After the wet outside, she had washed or wiped them clean. She had nice toes.

She glanced up to him then, smiled at his scrutiny.

"I could have been anyone," he said, repeating his earlier caution. "Inviting me in at this time of the night was taking a chance." Now that he'd made up his mind that she was Dalgleish's lover, he felt less suspicious of her; but he did not relax his guard.

She handed him his cup. "It was no chance. Uffa described you well enough." One corner of the mouth deepened briefly. "I would hardly think Uffa knows of another like you in his kind of business."

Gallagher wondered how Dalgleish had described him and what Lucinda's reaction had been.

"I suppose not," he said, watching her above the rim of the cup.

She picked up her milk, curled herself into the far corner of the chesterfield and tucked her feet beneath the folds of her dressing-gown, which effectively hid her body, but not so well that Gallagher could not imagine what was beneath. There was, however, no lust in his mind. He was observing her, waiting to hear the explanation for her place in the scheme of things.

She took a sip of her milk. The blue eyes looked at him frankly.

"You're wondering," she began, "whether I'm really Uffa's cousin. You think I am probably someone he sleeps with. A spinsterish country girl, conveniently away from the mainstream of his life."

"You're very direct. And I don't think you're spinsterish at all."

"The MacAuslands have always been direct." The obvious pride in her voice brought forth an overlying hint of a Scots accent that was very attractive. "Neither Uffa nor I knew we were cousins," she went on, "until about three years ago. Our family history is like many in Scotland. Ancient animosities had split ours and the branches grew apart. I will not deny that when we first met we were attracted to each other. We met at a party. We talked about ourselves and our families, although naturally Uffa said nothing about his real job. During our chat that evening we began to realize we were actually related. It stopped us going to bed, which was a shame, because Uffa was the only man there worth considering." She drank some of her milk, smiled at him. "Shocked?"

"Why should I be? Stranger things have happened. People have gone to bed together only to wake up in the morning and find themselves brother and sister."

"You can understand our astonishment." She seemed pleased he had taken it that way. "We're related on my mother's side. She was not a Dalgleish but her mother was. Married wrongly, and totally cut off, in every way. Uffa is the first contact the two branches have had since that time. He said we should keep it our secret. I went along, thinking it rather amusing but not understanding why. Now, of course, I know."

"You seem to have taken it quite calmly."

"I've had three weeks to settle down. Uffa and I kept in touch, of course. He came here a few times and was introduced to my father as a friend. The name did not cause any particular ripple, since my mother had never really discussed that side of the family with my father. She'd died when I was quite young and my father remarried some years later. I rather enjoyed our little game.

"Then suddenly, no Uffa. A complete silence for over two years; then one night he reappears, looking as if the entire world were on his heels."

"It might as well be," Gallagher said grimly.

"He would not tell me much; only that he

was in great danger, and that I must contact you at all costs. He gave me the message which he said you'd recognize as being specifically from him. I tried several times but got only your machine. I assumed you were away."

Nodding, Gallagher found he had eaten all his toast. "I was. I called the machine from time to time and got some clicks on the tape."

"Some of those were certainly mine. I hate talking to machines. Uffa said that I should never make two calls from the same area, and that if I got you, I should give you at least half an hour to get to a public phone. He knows you well."

"He knows how to survive well. I'd have done exactly the same."

She smiled suddenly. "Thanks for saying I'm not spinsterish."

He'd thought she had chosen to ignore that. "I spoke the truth. And where is he now?"

"On Skye."

"*Skye?* Jesus! Why up there?"

She shrugged. "He says it's important, and also the safest place at the moment."

"I agree with that part at least." Skye. The Department would never think of looking there. Clever Dalgleish. "I take it I'm supposed to meet him there?"

"Yes."

"Well, I've dodged people to get here. I can dodge them up to Skye."

Her eyes widened in alarm. "You were followed?"

"Very briefly. I lost them in London."

The alarm subsided, but there was still anxiety. "But if they know. . . ."

"They know nothing. I was being watched out of habit. It gets like that these days. In a way it helps. You expect to be watched, so you always assume it and act accordingly." He did not mention the Mercedes or the Escort. No need to frighten her needlessly. She was vulnerable enough as it was.

"I thought this only happened in other countries."

"It's a nice thought but not very realistic, I'm afraid."

"It makes one wonder."

"About what?"

She didn't say. Instead, she passed on the instructions Dalgleish had given for making the rendezvous on Skye. As he listened, he wondered whether Dalgleish was really there. But he had to find out. At the back of his mind was the constant feeling that Dalgleish would have done the same for him.

Thinking of his loyalty to Dalgleish made him remember O'Keefe, another person from another time whom loyalty had eventually killed. O'Keefe had been an RAF Warrant Officer who had physically trained Gallagher and had subsequently accompanied him on many missions abroad. Loyal O'Keefe had died when Gallagher's gun had jammed during a fierce gun battle. O'Keefe had been quick enough to save Gallagher's life but not his own, on the borders of an African state. The death still haunted Gallagher. Sometimes, during moments of intense battle stress, O'Keefe's dictums would come to him.

When Lucinda had finished, Gallagher said, "I'll leave later today, about four o'clock. It will be getting dark by then. Best time to start."

"Less chance of being seen?"

"Exactly. But don't worry. No one knows of your connection with Uffa, except the three of us. Did your father see him when he came?"

She shook her head. The red hair seemed to catch fire in the light. "No."

"Good! As I said, don't worry." But he was worried. "Is there somewhere out of sight I can put the car?" He should have done that at the beginning. "Best not to take chances."

She nodded and stood up. The movement was graceful. "I'll show you. I've also prepared a room."

He stood up, looking at her. "Why are you doing so much for him? It can't be just because he's your long-lost cousin."

The blue eyes were steady on his. "Perhaps it's because I know what it feels like to be very much on your own. When my mother died. . . ." She stopped, unwilling to continue.

Gallagher could imagine it. Mother dying, father retreating, eventually to marry again. Little girl left to grow up by herself. It explained, in part, the study.

"It's all right," he said. "I think I understand."

"Thank you." Softly said.

When he went out again, he checked the car, although there was no need to. She watched him from the doorway. It was now 5 a.m. The hour had fled. He drove the *quattro* into a wide garage that was empty. It had a concertina door which he pulled shut before hurrying back into the house.

She showed him into a large bedroom with a low, comfortable-looking bed. "Sleep well. Breakfast?"

"More like lunch," he said. "A late one at that."

She smiled. "There's plenty of food. Goodnight." She almost giggled. "Perhaps I should say good morning."

"Perhaps."

They stared at each other, then she said again, softly, "Goodnight."

" 'Night," he said, as the door closed. He stared at it for a long time, before removing his clothes and climbing into bed.

He was still looking at it when he fell asleep.

9:30 a.m. in Moscow. General-Major Dmitry Vasil'evich Ulvanov of the KGB looked at his opposite number, General-Major Vladimir Mikhailovich Skoryatin of the GRU. Both men were in civilian clothes. Ulvanov's almost rough-cut double-breasted suit contrasted sharply with Skoryatin's sleek, Western-style single-breasted affair. The two could not have been more physically different. The KGB man was squat, bullish. Skoryatin's sleekness was almost effete by comparison; but that was illusion. Both were big men, and few would put bets on who was the most dangerous.

"It was kind of you to come in so early, Comrade," Ulvanov said. "A warm bed is infinitely preferable to a journey in the cold, even by staff car."

Outside, Moscow froze at minus twelve degrees. Skoryatin was not fooled by the pleasantry. Nothing would have kept him away, and Ulvanov knew it.

"I know you like English tea," Ulvanov went on, "so I have had some prepared."

This Skoryatin read as another oblique reference to his previous trips to the West, before he had reached the rank of general. He had once been a highly successful operative in the field, and a member of the Spetsnaz. Some quarters liked to believe he had picked up a few Western tastes rather too eagerly.

"It is kind of you to consider my simple pleasures, Comrade," he said.

The ritual sparring over, they relaxed. Ulvanov poured the tea out of a silver samovar, passed it to Skoryatin and poured a cup for himself.

They were in neutral territory. The small conference room was neither KGB nor GRU property. Not that it mattered: the KGB could commandeer anything it wanted. Skoryatin would not have been surprised to find it bugged. Equally, he knew, Ulvanov would have the same distrust of the GRU. At the start of the operation they had tacitly agreed to their joint meetings on neutral ground; but each had his troop of security men waiting outside. Each would know if the other mounted a bugging operation. Skoryatin had long reached the conclusion that the room was clean, if only because of that; but he was not complacent.

The conference table was long and bare, save for the tea. Neither had brought papers with them. They never did. They sat in the middle of the long table, opposite each other, eyes never wavering. Nature had played a curious trick on them. Ulvanov's heavy face was graced by delicate eyebrows, while the sartorially elegant Skoryatin, against all expectations, sported bushy brows that matched his dark hair.

Ulvanov said, "I am very pleased indeed with the Tu-22P flights. The crew perform well, and the reports from Greece and Spain confirm your predictions. We should work together more often, Vladimir Mikhailovich."

The good-natured familiar use of his name did nothing to dispel Skoryatin's healthy distrust of the KGB man, but he played the game.

"I thank you for your good words, Dmitry Vasil'evich. As for working together, that is of course dependent upon circumstances."

Ulvanov briefly lowered his head graciously. "Naturally, I accept the proviso. However, we have a more pressing problem to solve."

And here it comes, Skoryatin thought drily.

"The Englishman Dalgleish," Ulvanov continued.

"Scots." Skoryatin could not resist it.

"What?"

"I believe he is Scottish. The Scots hate being called English."

Ulvanov regarded the GRU man balefully.

"Do you laugh secretly at me, Vladimir Mikhailovich?"

Skoryatin took the level higher. "I was being precise, Comrade."

Ulvanov paused, seeming to give way. "Very well. Let us call him British. You have no objection?"

"None at all," Skoryatin said mildly.

"Very well. Dalgleish appears to have evaded the British quite successfully so far, *and* your Spetsnaz. The British, for their own reasons, have withheld the fact that the two he killed were GRU."

"Equally," Skoryatin said, still mildly, "the British have not had any information from him. Your disinformation has obviously worked." No harm in a little judicious back-patting.

"We have still not been able to find those responsible for getting him in, and for engineering his subsequent escape."

"I do hope, Comrade, I do not detect a note of accusation." Skoryatin smiled.

Ulvanov, no fool, knew that when the GRU man smiled he was at his most dangerous. Ulvanov had no intention of being trapped into making a false accusation.

"I assure you not, Comrade. Your men are out there, bearing the brunt of the action and gathering most important information. I merely wish to stress the need to find the culprits swiftly."

Skoryatin stood up. "Then we are in accord, Comrade. Thank you for the tea." He went out, smiling.

Ulvanov was quietly furious. He knew he had lost the engagement.

Midday in London, Fowler studied the reports that had been brought to him. Gallagher had vanished after having given the Branch a quick tour of north London. Kingston-Wyatt was gone too, truly for good. A quiet morning burial was what his wife had wanted. No fuss. Fowler felt briefly saddened that Gallagher had not been there. Gallagher had been Kingston-Wyatt's protégé. Pity about the death of his girl.

Fowler pursed his lips. He had sent the contrite Branch man back to his own patch. There were other ways of handling this. He did not tell Winterbourne, who was hoping to play a round of golf. Fowler cheerfully wished him a waterlogged course. Winterbourne had not come in but had gone straight to the club from the funeral.

"Call me if needed, Fowler."

Not even for World War Three, Fowler thought nastily.

He put the report on Gallagher to one side, picked up another, this time about a sudden and inexplicable failure of communications and military radar in Greece, ominously similar to the report he'd also had about the one in Spain.

Fowler pondered. Was this the secret weapon the Windshear Group had hinted at? If so, how had it been placed? What and where was it? Nothing had been found, despite thorough searches of the affected area. To be able to "blind" all radars and jam all communications at will was a potent enough advantage; but something told Fowler that was not all there was to it. There was more to come. Dalgleish had the key.

Dalgleish had to be found.

Gallagher finished the quite lavish meal Lucinda had prepared for him. He had eaten enough to last him the long journey to Kyle of Lochalsh in the western highlands of Scotland, the jumping-off point for Skye.

She had astonished him when he had awoken at about two in the afternoon by walking into his room dressed in tight jeans and a sweater. Her legs appeared to go on for ever, and her hair, brushed loosely about her face, was a fiery cascade.

"You're dangerous looking like that," he'd said to her. "Do you know that?"

She'd been barefoot too. She still was.

She had smiled with pleasure, telling him that lunch would be ready in half an hour.

Now, as he finished, she passed him what looked like a binoculars case; but the shape was markedly different. It was a binocular camera. She also handed him a thick sweater.

"What are these for?"

"Uffa said to give them to you. You might need them, he thought."

Gallagher said, "I've got a camera with me; but I'll keep the sweater.

"This might be more practical, and you won't have to change lenses all the time. Have a look. They're very powerful glasses, with night lenses."

Gallagher opened the case and pulled the

massive thing out. It was Russian. He stared at her. "He brought that across?"

She nodded.

"Did he have exposed film?"

Again, she nodded. "But he's got it with him on Skye."

No wonder the GRU were after him. "Did he say why he thought I might need this?" Gallagher put the binocular camera back in its case.

"No. But I expect he has a good reason."

"All right. I'll take it with me." Gallagher glanced at the wall clock in the classically furnished dining-room. "Nearly four. Time I was going." He stood up. "I don't like leaving you here all by yourself; not while this thing is going on. Aren't there friends you could go to until it's all over?

She stood to join him. "Don't worry about me. I've lived here long enough. The house and I are friends." She smiled, tucking her hands in the pockets of her jeans. They barely made it.

He looked at her, enjoying the moment. "Thank you for the bed and the good food. I suppose, since you won't take my advice, I can but hope that you'll be careful."

"I'll be careful," she promised. "MacAuslands always are."

"The MacAuslands always seem to have the answers."

The corners of her mouth deepened. "Sometimes they do. Both of you be careful up there," she added softly. The blue eyes seemed larger somehow.

He smiled back at her. "Gallaghers always

are, and I'm sure the Dalgleishs are too." He hoped.

She walked with him to the door and opened it. Heavy cloud had brought the darkness early and it was raining.

Gallagher looked out at the gloom. "Lovely. Just my kind of weather." If anyone chose to follow him north, an isolation switch in the car would turn off all rear lights, even indicators, while leaving the front fully operative. Translucent black coating on all the rear lenses and even on the full-width rear reflector strip ensured that, with the lights out, a shadower would see nothing up ahead.

He turned, sticking out his hand. "Thanks again."

The hand she gave him was soft yet strong, and warm. "It would be nice to see you again."

"I'd like that."

They both knew why.

He went out into the night to the garage and slid the door open. He had already checked the *quattro*. Now it waited for him, a dark shape that emanated power, even in repose. He unlocked it, put his bag and the big camera in the back and climbed in.

The engine roared deeply into life at the first turn of the key. Gallagher switched on the lights, reversed slowly out and pointed the nose towards the drive. He looked to where Lucinda was standing in the doorway. She seemed dwarfed by the huge house, a tiny creature in its open maw.

She didn't wave as he drove slowly away, the wheels crunching on the unpaved drive. He

eased the *quattro* on to the road, drove back
through Bleasby, heading across country towards the M1 motorway that would take him
north.

As the car thrust itself along the darkened
Nottinghamshire back roads, Gallagher suddenly remembered that Kingston-Wyatt had
been buried during the day. The rain spraying
towards the windshield from the darkness
seemed a fitting elegy. Hell of a way to go.

Momentarily, he felt a twinge of sadness
for the man he had once respected so highly, it
had been dangerously close to hero-worship.

It was six o'clock in London. She walked briskly
towards the steps, fumbling in her handbag for
the keys to her flat. She paused, wondering
whether he was back; she decided to look. Instead of going up the short flight to her door she
bypassed the steps, heading for the side of the
building where Gallagher usually parked his
car.

The carport was empty, but there appeared
to be someone at his door. She couldn't see
clearly. Perhaps he was on his way out and had
left the car in the street.

"Mr. Gallagher?" Hesitantly.

The figure jerked erect as if startled.
Frowning, she went forward.

"Mr. Gallagher?" Then realization dawned.
"You're not . . . ! Who are you and what do you
think you're doing?" she shouted.

She never saw the blow coming. It was
delivered by another man striking from behind.
The edge of a savagely slashing hand struck her

just beneath the jawbone, shattering it and sending slivers of bone into her brain. She fell without a sound.

The men ran silently off, leaving her where she had fallen, after deliberately scattering the contents of her purse.

The report on the incident arrived on Fowler's desk two hours later. He read it twice, forcing under control the anger he felt rising within him. He then contacted Winterbourne at home, choosing his words carefully so as not to be later accused of insubordination, yet leaving his superior in no doubt that he should come at once to the office.

Winterbourne arrived forty-five minutes later in a state of high dudgeon. He was in formal evening wear, braid and medals included. He stomped into Fowler's office.

"Dammit, Fowler!" were his first words. "I was on my way to an important function! I do hope you've got sufficient reason for this! We don't all like to live here as you do, you know!"

Fowler walked over to him, wordlessly handed him the report and stood back to watch his face. Everything relevant was on the single page.

Winterbourne's hand shook slightly as he read, his face paling. Finally, he forced himself to look up at Fowler, his eyes seeming to pop.

"They over-reacted! A quiet break-in. That was all!"

Fowler's glacial silence was more damning than the choice words he could feel forming in his mind. Winterbourne's stupidity had brought unpleasant and possibly damaging dimensions to the entire operation.

"They were ordered to be careful!" Winterbourne continued. "They were ordered!"

"They killed an innocent bystander, Sir John," Fowler at last said with barely disguised contempt. "People heard her initial shout and called the police. The straight boys were all over the place by the time we got someone down there. It will be in the papers tomorrow."

"Then they must be given a story; a plausible one."

"I have already seen to it." Fowler's contempt was even more in the open. He was not worried about what Winterbourne might try to do to him. Winterbourne had blundered quite seriously and would not be let off the hook easily. "You used those men without my knowledge, Sir John, I do not have to remind you that I expressly opposed the use of outside help—"

"Yes, yes, Fowler! You have repeated yourself *ad nauseam* about it!"

"This is a very carefully set up operation," Fowler went on with icy calm. "Years of planning. You, Sir John, with respect, have only recently taken over command of the Department. It is natural to expect that there would be several operations running with which you would not as yet be fully acquainted. Such thorough knowledge is bound to take time. It would therefore help if you gave me your co-operation, considering that at this juncture I am more familiar with the details than you are. I am the executive officer of this department. It is my job to be in control of all aspects of operations which are the responsibility of the Department."

Winterbourne said nothing for a full minute. He had been given a roasting as if he were a mere junior sub on his first ship, by a man who was his subordinate. Yet it had been done in such a way that no disciplinary offense could justifiably be taken. It infuriated him even further.

Watching him, Fowler knew precisely what was going on in Winterbourne's mind. Winterbourne would come back at him, he knew.

At last Winterbourne said, stiffly, "Your point has been well taken, Fowler; but do remember at all times that I am the senior officer here. My predecessor shot himself, for reasons that we are still unaware of. You would do well to address your noted diligence to that fact, as it may well have serious bearings upon the very operation which you hold in such jealous regard. Now I must leave for my function. I shall be forced to make excuses," he finished petulantly.

Fowler watched him go. There had not been a single expression of regret at the untimely death of the unfortunate woman. Fowler stared at the offending report that Winterbourne had returned to him.

He wanted to tear it to pieces.

Gallagher made it to Kyle of Lochalsh, with one stop for gas, just after ten o'clock. He had pushed the *quattro,* giving it its head, the increased power of its modified engine enabling it to treat the miles with disdain.

Traffic had been practically non-existent, and no one had followed him; no Mercedes coupés, no Rovers, and no Escorts. He hoped they were all still looking for him in London. He had not seen a single patrol car which, all things considered, was good news. He had enjoyed the solitude of the long drive, feeding cassettes into the stereo, part of his mind tuning itself to the swirl of the music coming from the four speakers as he hurtled northwards into the night. The other part had remained sharply alert, wary, hunting like radar for the unexpected.

But there had been no hostiles. His only follower had been the rain which, at last, he had left in Glasgow. From the moment the A87 had hugged the coast on coming out of Glen Shiel, the smell of the sea in the waters of Loch Duich and Loch Alsh had come to him, bringing a strange excitement with it. He had driven along the edge of the darkened waters, feeling as if he were entering an eerie, enchanted land. Now, as he pulled up before the hotel that Dalgleish had named in his instructions to Lucinda, there was no rain, though the road was still wet.

Gallagher turned off the lights, shut down the motor and stayed where he was for some moments. Lights were still on at the front of the building. Three parked cars had appeared in the headlights as he'd swung into the forecourt. None was any of the cars that had been following him. There was an Escort, but it was not an XR3.

He remained· in his seat as the car hummed, clicked and whirred softly as it wound down from its high-speed dash. No car came hurrying up to the hotel.

At last, satisfied, he got out, reached for his bag, locked the car. There was a gentle, cold breeze and the smell of the sea was stronger. Now he could see its dark surface separating him from the lights of Kyleakin.

From what he could see of it, the hotel was smallish, more like a large private house which it undoubtedly had been before its present incarnation. He walked slowly towards it, still alert. No one came at him.

He entered. A pretty, slim girl was at the reception desk. She smiled a welcome.

"Good evening," he began. "I'd like a room, please."

The smile was even more welcoming. "Ah. You must be the gentleman." Her Ross-shire accent was strong.

He would have found the modulation of her voice pleasing had her words not made his insides tighten. He kept his expression calm. "I am?" Someone looking for him? *Here?*

But she said, "You're Mr. Thompson, aren't you? From Nottingham. The young lady, Miss MacAusland, rang earlier to tell us to expect you."

Jesus. Lucinda. She might as well have broadcast it.

Then Gallagher paused. She had given him a false name. She had obviously reasoned that for him to arrive unannounced at this hotel might excite undue interest. People always viewed strangers with curiosity, especially if they turned up at night. A reservation would help temper such curiosity. Less chance of gossip, particularly to police patrols.

It had not been a bad idea, Gallagher decided. He felt sure Dalgleish had put her up to it. Still, it had been a risk, and that did not make him feel happy. He wondered why Dalgleish had done it.

"Yes," Gallagher said, "I'm Thompson." He hoped she wouldn't ask for proof. He wasn't too bothered about credit cards and the like. He'd intended to pay for everything in cash, anyway. This was just a quick trip.

He signed himself K. Lee Thompson, permitting himself a private smile. The receptionist read the name silently.

She looked at him interestedly. "American, are you, sir?"

Which, Gallagher thought, was quite an amusing way to describe a man who was London-born and the son of a Jamaican mother of half-Scottish parentage and a Christ Church Irishman from County Clare. The feeling of amusement left him as he remembered the deaths of both parents. Mother dying of illness, leaving a shattered, loving husband who years later had in turn been blown up in his own car in Oxford a short distance from his beloved college, by the same people who had killed Lauren Tanner, Gallagher had taken his own revenge for that too. Thinking of it brought the hate he had felt rushing back. He fought it down. That part of his life was over. Nothing of the past mattered now. He did not allow his feelings to show.

He smiled at her. "I'm a Londoner, but my mother was American." What the hell. Jamaica was nearer the States than the U.K., so it was only a small lie.

"That must be it." She looked pleased. Being half-right was better than being totally wrong. "Would you like a bite to eat, Mr. Thompson? You'll just about make it before we close down for the night."

"Yes, please. It's been a long drive."

"Fine. If you'll go through there—" she showed him—"someone will come to you." She handed him a key with a number tag. "Your room. It's got a fine view of Skye."

"Thank you." He wanted to get on. She'd soon be asking questions he did not want to answer. "Well, I'd better go in, or I'll be too late."

"Yes. Of course, Mr. Thompson. Oh . . . would you like the papers in the morning?"

Why not? Might as well play the role to the hilt. "Yes, please," Gallagher said. *"Times* and *Observer?"*

"Right you are, Mr. Thompson."

Her eyes followed him out. At least she hadn't asked for proof.

Sunday

Gallagher awoke early. Some hotels ap-peared to pitch the breakfast period at dawn. Probably hoping, he thought wryly, that the guests would be too lazy or worn out to make it. But breakfast at his hotel sensibly commenced at eight; by which time he'd be fully prepared for the day. He intended to have a full meal and to take his time about it.

He'd had a good sleep in the surprisingly comfortable bed, though his senses had remained alert for intruders. No one had disturbed the stillness of his room. Having had a quick shower, he got dressed, then stared out of the single large window. The "fine view of Skye," a mere kilometer away across the narrow Kyleakin, or Strait of Haco—as Lucinda had told him it meant—was hidden by a fine mist of rain. Haco, an ancient Norse king, had sailed through the strait with a vast fleet to do battle in the south. He had not counted on the weather. A storm had mauled him, leaving his decimated fleet to the mercy of his enemies.

Gallagher turned away from the window. He was quite happy with the weather. He didn't know what the roads of Skye were like but the rain would give their surfaces just the kind of environment the *quattro* would thrive in if he had to outrun any followers.

He glanced about him. The room was quite spacious, reinforcing his belief that this was a converted private house. The carpeting was of a higher standard than would have been expected in such a place, and the items of furniture were not warehouse stock. He'd asked for a double room. He liked space about him. Easier to move when trying to stop someone from killing you.

He studied the door. It wouldn't stop a determined child. He decided to take his bag with him. No point leaving anything for someone curious enough to poke an enquiring nose into.

He put his key on the reception desk as he went down to breakfast. The same girl was there, looking bright and chirpy.

She stared at his bag, then looked up at him. "Good morning, Mr. Thompson. Are you leaving us?"

"Good morning. Leaving? Oh, I see. No. I'm going to do some location photography. My cameras," indicating the bag.

She brightened. "Oh . . . you're a photographer! You'll not find a better place. It's the best in the world. Even if I say so myself." She pointed to the key. "No need to hand it in."

"I'd rather. In case I lose it."

"All right, Mr. Thompson. Have you picked anywhere in particular?"

"I was thinking of just driving around until I find something worth taking."

She was sizing him up. "You'll be spoilt for choice up here. You won't know where to start. There's Eilean Donan castle near Dornie. It's out in the loch. People always go there. Very popular; and, of course, if you prefer to go across the water, there's all of Skye itself."

Gallagher smiled at her. "I'll take note of your advice. But I'm looking something really special."

"We're all special up here." Her eyes dared him.

"Hm," he said and went in to breakfast. If anyone came to question her about his whereabouts, it would look as if she'd suggested where he should go.

He hoped.

Gallagher drove down to the little port. The wide car-park reached to the water's edge, and tethered midway along it, ramp down, was what looked like a mini aircraft-carrier. The first ferry of the day. It was nearly ten o'clock, and there were just three cars on the flat, open deck. Along the full length of one side, a narrow superstructure ran, with the wheelhouse sticking out of it like a control tower.

Gallagher eased the *quattro* up the ramp and on to the deck. He stopped behind a white Volvo with Finnish plates. He wondered why Finns would come to Skye in November. From what he could see of the Volvo's passengers, they appeared to be a family; hardly a chase group. He put them out of his mind. Beyond the

Volvo, he could just about see a big red motorcycle on its stand. It looked like a fancy Japanese job. He saw no one near it.

The rain had become heavier, and Skye was still hidden by the mist that had now come right down to the water. A man in oilskins came up to the *quattro* to collect the fare. Gallagher lowered the window.

"Are there many sailings today?" Gallagher asked as he paid. "I'll be going back across."

"Oh, yes, sir," the man answered. He seemed unperturbed by the rain. "Frequent sailings; but today, the last trip from Kyleakin's half-past five. Mind that you make it, or it will be the island for you till tomorrow." He was friendly and gave a quick smile. "I would not worry. Plenty of places to stay on Skye."

"I see. Thank you."

The man nodded and went off to see to another car that had just come on.

Gallagher pressed the switch to raise the window as he stared in his mirror at the oncoming car. It was not one he recognized as having followed him. As it drew closer, he saw a middle-aged couple in it. He relaxed, staring out at the mist.

Then the ramp was raised and soon the ferry was pulling away on its five-minute journey across the Strait of Haco. The mist was immediately upon it. The unwelcome thought came into Gallagher's mind that he was being ferried across the Styx. He grimaced at the morbid thought.

Suddenly there was no more mist; no more

rain. Disbelievingly, he stared at the brilliantly sunlit island, its stunning peaks seeming black and ocher with the distance, and appearing to gleam wetly.

The mountains of the moon, he heard himself say in his mind.

He turned to look behind him. The mist now hid Kyle of Lochalsh. It was as if the ferry had taken him through some kind of elemental gate. He wondered if he were the only person to notice.

But no. The people in the car behind were looking back too, and when he had looked round again, he saw that the family of Finns were gaping.

The friendly crewman was at his window again.

Gallagher lowered it. "Does this always happen?"

"I saw you looking," the man said. "No. Not quite like this. You must have brought it with you." He smiled.

He looked about fifty, small and wiry with a skin polished leathery-smooth by the winds of countless crossings. There was a lilt in his voice that was not Scottish yet held a hint of Scotland. Gallagher assumed he was an islander.

The man was admiring the *quattro.* "Never seen one like this before. It's a fine car. Very fine." He seemed to want to talk.

"Thank you."

"Meeting some people, are you? This not being the holiday season."

"Oh, no," Gallagher began easily. "I'm not

meeting anybody. I'm a photographer. This time of the year is perfect for what I want."

"Oh, well. You've come to the right place; but you'll be needing more than a day to do justice to it."

"From what I can see, I would say years."

The wiry man seemed pleased by this. "I'm sixty-two and, save for the War, I have never been away from Skye. Never will again." It was said with love. "Well. We're nearly there. Got to see to the boat. Good day to you, sir. Hope you find what you want."

"Good day," Gallagher said and watched him move forward.

Thinking about their conversation, Gallagher decided there had been nothing in it. The boatman had merely wanted a chat because of the car; which wasn't so good if anyone spoke to him later. He'd remember the *quattro*.

Not that it would really matter, Gallagher felt. By the time anyone had worked out enough to make it to Skye, he expected to be long gone. He'd meet Dalgleish, listen to what his exuniversity friend had to say, then make a quick exit. That would be all. He'd help if he could, but within certain limits.

The ferry eased itself up to the concrete shore of its terminus and dropped its ramp. The cars began to move off.

Gallagher watched each one. Nothing to worry about. The motorcycle remained where it was, parked close in to the superstructure. The narrow superstructure was itself made up of two decks, the lower of which was enclosed, while the upper, out of which sprouted the wheelhouse, was open to the elements, with a surrounding guardrail. Metal steps led up to it. A few people had been sitting there admiring the view. Now they began making their way down to the car deck. None of them approached the motorcycle.

Probably someone waiting to collect it, Gallagher thought as he drove the *quattro* down the ramp and up the concrete slope. The friendly boatman gave him a wave. Gallagher raised a hand in acknowledgement, but his mind was already concentrating on the directions Lucinda had given him for the rendezvous with Dalgleish.

The stark basaltic beauty of the hills and peaks made him catch his breath as he drove away from Kyleakin. Lucinda had warned him about what to expect, but he was none the less totally unprepared for what he saw. It was a strange scenery, belonging completely to another world.

He cruised the *quattro,* enjoying the feel of the car in this unreal land. Perhaps there was nothing especially fantastic about it, he told himself. Perhaps the mist the ferry had sailed through had seduced his mind. But he did not believe that. The seduction was being carried out by the island itself.

Following Lucinda's instructions, Gallagher drove on through Broadford, heading for the north of the island, identifying the landmarks she had given him. At the head of Loch Ainort, the A850 began to climb and he saw, to his left, the imposing black and red mass of the Cuillins. At least he was on the right track.

He stopped briefly in Portree to fill up with gas, then took the A855 out of the little painted capital, heading further north into the unearthly peninsula of Trotternish. Here, Skye began to play with him.

The bright sunshine that had accompanied him since Kyleakin suddenly gave way on a gentle bend to a swirling mist that cut visibility almost to a hundred meters, about five kilometers or so out of Portree. As he drove on, eerie columns and cliffs played hide-and-seek in the mist until, just on a right-hand bend, he saw his next point of reference.

For a brief second, to his left, he saw in brilliant sunshine a good two kilometers away the 150-foot-tall column of basalt that was the Old Man of Storr. Centuries of demonic erosion by Nature in all her savage fury had shaped it into a precariously balancing cone. Then, as suddenly as he had come, the Old Man was gone. There was only the road, and the mist; and the low growl of the *quattro,* and the hiss of its wheels. Gallagher wondered whether he'd actually seen the column. It had been like a mirage.

He drove on to Staffin. Now and then, he passed the scatter of isolated communities, pretty dolls' houses pockmarking the emptiness of the bracken-strewn landscape. He saw a pink one squatting in solitary splendor, stared at it in his mirror as he drove past. He took the opportunity to check for shadows. No one on the road behind him. No one in front. The mist closed in, accentuating the feeling of unworldliness. He cruised cautiously. Imagine coming all this way just to hit a wandering sheep.

But no sheep strayed in his path. He drove through Staffin and about two and a half kilometers later, at Brogaig, he turned left on to the narrow, twisting old road to Uig on the west coast of the peninsula.

He was not going to Uig. The narrow road climbed in the mist, taking him into the haunting landscape of the Quiraing. The mist prevented him from seeing the great slabs of ancient rock squeezed from the bowels of the earth millions of years before, to form the awesome battlement that had been chiseled and carved into bizarre shapes; that had had secret passages channeled into them; that had in places been polished smooth by demented winds and, in others, scoured and pitted by nature's sculptors.

Gallagher saw none of this as the mist closed in and the road continued to climb. He put the wipers on intermittent. The road was too narrow for two cars to pass each other safely, but here and there rough spaces at the verge denoted passing areas.

He glanced in his mirrors. Nothing. He'd had his lights on for some time now. He wondered if a follower would bother. Unless whoever it was knew the road well, Gallagher decided he would. No lights meant no shadow. He did not relax his guard, but neither was he unduly worried. He'd not used the stereo at all, enjoying listening to the car as he drove. It gave him a feeling of peace in the enclosing mist.

Suddenly, on a left-hand sweeping bend

that took the road to the foot of a towering escarpment, the mist vanished before him, and the *quattro,* like some gleaming creature emerging from a cocoon, entered bright sunshine. Gallagher felt as if he had come through another gate, and the sight of the Quiraing range, a twisting spine of surreal shapes that marched southwards, made him gape momentarily.

But that was not all. The road was beginning to curve tightly back on itself on the very edge of the spine and appeared to have fallen over the lip of the world and out of sight. It was like coming to the end of bridge when you're only half-way across it. A very tight 1:7 climbing turn to the left followed; then the illusion ended as he breasted the rise.

But a new illusion had taken its place.

Gallagher pulled off the road to the left, where there was enough room for about three cars, and stopped. He climbed out as the car whirred to itself, and gazed about him in wonder. He was parked on the very peak of the range of hills and stretching before him to westward, limitlessly it seemed, was a rolling surface of dazzling white. He was above the clouds. It was almost like flying; except he was not in an airplane but standing still, transfixed.

In the distance, the higher peaks poked out of the soft billows like dark, mysterious islands. It was as if half of Skye had disappeared. The air was still and, he felt, at least ten degrees warmer. Further west, the Isle of Lewis was nowhere to be seen in the whiteness. Nothing showed beneath the all-enveloping blanket.

I could stay here for ever, he thought. The clouds looked solid enough to walk on.

"Beautiful, isn't it?" someone called.

Gallagher whirled. The faint voice had come from behind and to his right. A track led steeply up along the spine towards the Quiraing itself. A man was standing a good two hundred meters up, and perhaps another three hundred meters or so away, his bulky form indistinguishable in the distance. Some distance to the right from where Gallagher was standing, a lone wooden bench stood vigil at the edge of a precipice.

Gallagher did not move. He could not tell whether the man carried a rifle. He waited. If the stranger had wanted to kill him, he could have done so with ease.

Gallagher felt a slight chagrin. He had allowed nature to enchant him; dangerously.

The man began to descend as Gallagher continued to watch, his entire being now on full alert. As the man came nearer, Gallagher realized that his bulkiness was due to the clothes he wore; padded and camouflaged garb that blended perfectly with the scenery. Every now and then, the man would seem to disappear completely, even to Gallagher's trained eye. Marvelling at the man's effortless use of virtually non-existent cover, he knew it to be Dalgleish.

Incongruously, Gallagher suddenly remembered that he had not picked up his newspapers.

He watched Dalgleish's downward progress. A path went steeply up along the crest of

the ridge; but Dalgleish ignored it, making his
way down its side with all the swift confidence
of a mountain goat, never exposing himself for
long. It was almost as if Dalgleish was expecting
someone to take a potshot at him.

As he watched, Gallagher remembered
how they had met up again after university.
Like many friendships born in academic insti-
tutions, theirs had drifted apart until they had
eventually ceased to get in touch with each
other; then one day, they had met again on a
special training course.

Gallagher had been stunned to find Dalgleish in the Air Force. Dalgleish, however, was
not a pilot; not even aircrew. Dalgleish, to Gallagher's consternation, had joined the RAF
Regiment, the Air Force's Infantry—then un-
charitably called the Rockapes, after the famed
simians of Gibraltar. Gallagher smiled, remembering. He wondered whether they were still
called that.

For reasons Dalgleish had never made
clear, he had failed to make it as aircrew; but
Gallagher could still not understand, even to
this day, why his former university friend had
joined the Regiment, a more unlikely candidate
could not have been found.

But in the Regiment, Dalgleish had pros-
pered and had risen rapidly to Flight Lieuten-
ant by the time he and Gallagher met up again,
by which time Gallagher had himself been
taken into the embrace of the Department.
Their training course had been under the control of the Department and had been an inten-
sive one in guerrilla warfare, given by a

ferocious Regiment Squadron Leader called McQueen who had seen service in the jungles of Malaya. O'Keefe had been there too.

Dalgleish jumped down from the exposed tip of an entombed boulder and walked up to the *quattro*. He moved with the alert gait of a wild animal. Gallagher recognized something of himself within Dalgleish's manner. It was hardly surprising. They had passed through the hands of the same tutors, the same system that had turned each in his own way into a killer.

Dalgleish was slightly shorter than Gallagher but seemed thicker, because of the bulkiness of his clothes. As he drew closer, Gallagher could see how the reddish beard that practically hid his face gave him the fierce look of a Viking. A commando-style knitted hat was worn over his balaclava.

Dalgleish stopped a few feet away. Pale blue eyes stared quizzically at Gallagher. They stood looking at each other for fleeting moments, silently.

Then Dalgleish said, "So. You came."

"As you can see."

Dalgleish glanced at the *quattro*. "Very inconspicuous." Drily. "Doing well for yourself."

"HMG doesn't pay very well."

Dalgleish appeared to smile. "At least you'll give a shadow a good run for his money in that thing. Anyone follow you?"

"No."

"You haven't forgotten then."

"Not that much."

Again the hint of a smile. Dalgleish held out a hand. "Good to see you, Gordon."

They shook hands, eyes never leaving each other. "You too, Uffa. News was you'd been careless."

"Ground clutter, old son. Ground clutter."

Gallagher thought he detected bitterness, but wasn't sure.

"Let's get out of here," Dalgleish was saying. "You may not have been followed, but someone could drive up."

Inspecting the car briefly as they climbed in, he commented, "Pretty." He fastened his seatbelt. "Sorry about the clodhoppers on your nice new carpets."

Gallagher wasn't sure whether Dalgleish was being serious. He clipped on his own belt and started the engine. It growled powerfully.

"Oh, very nice," Dalgleish said approvingly. He was looking at Gallagher.

"Where to?" Gallagher asked. He stared through the windshield.

"Back into the mists," Dalgleish said. "To Uig."

Gallagher eased the car back on the narrow road which plunged down towards Uig. The mist took them immediately, blotting out the world, save for the briefest of stretches of road ahead of the *quattro*. They traveled without speaking for a while, as the track twisted itself for about a mile or so before becoming a relatively gentle sweeping curve.

Dalgleish said into a silence broken by the subdued hum of the car and the intermittent swish of the wipers, "Do you remember McQueen?"

"Could I ever forget that sadistic bastard? Funny." Thoughtfully.

"What is?"

"I was thinking about him while I was waiting for you to come down from your mountain."

Dalgleish seemed to be looking at him intently. "Why?"

"Just watching you come down triggered the memory. I suddenly remembered when he'd taken us into north Wales."

"I see." Dalgleish appeared to relax. He gave a chuckle that held no humor. "He certainly was a bit of a bastard. Remember those pictures of the people he'd personally blown away in Malaya? What did he call them? Er. . . ."

"CTs."

"Oh, yes. CTs."

CTs. Communist Terrorists. Gallagher remembered. Pictures of obscenely destroyed heads, some blown half away like disfigured melons. And the captions. "Effects of a Bren from six feet." Christ.

"I remember," Gallagher now said. McQueen's Trophies, they had been called. McQueen had gloated over them. "He was a sick bastard." Heads shot by a Bren from an ambush position. Jesus.

CTs, VCs, Terrs. When the Establishment killed, it dehumanized its opponents. The country was immaterial. The Russians called the Afghan rebels terrorists.

"Bit too old, really," Dalgleish said after another silence. "McQueen."

"Not when he was teaching us, he wasn't."

"Oh, I don't mean then. I'm talking about two years ago. He was pushing fifty; at least. Bit old to be in the field, I'd have thought. Not our type, anyway. Too . . . bullish."

Gallagher could smell something coming. "What happened to him?"

"Got his head blown away in Sharjah. Shouldn't have happened, really. But there's a kind of poetic justice in it, don't you think?"

Gallagher kept his mouth firmly shut while he thought about this piece of news. That was not what Fowler had said. Fowler had said that the person who had been killed in Sharjah had been a KGB friendly. What the hell was going on? *McQueen?*

"What was McQueen doing out there in the first place? I thought they'd put him out to grass a long time ago, or that he was still taking out his nasty temper on poor sods, in the Welsh mountains."

"Ah. Thereby hangs a tale."

Dalgleish said nothing further and their silence took them all the way to Uig. Dalgleish directed Gallagher out of Uig and on to the A856, back south to Kensaleyre. Just after Kensaleyre, they took a B-class road to the right that took them for two miles across bleak undulating country, before it joined the A850. Under Dalgleish's directions Gallagher turned right again, heading towards the Waternish peninsula. The mist was still with them, but Gallagher found that visibility was appreciably better. He could see a good hundred meters ahead. He used low beams.

Since leaving Uig, Dalgleish had taken to turning to look through the back window from time to time. Now and then, he'd lean sideways to check the passenger-door mirror as well.

A ninety-degree bend came up near Clachamish. Gallagher took the *quattro* easily through it. He was in no hurry and allowed the car to cruise at its leisure. He did not prompt Dalgleish, deciding his companion would choose his own time to say what he wanted to.

Dalgleish leaned over to peer into the door mirror. "Is this adjustable?"

Gallagher showed him, using the switch set into his own door.

Dalgleish said, "Electrically-operated. Flash. Photography pays you well."

"I had to trade in my old car." Gallagher re-set the mirror, glanced into the others. Nothing.

"Even so. It didn't cost peanuts."

Gallagher said nothing.

After a while, Dalgleish said, "That wasn't why you left the Department though, was it? Not because of the money."

"No."

Dalgleish, Gallagher knew, was gearing himself up; testing the waters before committing himself.

The road began to curve to the south west.

Dalgleish said, "Pity about this mist. That road to Uig is quite spectacular." It was almost as if he were speaking to himself. "What was on the ferry?"

"Nothing to worry about, unless you want

to count a Finnish car." Gallagher explained about the Finnish family.

"Too obvious," Dalgleish said. "Even the Russians wouldn't try that. Besides, they were probably visiting relatives."

"Finns?"

Dalgleish gave a sudden, sharp laugh. "Why not? The history of this island has strong Scandinavian links; but, mainly, the people are Celts, the last true ones, they'll tell you. Who knows? Even you might have a link."

"You've got to be joking."

"Why? Your mother was half-Scots. . . ."

"Transplanted to the Caribbean. . . ."

"And your father's Irish," Dalgleish went on as if uninterrupted. "There's more than a touch of the Celt in you, old son. A little dark, of course, but still Celt." Dalgleish was again looking at Gallagher. The beard seemed to be smiling.

Gallagher remained silent.

"Come on, Gordon," Dalgleish said in mild reproof. "Not prejudiced, are you? It's not that bad. And I speak as a man in whose veins flows Gaelic blood."

"My father's dead," Gallagher said at last.

"My God. I'm sorry. How?"

"He was an innocent bystander," Gallagher said grimly, remembering.

Dalgleish looked away. "The Department?" he eventually said, softly.

"Only in an indirect sort of way."

Dalgleish seemed to think about that. The silence came again.

They drove past Edinbane, took the sharp curve at the top of Loch Greshornish.

Dalgleish said, "Want to tell me?"

"No."

"I understand."

More silence.

The mist began to lift, and Gallagher saw the silent peaks on either side of the road, their tops still hidden, giants with their heads in the clouds.

"Bròn nan Aighean." Dalgleish spoke reflectively.

"What?"

"That peak there, on the right."

Gallagher glanced at it. The road ran along its base. He checked his mirrors. Nothing.

Dalgleish said, "Did you ever betray your house at school?"

Wondering about the question, Gallagher said, "No."

But he had let it down, once, in an odd way. He had been picked for the cricket team. Hating cricket, he'd said no. The housemaster had been scandalized. Someone with Caribbean blood who hated cricket! Sacrilege! It was like the rhythm all such people were supposed to have. But he'd been forgiven. He'd joined the shooting team instead and won the House a trophy. Forgiven, but not forgotten. Years later, when on a nostalgic whim he'd visited the school, the same housemaster had greeted him with, "Ah, Gallagher. I remember you. The one who wouldn't play cricket." It had cured him of ever wanting to go back.

". . . never betray the House," Dalgleish

was saying. "Once, we had some visitors from a school for young ladies. Pretty things, they were. When they came into our form, someone whistled. The Head was with them and was furious. He demanded the identity of the culprit. Of course, no one spoke. So we were all punished. He asked again. Again we refused to tell. We were all punished a second time. Later, we carried out our own punishment of the culprit. We knew, of course. We gave him no warning, allowing his guard to relax. Then one night, while his attention was kept diverted, I soaked his bed with water; thoroughly. The entire House heard his screams when he got in. It was February."

Unsure of what the story held as a lesson, Gallagher said, "What happened to him?" A soaked bed in February. Poor little bastard.

"Caught a chill of course, the silly sod. Expensive whistle. But we didn't betray the House. We carried out our own punishment. We didn't betray the House," Dalgleish repeated. "That was the main thing."

Gallagher said nothing. Dalgleish would get to what he really wanted to say in his own good time.

The road began to fork. To the right, it was untarred, curving towards Fairy Bridge. The main tarred route curved left, towards Dunvegan.

"Go left," Dalgleish instructed.

Gallagher swung the car round the bend. Just past the apex, a side road joined it from the right. The fat tires of the *quattro* hissed on the damp road surface. He wondered when Dalgleish would decide to stop. Another check of his mirrors showed no shadowers. Throughout the journey, they had seen very little traffic.

Dalgleish, noting his scrutiny of the mirrors, said, "Most things stop on Sundays. Anyone following will stick out like a sore thumb."

While Gallagher was prepared to accept that, he did not relax. They had passed two nondescript cars and a very dirty Landrover. Forestry Commission, Dalgleish had said, as the vehicle had receded in the distance. That had been all.

Even so.

Before they'd got to Dunvegan and about two kilometers later, Dalgleish said, "Here. Take this track."

The road had been skirting an extensive wood just under half a kilometer away. Now, Gallagher swung the *quattro* on to the track that led into it.

Dalgleish looked at him. "This thing won't get stuck, will it?"

"Not a chance. Four-wheel drive."

"On a car like this?" Dalgleish was disbelieving.

"They've had it on the market for close on three years."

"You forget. I've been away." There was a sudden tightness to Dalgleish's voice.

They'd gone about a kilometer along the track when Dalgleish decided to speak again.

"I suppose you're wondering if I'm carrying a gun."

"In the circumstances," Gallagher began, "I would consider that a very prudent thing to do . . . so long you're not thinking of using it on me."

Dalgleish made a sound that seemed like a chuckle. It was difficult to tell. "Pull off the road here. Drive far enough to put it out of sight."

The track had climbed gently, but now it leveled off. Gallagher turned the *quattro* off it and entered the wood. The car took the terrain with equanimity. Gallagher stopped when he thought they were a sufficient distance from the track. He cut the engine. The car sighed and ticked to itself.

"Right," he said. "We're far enough from your bolthole, I take it. Now tell me why you've brought me all the way to Skye."

"Let's take a walk. I don't like staying in one place when I'm away from my base."

They got out. Gallagher locked the car. Dalgleish led the way as they began walking. A cap of mist shrouded the top of the wood, but visibility was good, though the day itself was gloomy.

They had walked in silence for about five minutes when Dalgleish said, glancing to one side, "I see you've put on the sweater. Warm enough?"

"Yes."

"Good. Did you bring the camera?"

"It's in the trunk."

"Good," Dalgleish repeated. "You'll be needing it. I hope it will do the job."

"Job? What job?"

"All in due course. What did you think of my cousin, by the way?"

"I didn't really. . . ."

"Liar." There was a definite chuckle.

"She's stunning, and you know it. Thought you'd like her." Before Gallagher could make comment, he went on, "See much of Celia?"

Celia, God. It seemed so long ago. The wife who had betrayed him. Then he'd found Lauren. Now Lauren. . . .

"No," Gallagher said.

That earned another sideways glance from Dalgleish. "You sound as if a hundred years from now would be too soon."

"Make it two hundred."

"Bitterness?"

"No." That was true now. Lauren had made Celia irrelevant. "Indifference."

"Which means another woman."

"There was."

"Was?"

"She's dead. Someone shot her. Months ago." He'd never forget.

"Good Christ," Dalgleish said softly. "What did you do?"

"I got the bastards responsible, but I think the Department knew about it. At least, I'm sure Kingston-Wyatt knew. Not that it matters now."

Dalgleish stopped suddenly. "What do you mean?"

Gallagher had gone on a little way ahead. Now he stopped, turned and leaned against a tree. They were on a slope. A short distance away to Dalgleish's right, and just behind him, was a fallen trunk that looked as if it had been there for years.

Gallagher said, "The Boss is dead. Blew himself away."

Dalgleish was very still. The wood now seemed unnaturally silent. At last, Dalgleish said, "Well, what do you know." He appeared strangely thoughtful. "How did you find out?"

"Fowler—" Gallagher stopped. Dalgleish was pointing a big automatic at him. "What the hell . . ." he went on slowly.

"Fowler?" Dalgleish said tightly. "You *saw* Fowler before you came up here?"

Gallagher stared at Dalgleish, stared at the automatic, body tensed. "Yes. I—"

"You bastard. You *bastard!* No wonder no one followed you. Why would they? The Department pointed you like a gundog at me and I let them! They've sent you to do what the others couldn't. The man who won shooting tropies at school. Kingston-Wyatt's brown-eyed boy. But the eyes are not really brown, are they? Somewhere between green and gray. Well, they've failed, old son. . . ."

"Uffa," Gallagher began carefully, "what are you on about?"

"They've sent you to kill me."

"Is that your bright thought for the day?"

The gun did not waver. Dalgleish, Gallagher knew, was one of the best, and unless he could be convinced he was wrong, it would be all over. The distance was too great for a lunge. With someone like Dalgleish, more than three feet was fatal.

The pale blue eyes were blazing. "You deny it?"

"Of course I bloody deny it!"

"Don't come any closer! I know all about you."

"I haven't bloody moved!"

"Then don't even think about it." Dalgleish backed warily away, and made his first mistake.

He trod on the log.

As Gallagher leapt forward, several things were happening. Dalgleish, taken completely by surprise, tried to regain his balance and keep his eye on Gallagher at the same time. He failed, stumbled, toppled over and began to slide down the slope. The gun flew out of his hand, bounced on the tree trunk, fell on to the carpet of wet, dead leaves and disappeared. Gallagher marked where it had gone even as his body hit the tumbling, rolling Dalgleish.

But something else had concentrated his mind sharply. As Dalgleish stumbled, a long gouge had appeared in the tree trunk, pieces of dead bark flying off it.

Rifle! Gallagher thought as he grappled with Dalgleish.

"Don't be stupid, you rockape!" he panted as they continued to roll, struggling. They fetched up against the bole of a tree. "You should be worrying about someone who's out there with a bloody rifle! Not about me."

Dalgleish did not relax. Gallagher held on to him as their bodies strained to gain the upper hand.

"Uffa! *Listen,* you prick! A *rifle.* Someone's out there with a rifle. If I'd come here to kill you, why would I be trying to hold you down so you don't get your stupid head shot off?"

Dalgleish relaxed a little.

Gallagher did not release him, but spoke quickly, "I've been away for months. I only got back on Friday. Within minutes, now I think of it, I was being shadowed. I went to the Department to have it out with Kingston-Wyatt. I didn't know he was dead. Fowler told me. He also said the Department was not having me followed. I didn't believe him. I wouldn't believe that lot if I were standing in a downpour and they told me it was raining.

"It was then that he told me about you, and about the Windshear group. He wanted me to contact you and to ask you to come in. I told him to piss off. When I eventually got home, I got your message via Lucinda. I came because I felt you would do the same for me, *not* because of the bloody Department. And that's it. If you don't believe me, you can piss off and face that sniper by yourself."

Gallagher released him.

Dalgleish made no move as they stared at each other. Finally, he said, "Rifle, did you say?" It was almost conversational.

"Yes."

"And how did he or they get here?"

"You tell me. I certainly didn't bring them."

"What's that supposed to mean?"

"I shook my shadows in London. They probably think I'm still there. I'm registered at the hotel as Thompson. Lucinda booked."

"I told her to do that."

"There you are. Which still leaves the question: who brought them?"

Dalgleish turned his head slowly, searching up the slope.

"Which direction, do you think?" he asked eventually.

"From behind, and to the left of where you were standing. He won't be there now."

Dalgleish's eyes were still searching. "If he's got an infra-red scope, our body heat will register."

"He'll have to make it to a new position first. I pulled you well out of line. The slope's helping, but we don't have much time."

"You mean flush him?" Dalgleish was already in his element, turning into the hunter.

"It's the only way we're going to get out of here alive."

"What if there's more than one?"

"Count on it."

"Well, I've been dodging them in Russia. I can do it here. I could do with my gun."

"I know where it is." Gallagher was moving before Dalgleish realized what was happening. He crabbed swiftly to where he'd seen the weapon fall, felt quickly with his hand and found it. He returned and handed it to Dalgleish.

Dalgleish gave him a neutral stare while balancing the gun right-handedly, as if testing it for feel, before wiping the moisture lovingly off it. It was a massive Stechkin APS twenty-shot auto.

"All right," Dalgleish said. "How do we do this?"

"We hunt. We'll split up, work in opposite directions and up and round him . . . or them. We'll each be our own decoy, if need be."

"I know the island terrain. I'll flush him, you catch. Would you like the gun?"

It was a vote of trust. Gallagher said, "No. I'll find something."

Even as they spoke, both of them were searching the autumnal wood for signs of movement, eyes lively in slowly tracking heads.

"Right," Dalgleish said. "I'm off. See you later, I hope."

"You'll see me."

Dalgleish nodded before scuttling away.

Gallagher watched him go. The mist had decided to lower itself and was now threading its way through the trees. In seconds, Dalgleish had disappeared, moving to the left and upwards.

Gallagher moved cautiously to the right, searching for a particular item that could be turned into a weapon. He knew exactly what he wanted. After a minute, he found it: a short, branched dry stick. He pushed the stick beneath the carpet of leaves and carefully broke the branch about two inches from the joint. The leaves effectively muffled the sound. Next, he broke the stick at each end. Satisfied, he lifted the shortened stick from the leaves and inspected his handiwork, holding it before him like small handlebars.

The stick had a slight indentation behind the joint so that it looked like a shallow vee, the sharp stub of its amputated branch protruding wickedly from its apex.

"You'll do," Gallagher said softly; then he went into the swirling mist to commence his hunt.

* * *

Three p.m. Moscow. Ulvanov and Skoryatin were in their room of neutrality, and in full uniform. Neither had known of the other's intention to attend in military splendor. Each had decided to do so in a desire to create a greater sense of presence over the other. Each was wily enough to greet the other with studious indifference to the uniform. Skoryatin knew, however, that he was the more elegant and took a quiet pleasure in that. He was as determined to keep up the psychological pressure as Ulvanov, whom he knew was equally determined.

Skoryatin smiled in his mind. Ulvanov would never succeed in tripping him up.

Ulvanov eyed Skoryatin speculatively as they sat down in their usual places. On the table between them were all the British national Sunday newspapers. Within the pages of each, certain sections had been bordered in blue ink, demanding more than normal attention.

There was also vodka on the table, a bottle between them with a glass at each place. Skoryatin's held ice. Ulvanov poured, then downed his with one gulp. Skoryatin swirled his ice once before taking a generous mouthful of his drink. He replaced the glass with studied care.

Ulvanov gave the offending glass with the ice melting in the crystal-clear liquid a baleful stare. Ice in vodka was an abomination, effete, and a typically degenerate Western habit. He did not voice his thoughts. It would only have given Skoryatin the satisfaction of knowing he had been irritated. Besides, it was certain that Skoryatin already knew it.

Ulvanov thumbed through the newspapers. Many of the articles concerned the siting of cruise and Pershing missiles in Europe and focused on the British angle with the attendant demonstrations. The death of a soap-opera actress in Holland Park was prominently reported, but it had no blue border.

Ulvanov smiled without humor. "These British. They give more importance to the death of a second-rate performer than to the imminence of their own destruction."

"We must not forget dogs," Skoryatin said. He took another drink.

"Dogs?"

"The British love dogs. They'll do almost anything for dogs."

Ulvanov was not sure whether Skoryatin was kidding. "I would appreciate it if you would share the direction of your reasoning with me, Comrade," he said with mild sarcasm. What he really wanted to do was yell at the insufferable dandy before him. These meetings, born essentially of mistrust, frequently bore little fruit. But it was necessary that they continue. It was a way of checking up on each other. Neither would suggest ending them, even though they would both prefer it.

On Sundays, ever since the activating of the joint operation, the newspapers, with their outlined sections, were brought in for joint scrutiny. Neither paid much attention. It was so much window dressing. Everyone knew that the departments within their respective organizations responsible for dissemination of the foreign press had already done their homework, and any relevant information would have been acted upon. But the charade had to go on.

Skoryatin said, "My reasoning is not directed towards dogs, Comrade. I merely thought I'd mention it as an indicator."

"Of what?" Ulvanov tried not to snap.

"The British character."

"You have come here today to tell me about the British character, Comrade? I *know* all about the British character. I have been studying it for years." Ulvanov was looking exasperated.

"The thing," Skoryatin began mildly, "about the British character is that they don't understand it themselves."

"Ice in vodka is bad for you," Ulvanov said. He'd been wanting to get that in. "You speak in riddles, Vladimir Mikhailovich."

Skoryatin found himself staring at a picture of the dead woman. It had been taken when she was considerably younger. Quite pretty, though with a slightly vacuous smile. Necessary in her profession, he reasoned. He knew it was a picture of her youth because the other papers carried less flattering, more recent photographs. Someone, somewhere, had chosen to be kind.

He continued to stare at the picture, wondering why the story of a simple mugging should intrigue him. It had not even been marked out.

"You like the type, Comrade?" Ulvanov asked with the merest hint of malice. Another vague reference to Skoryatin's trips to the West.

"Not particularly. I was thinking, Dmitry Vasil'evich, that suppose the British were siting dummy missiles at Greenham Common while preparing to site the real ones well away from our present target areas. . . ." Skoryatin paused deliberately.

Ulvanov stared at him. "Are you saying you believe them to be doing with the missiles what we're doing with the Tu-22P?"

"Why not?" Skoryatin had thought that most likely for some time now. "We let the West take a photograph of something at Ramenskoye, placed neatly between two Tu-144s. It's given them a fright. They call it Blackjack, and it's big enough to give them nightmares. We have even let them see it flying off North Cape. While they concentrate on it, our mission continues in peace and in total secrecy."

"And you believe the British to be carrying out the same kind of bluff?"

"Why not?" Skoryatin repeated.

"They would not be so devious."

"At times, they can quite surpass themselves."

"But the Americans. What about them?"

Skoryatin smiled. "Perfect foils."

Skye, 1300 hours. While Skoryatin and Ulvanov, thousands of miles away to the east, had been busy scoring points off each other, Gallagher and Dalgleish had been carrying out a deadly game of hide-and-seek; their quarry, the unknown sniper. They had just spent an hour carefully moving from one position to another, using every aspect of the terrain as cover as they moved relentlessly upwards.

Now, Gallagher found he had reached the edge of the wood, a good kilometer from where he and Dalgleish had parted company. During the interim, he had neither seen nor heard anything to betray the hidden gunman. He wondered how Dalgleish was doing.

The mist was patchy so that while a few yards to his left the trees were wreathed in the stuff, up ahead, up the bracken-covered slope, there was a clear patch of ground that made him feel positively exposed. From his position, where he lay as close as possible to the cushion of dead leaves and still within the wood, he scanned the slope apprehensively.

"I don't fancy going up that bastard," he muttered softly to himself.

The top of the peak, he decided, was a good two hundred meters from where he lay, but it was hidden by a forbidding outcrop. He wondered if the sniper had made it to that position. Plenty of places to hide and wait.

Gallagher remained where he was. Minutes passed. There was no sign of Dalgleish. A series of outcrops girded the hill in storied ranks. The nearest, he gauged, was less than twenty meters from the edge of the wood some distance to his right. It had the added bonus of being still partially hidden by mist.

I can do it, he told himself.

He inched himself backwards until he was well into the wood again, then made his way at a swift crouching run to the spot he had selected. He moved with feline silence, a dangerous animal on the prowl.

From his new position, he watched the outcrop. It was closer than he'd judged. All the better. He remained where he was for another ten minutes, his senses pulsing out, testing the area about him. Nothing moved, and nothing made a single sound. The wood seemed to be waiting for something to happen.

The mist around the outcrop was shifting like a living being, as if teasing him with a siren dance. It shifted, twirled, split itself into several tendrils before joining them all together again. It did this in a slow-motion sequence that Gallagher found dangerously mesmerizing, so that when long minutes later it parted a section of its amorphous body like a teasing curtain, he almost missed what it displayed to him.

A man was standing on a narrow ledge, pressed hard against the rockface. A man with a rifle.

Gallagher realized he had been holding his breath only when he began to let it out again slowly, as if expecting the man to hear. He remained perfectly still, not a single part of his body moving.

The rifle was pointing upwards, and the man's attention was riveted on the curvature of the rock structure above him. Gallagher wondered why, following the gaze. No one was there. The mist was beginning to close its curtain.

Had the man heard something? Was Dalgleish even now crawling straight into a high-power bullet at close range?

Gallagher stayed where he was, eyes fastened upon the gunman's point of interest, as the mist slowly drew itself together. Strangely, it remained open where the man stood, as if to say to Gallagher, "Look, look, see what I've brought you."

Gallagher saw something else. He knew now what had captured the man's attention so fixedly. Scrapings of rock surface fell intermittently down the sides. A sizeable piece struck the man on a shoulder. He might himself have been made of stone, so little was its effect. The spill was exactly what one would expect of someone moving cautiously, though a trifle clumsily, on top.

Dalgleish? Would Dalgleish be so clumsy?

Gallagher waited. The man with the rifle waited. The mist continued to draw its veil.

More spillage. The man did not move. Gallagher continued to wait, but his eyes now roved along the top curvature of the outcrop.

And stopped. He had seen movement. He waited.

The movement came once more, so minute that it could easily have been missed by someone not on the lookout for it. A head had been raised briefly, before disappearing again.

Dalgleish.

The man had not seen him, for the simple reason that Dalgleish had not appeared where the man had expected him to.

Gallagher felt his stomach tighten. When Dalgleish had raised his head for that briefest of instants, he had stared directly at where Gallagher lay. Gallagher knew the other could not have seen him; but Dalgleish had *known*. He knew with a sinking feeling what Dalgleish wanted.

Shit, he thought.

As if to prove his worst fears correct, the rockspill began again. Dalgleish was suckering the gunman.

Shit, Gallagher thought again. He was to be bait.

The mist had almost closed in on the man when he made his move; a sudden darting lunge to the right into deeper cover. He made a sufficient production of it so that the man on the rock, efficiently trained killer that he undoubtedly was, could not have missed the fleeting movement out of the corner of his eye.

He was almost too good; but he made a mistake.

He turned suddenly at Gallagher's movement, bringing the rifle on target with a deadly swiftness and firing almost at the same time. He hit the exact spot where Gallagher had been. The rifle made no noise.

Silenced, Gallagher thought even as he was lunging.

But something else was happening. In the same fleeting instant, Gallagher had a vivid image of Dalgleish launching himself off the top of the outcrop. When Gallagher again could look properly, both Dalgleish and the man were on the sloping ground. Dalgleish was getting to his knees, the man's rifle in his hand. The man himself lay still. Gallagher watched as Dalgleish searched the body quickly. Then Dalgleish was crouch-running towards the wood in Gallagher's direction, carrying the rifle.

At the edge of the wood, Dalgleish paused briefly, uncertainly. Gallagher did not move. Sudden movement could bring death. Dalgleish was holding the rifle at the port. Swinging it into action would take the merest fraction of a second.

Gallagher said softly, "Uffa!"

Dalgleish located the direction and relaxed visibly. Gallagher moved so that the other would see him. Dalgleish came on swiftly and hit the ground next to Gallagher.

"You're still quick," Dalgleish said. The beard appeared to smile fleetingly. "All that soft living hasn't slowed you down. For which," he went on, to a God he didn't believe in, "thanks."

"That bastard was quick too. He nearly punctured me. For good."

Dalgleish's pale blue eyes were lively. "He didn't . . . which is all that matters."

"Next time you want me to play chicken, let me know, won't you?"

"You had it easy, old son. I had to do my flying bit. Brain salad if I'd hit that rock instead of our friend out there."

"He's dead, I take it?"

"As the proverbial doornail." Dalgleish looked at the rifle closely. "You were right about the infra-red. Recognize it?"

Gallagher stared at the weapon with the familiar balefully-red searchlight eye perched atop the telescopic sight. The make surprised him.

"A bloody Dragunov."

Dalgleish showed his teeth in a grin without humor. "That's what I thought. I was as surprised as you are."

Just over four feet from its skeleton wooden butt to its muzzle, its long slender barrel giving it a predatory look, the Dragunov SVD was the classic sniper's rifle.

"Would you," Dalgleish continued thoughtfully, "if you were a Russian field man operating in a foreign country, use a Russian weapon?"

They stared at each other for some moments.

"No," Gallagher said after a while. "But then, that's my own personal opinion."

"You don't want to admit it."

"Admit what?"

The beard twitched. "That the man out there could be one of ours. Naturally, there was nothing on him to tell us anything."

"You're crazy," Gallagher said. But he wasn't so sure. The whole affair was getting messier by the second and he wanted to get out of it.

Dalgleish was still looking at him. "More of them, do you think?"

"At least one more, possibly two. Somebody will be watching the car by now."

"What I'd like to know," Dalgleish went on midly, "is how they knew where to look." The pale blue eyes were dancing with a strange fire.

Gallagher knew exactly what Dalgleish was driving at. What was more, Dalgleish held all the weapons.

Gallagher said, with a calm he did not feel:
"You're not back on that tack, are you? Are you
accusing me of bringing them here?" He made
his own eyes look angry.

"If not you, who?"

"Are you quite sure you've checked your
own lines of communication?" Gallagher re-
joined sharply. "I am here because I obeyed
your instructions. It was your responsibility to
ensure all your lines were secure. Now you can
either lie here all day accusing me of blowing
you, or we can get on with the rest of the job.
I've just about had it. Once I've returned to my
car, it's back to London for me. Sort out your
own bloody problems."

Dalgleish said nothing for a few seconds.
Then, "All right. Let's get the others."

"I'll head for the car," Gallagher said. "Use
the infra-red to find the third man, if there is
one. I don't think the one by the car will be hard
to locate." He hoped.

During their conversation, they had kept
their voices low. Now, Dalgleish nodded, rose
silently and made off into the mists.

Gallagher watched as the crouching form
moved away. Dalgleish had kept the automatic
too.

Gallagher made a face. He was not totally
unarmed. He still had his bent stick. He rose
and made his way swiftly back to where he had
left the *quattro*. He was absolutely certain their
adversaries, whoever they were, would have
kept a watch on the car. The trick was to find
the watcher or watchers and deal with the obstruction silently. He did not like to think he

would be killing Department men. He did not want to kill anybody.

The mist still helped him; but it would be helping the others too. The mist was neutral, above the stupidity of the humans who hunted each other.

Gallagher made another face as the thought came to him. This, among other things, was the very reason he had left the Department. Yet here he was, knee-deep in it.

It took him half an hour to come within sight of the car. He could see it through the trees, a shape made soft by thinning mist, some thirty meters away. He would go no closer. From his position, he scanned the area minutely. All his senses told him someone was waiting, despite the apparent evidence to the contrary. Another fifteen minutes went by. Nothing.

Had they wired the car? He would have to check. But first, the waiting ones would have to be taken out.

Then a single shot lived and died briefly in the misty wood. Gallagher had not allowed the sudden bark of the Dragunov to deflect his attention. As he lay pressed closely to the ground, he wondered whether whoever was waiting had been similarly unaffected by the abrupt intrusion of the rifle shot into the stillness of the wood.

The unseen person was very good. No movement betrayed his hiding place.

Gallagher remained perfectly still for another fifteen minutes, letting his entire being relax as he had once been taught, while keeping his senses alert. He had, he reasoned, been expecting to hear the Dragunov. Had Dalgleish succeeded? Just the one shot. But whoever was waiting couldn't know what had happened. Did they have radios? Dalgleish had not mentioned anything about it after he'd searched the first man. But even if they did have radios, they would not risk speaking, Gallagher felt. Not now. Even whispers on radio could carry far in such stillness.

He waited. The man would soon be wondering what had happened. The waiting man would have to do something. Anything.

He did.

Gallagher nearly missed it: the merest suggestion of movement. A head raised slightly, inquiringly, before lowering once more to become still.

Gallagher pinpointed the position. "Oh, you're good," he breathed at the hidden man, "but not good enough."

The concealment had been efficiently carried out. The man had made himself a shallow trough in the soft earth and had covered himself with the fallen leaves. His clothing, what little of it showed, blended perfectly with its surroundings. Until he had moved his head, he had quite successfully passed as just another anonymous undulation on the floor of the wood.

Now that he knew where the man was, the other's position was a veritable beacon to Gallagher.

Was there another? Gallagher allowed the slow passage of five more minutes before deciding to make a move. No surreptitious shiftings had betrayed the presence of a second watcher. That meant nothing, but he would have to take the chance.

From where he lay, the ground sloped gently down towards his hidden quarry, curving slightly upwards in the middle distance. A rampart mere inches high, the curve formed a shallow ridge that ran horizontally along the slope, each end disappearing into the mist. The man's position was about forty meters away.

Keeping the ridge between him and his target, Gallagher inched backwards into the mist until he felt secure in the knowledge that he would not be seen. He then rose to a crouch and began to work his way around to come up behind the unsuspecting man.

As he moved, he wondered who the man was. If not Russian, what team? Was Dalgleish correct in thinking they were British? There were some departments, he knew, who had a habit of using soldiers for hit jobs. The Department itself did not believe in it, and called such outside help Rogues. There was no way Fowler would employ Rogues.

Gallagher paused. Fowler wouldn't; but what about Winterbourne? It didn't feel good at all. He pushed the uneasy thought out of his mind. He had to concentrate on what he had to do.

It took him twenty minutes to get into position. During that time, the wood had remained deathly silent. Where, he wondered, was Dalgleish?

Then he put Dalgleish and everything else out of his mind, save for the unobtrusive mound of leaves a short distance directly ahead of him. He felt his whole being gather itself for what was to come.

The first indication the hidden man had of his fate was the presence of a sudden crushing weight upon the small of his back and of something unbearably savage forcing its way down into the neck of his thick polo sweater to tear at the vulnerable throat behind it.

He tried to throw the weight off, but the unrelenting thing was ripping into the soft skin, creating unspeakable havoc within the confines of that vital passage. It was suddenly no longer important to get the weight off his back. He had to fight that dreadful thing at his throat.

Hands that would normally have been used in defense were now trying to pry away the torment from his ravaged neck as blood began to gush out of him. The awful pain would not stop.

Gallagher leapt off the man, leaving the stick embedded. The man rolled, tore the stick away with a scream, put his hands to the wound in an ineffectual attempt to stop the inevitable. He tried to scream again, but only a bubbling sound came out of him. His body thrashed insanely on the wet leaves.

Sickened by what he had done, Gallagher knew he would have to complete the job quickly. It didn't matter that this man had been waiting, possibly to kill him, as well as Dalgleish.

A soft noise came clearly to his alert senses above that of the thrashing body. He whirled.

Dalgleish. Dalgleish with the rifle in one hand. In the other, the big Stechkin was pointing.

It roared. Once. The thrashing body arched, relaxed, lay still.

Wordlessly, Dalgleish approached, stopped to look down at the dead man. He stared at the throat where blood continued to pump a glistening coating on to the neck of the sweater. Then his eyes turned to the stick lying where the desperate man had thrown it, its bloodied single fang looking as if it had just drunk copiously.

Dalgleish turned to the silent Gallagher. "Jesus. I've heard you could be lethal. Did you have that thing on you when we were lying back up there?"

"Yes."

"Would you have used it on me if the need had arisen?"

Gallagher stared unflinchingly back at the pale blue eyes. "It never crossed my mind."

"Well, thank God for small mercies," Dalgleish remarked with some feeling.

Gallagher said, "Will you get it into your thick skull once and for all that no one sent me here to kill you? In case it has escaped your notice, I don't work for the Department any more and haven't done so for some time now. *You* brought me here. Remember that."

"All right. All right! Keep your shirt on."

"Well, bloody hell, Uffa."

"All right, Gordon. All right. So I'm jumpy. In my place, you would be." Dalgleish put the

Stechkin away inside his camouflaged jacket, then patted the Dragunov. "I removed the silencer to warn you."

"It worked," Gallagher said. He stared at the dead man. "He moved."

"Silly sod," Dalgleish commented disparagingly. There was no sympathy for the vanquished. "No point searching him. He'll be as clean as the others. One interesting thing."

Gallagher went over to pick up the lethal stick. "What?" He cleaned the wooden fang by stabbing it into the wet earth and twisting back and forth. When it was clean, he broke it in two and threw the pieces far into the mist, in opposite directions.

"I found their transport. The Landrover."

Gallagher turned to look at him. "From the Forestry Commission?"

"The very same. Has to be a fake, of course. I found something else."

They began to walk towards the *quattro*, leaving the body. Gallagher waited for Dalgleish to continue.

Dalgleish rested the Dragunov casually on his shoulder. "Two radios," he continued. "Hand-held. Russian. It's so bloody obvious, it screams at you. I can't believe they could be so clumsy. Someone's really fucking up."

"So you think they were Rogues?"

"I can't see what else. Those weren't Spetsnaz. I should know." Dalgleish's voice had become grim once more, as if with a particularly unpleasant memory. "Whatever I may think of Fowler and his lot, somehow I can't picture him using Rogues. It's puzzling."

They reached the car. Gallagher stared at it. "Not Fowler, perhaps. Stand back."

Dalgleish took some steps away from the *quattro*. "What do you mean, 'not Fowler'?"

"An idiot called Winterbourne has replaced the Boss. He and Fowler do not like each other. It wouldn't surprise me if Winterbourne tried to steal a march on him." Gallagher continued to stare at the car.

Dalgleish said, "Are things that bad?"

"Worse. I'm glad I'm not in that shit any more."

"It still doesn't explain how they got here."

"No. It doesn't. I think you ought to go over in your mind everything you've done since you got back. There's a weak spot somewhere. Well, here goes." Gallagher took out the single key that operated all locks on the *quattro,* inserted it into the door. "I'd move right back, if I were you." He pushed the key in slowly.

Dalgleish did not move.

Gallagher paused, looked round. "Feeling brave, are we?" He turned back to the car.

Dalgleish said nothing.

Gallagher turned the key equally slowly. The central locking system went into operation. No explosion. Gallagher went on to check the car minutely. He even tested the seatbelts to see if the inertia reels had been wired up as triggers. The *quattro* was clean.

"You're thorough," Dalgleish said approvingly as they climbed in.

"They were a bit cocky. I don't suffer from the same disease."

"A survivor."

"It helps to have a healthy instinct for survival. But I don't have to tell you about that, do I?" Gallagher shut his door carefully, clipped on his belt and inserted the key gently into the ignition.

Watching him, Dalgleish said, "I thought you were satisfied."

"I take nothing for granted."

"Oh, wonderful. All the way from Russia to be fried on Skye." Dalgleish grinned. "That was a joke."

"No. Really." Gallagher turned the key suddenly. The engine burst smoothly into powerful life. He gave a mental sigh of relief.

Dalgleish shut the passenger door and put on his own belt. He kept the rifle with him but lowered it out of sight.

Dalgleish said, "For a man who's been out of the trade, you're well on form."

Gallagher stared at the group of square-shaped warning lights at the bottom of the rectangular instrument binnacle. They winked out one by one, save for the orange glow of the brake warning. He tapped at the brake pedal. The light winked out. The digital units of the main instruments stared back at him. A quarter circle on the left marked out the rev range to seven thousand in single units, while within its radius the timer told him it was 1500 hours.

Christ, he thought. *Already?*

An hour or so of daylight left. Not that it mattered. The mist, though much thinner here, now had a top cover. Visibility was good, but there was now no brightness to the day.

He glanced at the fuel read-out at the right-hand bottom corner. Plenty of juice. He put the *quattro* into gear and began to turn to head back to the track.

"Uffa," he said quietly, "I've been away for about nine months, during which time I've had a reasonably quiet life; the kind I like. Within two days of my return, I find myself surrounded by corpses on a Hebridean island, one of which I am responsible for. I don't call that being on form."

"You could have fooled me. . . ."

"I call that stupid," Gallagher went on inexorably. The *quattro* eased itself on to the track. The fat digits in the center of the instrument panel began their read-out slowly, as the speed increased at a leisurely pace. "You're going to tell me what this is all about. I want to know why the Rogues were after you—if they *were* Rogues—as well as the GRU and the KGB. What the hell have you really been doing?"

"Where shall I begin?"

"Lucinda said you had a film. Begin with that."

Dalgleish seemed to give it some thought. "I'll go the standard way," he said eventually. "I'll begin at the beginning. The film comes much later."

"Go ahead then," Gallagher said, more grimly than he'd intended.

They cruised down the track towards the main road. No point hurtling out of there. A slowly moving car attracted less attention.

"How much do you already know?"

"Very little, so you'd better give me chapter and verse."

Dalgleish paused once more for thought. Gallagher wondered whether he was selecting what to divulge.

"For some time," Dalgleish at last began, "the Department had been getting odd snippets of information that there was a dissident organization within the Soviet intelligence services—not infiltrators fed in by the West, but genuine Soviets, people who wanted to change the order of things. Not for our sake, naturally, but for the Motherland. They were thinking of survival; the world's survival, and therefore their own."

So far, so good. Dalgleish was keeping to roughly the same story Fowler had told.

"So, of course," Dalgleish went on, "the news was suspect. It could easily have been a multi-layered KGB bluff. They're always setting up machiavellian stunts. But the news kept coming. Eventually the Department decided it was worth a try. Someone was to be fed in. Me."

Gallagher thought he detected the trace of bitterness once again, but kept his silence. Dalgleish was still following Fowler's line.

Dalgleish said, "My linguistic skills made me the prime candidate. I knew the risks . . . or so I thought." The bitterness was definitely there now. "The Department named the dissident organization the Windshear Group. We simply called them Windshear."

Still online. Gallagher said, "Do they really exist?"

"Oh, yes. They do, and the KGB wants them badly. But I'll come to that."

They had reached the main road. Gallagher swung the *quattro* left, back along the route they had come. More out of reflex than anything, he inspected the mirrors, and frowned. A speck had appeared in the interior mirror. He checked the wings. Nothing. Again the interior. The speck was there and had grown perceptibly.

Dalgleish noted his scrutiny, glanced behind. "Another Rogue?"

"Who knows?" Gallagher did not increase speed, but every so often he glanced into all three mirrors. "Bloody motorbike," he added tightly after a few seconds.

"Important?"

"There was a big red bike on the ferry when I came over. . . ."

"A bike? You never said. . . ."

"I didn't bloody think! I didn't even consider it. Jesus. I really am rusty."

"He may not be following us."

"You don't believe that any more than I do," Gallagher said. "A bike on the ferry is one thing. The same bike conveniently following us out here is a little too much for coincidence."

"It may not be the same bike." Dalgleish's voice did not carry conviction. Like Gallagher, he instinctively mistrusted anything that bore the merest hint of being out of pattern.

"We'll soon find out," Gallagher said. He gradually increased speed. The read-out said 55, and was climbing.

The motorcycle, which had been drawing nearer, receded temporarily before swiftly regaining the ground it had lost; then it began to catch up again.

"Need more proof?" Gallagher said drily.

"I could say he was trying for a race but, with those three we left behind, I very much doubt it. Can we outrun him?" Dalgleish was very calm. He began to check the Dragunov.

"Can we outrun him, the man says." Gallagher gave the rifle a glance. "And you can forget about that. You won't hit him. Besides, I don't want any loony bastard shooting back at my car. Anyway, I've got a better idea." He patted the steering-wheel. "We can handle him, can't we, Lauren?"

Dalgleish stared. "You talk to your bloody car?"

"Of course."

"I suppose it talks back?"

"I had it throttled at birth. I don't like my car talking back at me. They build voice synthesizers into these, you know."

"Jesus."

"Hold on," Gallagher said, then he shifted down into third and floored the accelerator.

The *quattro* raised its nose and hurtled down the road as if suddenly propelled off the deck of a carrier by a catapult. The exhaust roared. The digital speedometer went berserk, its numbers blurring as the speed climbed with a rapidity that left Dalgleish gaping. Gallagher shifted up. The scorching acceleration pinned them to their seats.

"Christ!" Dalgleish exclaimed. "What have you got under there? A 747?"

Gallagher gave a grin of pure pleasure. "There's one more gear to go."

"Well, don't hit a bloody sheep. Will this thing stop when you want it to?"

"Of course. ABS."

"ABS?"

"Anti-lock braking."

"I hope it's read the same book you have. This bloody road's still wet."

"Have faith, Uffa." Gallagher took a swift look in the mirror. The motorcycle, obviously taken by complete surprise, was a rapidly diminishing speck. "Take a look at our motorcyclist."

Dalgleish did so. "Pretty impressive."

The *quattro* seemed to be enjoying itself as it streaked along the narrow ribbon.

"He'll be winding up to come after us," Gallagher said.

"We're doing 110." Dalgleish's voice sounded uncertain.

"That's slow. I want a nasty bend, preferably with a nice precipice, and soon."

"The mist is closing in again," Dalgleish said, staring at the numbers on the speedometer read-out. They were still climbing.

"We'll be all right. Where's that bend?"

"Er . . . take this road just up ahead, to the left."

They were approaching the sharp curve in the A850, now a right-hand bend, coming from their present direction. Gallagher swung the *quattro* left into the feeder road, with hardly a drop in speed, it seemed. The road led to Lusta.

Dalgleish could not believe the car had

held itself firmly to the surface without the slightest twitch. Lateral G held him fast against his seat belt as the *quattro* took the corner.

The road forked towards them at Fairy Bridge.

"Keep on," Dalgleish said, forcing his voice to remain calm.

"Nervous?" Gallagher asked.

"Who me? Why should I be? Didn't I just throw myself off a rock?"

Gallagher smiled briefly. He held the wheel with a light but firm touch, sensing the power of the car flowing through him. It felt good. The mist had closed in appreciably, forcing him to use the wipers. He turned on his lights, but then cut in the isolation switch to turn off the rears. No reason why he should help the motorcyclist.

Nothing showed in the billowing curtain behind.

Dalgleish stared at the speedometer. Gallagher had slowed down a little, but the figures stubbornly hovered around the hundred mark. Dalgleish wondered what was keeping the car on the rough road. He preferred not to think of it.

"That bend's coming up soon . . . and God help us if some poor sod's coming the other way."

"Have faith, Uffa. Have faith."

"I gave up praying a long time ago."

What was meant to be a light-hearted remark carried within it a touch of grimness. Gallagher gave the mirrors a swift scrutiny. Nothing as yet. And nothing came at them from the mist ahead.

"This is it," Dalgleish said.

It was an S-bend, not as tight as Gallagher would have liked but it would have to do. He took the *quattro* through it then hit the brakes. The wheels bit into the road as the anti-lock system went to work, keeping them turning, but slowing them down with an efficiency that flung the car's passengers against tightly locked belts. The *quattro* stopped without drama.

Dalgleish looked slightly pale. He stared disbelievingly into the mist, as if doubting he had actually survived the experience.

Gallagher quickly turned the car round. Now it was pointing the way it had come. He unclipped his belt and climbed out, leaving the engine running. He had turned off the lights.

"Quick!" he called to Dalgleish. "Out!"

He peered through the mist as Dalgleish complied, carrying the Dragunov. Nothing coming yet.

"Leave the bloody rifle. We won't need it." He sensed Dalgleish hesitating. "For Christ's sake, Uffa! We haven't the time to argue about it!"

Reluctantly, Dalgleish put the rifle back in the car; but he moved with commendable swiftness. Gallagher's attention had already moved elsewhere, and by the time Dalgleish had come up to him, he was carrying a large rock which he placed in the road ahead of the car. He hurried for another.

"Come on, Uffa. Help me with these rocks. We want a curving line right across the road."

Gallagher placed the rock next to the first, went back for another.

Dalgleish, realizing what he was doing, went to gather rocks.

Gallagher had parked the car beneath another of Skye's many escarpments on the left side on the road, in the direction in which it was now pointing. This hid it from oncoming traffic until the last possible moment. Together, both of them worked quickly to build a low curving rampart that would be high enough to deflect the approaching motorcycle's front wheel. The rampart led to the edge of the road, beyond which was a steepish slope that disappeared into the mist.

"I'd hoped for more of a sheer drop," Gallagher said when they'd finished, "but beggars can't be choosers. There should be some nice boulders down there to finish him off. What's at the bottom?"

"Bay River," Dalgleish replied, staring at him. "The slope seems relatively gentle up here, but nearer the bottom, it gets pretty steep; more like a cliff."

"Lovely. If the cliff doesn't get him, perhaps he'll drown."

Dalgleish was still staring. "You expect this to work?"

"Of course." The sound of a high-revving motor came on the mist. "And here's where we find out."

Gallagher ran back to the *quattro,* got in and strapped himself to the seat almost in one motion. Dalgleish was running towards the car; but already Gallagher had put it into reverse.

Gallagher pressed the switch to lower his window. "Stay out of the way!" He raised the window, continuing to reverse while Dalgleish stood in the misty road staring at him.

Then Dalgleish was moving swiftly towards high ground.

Gallagher stopped the car when he'd positioned it to his satisfaction and waited. He did not have long.

Almost immediately, it seemed, a single bright headlight pierced the mist as it swung into the first half of the S-bend. Gallagher hit the lights and the horns simultaneously. The sudden blaze turned the mist into a blinding glare that shocked the rider into snatching his mount upright at the worst possible moment.

He lost control.

The motorcycle began to lean in the opposite direction. Its front wheel hit the prepared barrier and began to travel along it, guided involuntarily towards the waiting edge of the road. The rider, as if suddenly realizing his fate, made a frantic effort to get off. This further increased the machine's instability. With a seeming mind of its own, it took its rider towards oblivion, singing raucously as it took to the air and its driven rear wheel finally lost purchase.

The big motorcycle spun into the enveloping mist, flinging its rider clear like a disjointed rag doll. Machine and man came back to earth far apart from each other. The motorcycle landed with a grating banging and slamming of metal that was deadened by the mist; then there was a silence that seemed poised, waiting for more. The rider had made no sound, not even of falling.

From below came a dull boom as the stricken machine exploded. A reddish orange bloom painted the mist briefly.

Dalgleish was running down off his perch and into the road to clear the rocks away even as Gallagher drove up and stopped, hurrying out to help. In seconds, they had made that stretch of narrow road as safe as it had been; which wasn't saying much.

They ran back to the car, got in, and Gallagher had it moving almost before Dalgleish had clipped on his belt. They did not speak until they were back on the A850 and Gallagher was powering the *quattro* along the wide sweeping bend that led towards Blackhill.

"Well, it worked," Dalgleish said.

"Yes. It worked the last time. No reason why it shouldn't have."

Dalgleish tore his eyes off the glowing numerals of the speedometer that seemed stuck at 120 to stare at Gallagher. "Last time? You've done a crazy thing like this before?"

"Yes. With a variation. The effect was just as devastating. But that's another story."

Dalgleish looked away. Here, the mist had practically disappeared. Skye was still playing with them.

"You can be a dangerous bastard when you want to be," Dalgleish said eventually.

"I wasn't always like this."

It was seriously said; sufficiently so to cause Dalgleish to look again.

"They did a good job on us," he commented reflectively.

Gallagher said nothing, so Dalgleish looked away once more.

They passed through Blackhill. Gallagher paid lip service to slowing down, urged the *quattro* on.

"Who do you think he was?" Dalgleish queried.

"You tell me. You've got the answers and I'm still waiting. You were going to tell me from the beginning, before our friend on the red bike interrupted us. I'm all ears again."

"As I've said," Dalgleish began after a while, continuing where he'd left off, "Windshear does exist, and the KGB wants them. Feeding me in to prove or disprove their existence had to be done in such a way that the KGB would not be alerted. That called for an elaborate smokescreen. We needed someone who could be used as a front to throw any KGB snoops right off the scent. That was where McQueen came in."

Gallagher retained his silence, concentrating on keeping the *quattro* moving at as high a speed as he dared. They were passing Clachamish, heading south towards Skeabost.

"McQueen," Dalgleish went on, "was in Oman doing what he knew best, for good pay. He was there in a private capacity, but you know with these things. The Department kept in touch."

"The Department always keeps in touch," Gallagher said with a wry grimace. No one knew better just how much.

"So, they hauled him in," Dalgleish went on, after a glance at Gallagher that could have passed as being sympathetic, "and gave him a story about a KGB man masquerading as an engineer, and who was a bit greedy for capitalist pounds and dollars. In his own way, McQueen was a bit of an old-fashioned patriot; blinkered and murderous, but still a patriot. At least, that was how he saw himself."

"I doubt that he saw himself as blinkered and murderous."

Dalgleish gave a smile that was devoid of humor. "Fanatical patriots never do."

"I almost feel sorry for the bastard."

Dalgleish shrugged dismissively. "He never knew what he was walking into. What he didn't know didn't harm him."

"You call dying on a spoof mission not being harmed?"

Dalgleish shrugged once more. "Ignorance is bliss and all that." The tinge of bitterness had again sneaked into the voice.

Once more, Gallagher kept his silence as he slowed right down for Skeabost. As if suddenly coming out to play, five cars passed, going the other way. He gave each a careful scrutiny. It was getting quite dark now.

Dalgleish said, "Islanders."

"That's what we thought about the Landrover." But he agreed in his mind with Dalgleish. He doubted whether there'd be others so soon; but you could never tell with these things.

The cars went on their way without stopping.

Dalgleish had turned to stare back at them.

Now he turned to his front once more. "How about the Finns?"

"Didn't you say scratch them?"

"Yes." Thoughtfully. "Really too obvious. Turn left here. Go back the way we came."

Gallagher turned the *quattro* on to the B8036, cutting across country to join the A856 back into Trotternish. He agreed with Dalgleish about the Finns.

"Go on about McQueen," he said to Dalgleish.

"Ah, yes. McQueen. The Department set him up as an import/export bod. . . ."

Gallagher made a derisive sound. "Import/export. Oh, the sins those two words cover. But I've interrupted you. Sorry. Go on."

"Oh, I agree with you," Dalgleish said, going on in a dry voice: "The Russians have their cultural attachés, we have our import/export merchants . . . who now and then come a cropper."

"To which list we can add the unloved McQueen."

"Precisely. So, the poor sod was sent out to the United Arab Emirates, to Sharjah, to set up shop . . . and to wait. Of course, he was totally unsuitable, but that didn't matter. In fact, it helped. Someone as brutish as McQueen would be instantly noticeable and, as his social manners left much to be desired, he stuck out among the expatriate crowd. In a bizarre way, therefore, he fitted his role perfectly. I believe he even began to enjoy it, jetting around the little desert kingdoms, being entertained— sometimes quite lavishly—by prospective customers who were rolling in it. As a salesman, he'd have made a good car mechanic, but his brashness saw him through.

"Three months later, our KGB contact came in from the Yemen, posing as a Swede. A pattern was established for another three months while we checked it out. It appeared to be a genuine attempt at a friendly contact. I went into the UAE and met him without McQueen's knowledge. It took two more meets over a period of another four weeks before he admitted he was carrying out a sounding for the Windshear Group; but he was not KGB, he said. He was actually GRU, though there were like-minded KGB."

By now the *quattro* was halfway to Uig.

"When we get to Uig," Dalgleish said, "don't go back into the Quiraing. Follow the main road right round the peninsula. I should have told you most of it by then. I think we can slow down a bit. It will be some time before anyone finds the motorcycle."

"What about the others? Whoever was running them will know by now that something's gone wrong."

"They've still got to find them. We've got a little time."

Gallagher was not so sure, but said nothing. The *quattro* loped along at 60. Even on such a road with the northern night having come early, Gallagher felt as though they were crawling.

Dalgleish continued: "Naturally, we were sceptical . . . but something like that could not be overlooked. It was worth a try. I agreed to go in. My contact said he was sure the KGB were suspicious of him. When is the KGB not suspicious? Christ. They're suspicious of each other, never mind the GRU."

"From what you're telling me, they've got reason. A faction inside the KGB *and* the GRU working together against their respective organizations would give any self-respecting secret snoop the jitters in a society like that. It should be giving us the jitters too. Nothing sends a nation to war faster than heavyweight dissension at home. It's not as if history isn't littered with precedents."

"That was considered . . . both by us and the Windshear Group. *They* felt that the more jittery their people became, the more likely they'd try to come up with a weapon that would give them a stunning advantage over the West so that *if* and *when* there came a need to strike, they could do it so devastatingly we would be in no position to retaliate. Don't forget that over there they still believe in the old blitzkrieg, the steamroller, the hammer, call it what you like. It boils down to the same thing: a surprise, unstoppable attack by sheer force of arms."

He paused as they drove into Uig, and did not speak again until Gallagher had negotiated the hairpin bend out of town.

"Talking of Windshear," Dalgleish said, "when the wind hits this place, it really makes a production of it. Until you've experienced a storm on Skye, in the Quiraing especially, you don't know what maddened nature can be like . . . outside Russia, that is."

He paused again, as if for reflection; then he seemed to rouse himself.

"On our final meeting," he went on, continuing his story, "I was given details of how I would be fed in, how I would be contacted, and so forth. I must admit that part of me still thought it was a KGB operation, but I couldn't see the motive; so I went back to the Department to say I'd go in.

"Meanwhile, our friendly kept up his meetings with McQueen. It would build a good legend, he insisted."

Gallagher nodded as he cruised the *quattro*. Legend meant cover story. Poor McQueen, the front man being set up for a hit. Bugger McQueen. The bastard had blown away enough people for the fun of it.

"So?"

"So he kept meeting McQueen and made it look as if he was selling for Western currency. He knew he was being monitored when he was with McQueen. He'd made sure of that. When they eventually came to take him, he fired on them, knowing quite certainly what would come next. There was no way he was going to let them take him alive. McQueen, who was conveniently with him at the time, also pulled out a weapon. In the battle that followed, both McQueen and our friendly were killed."

"Surprise, surprise."

"There was no other way."

"There never is."

"It took the KGB heat off," Dalgleish said, almost defensively.

"You don't have to justify it to me, Uffa. I

weep no tears for McQueen. I'm just having a touch of the there-but-for-fortunes. All this was set up by Kingston-Wyatt?"

"When he was certain the Windshear Group were worth investigation, yes."

"What a hard-nosed bastard."

"Tell me about it," Dalgleish said with a sudden tightness, slipping briefly into Americanese.

"Did he let the Americans know?"

Dalgleish said, "Ha! Kingston-Wyatt? Some hope."

"So they could be chasing you too."

"I doubt it. They can't chase what they don't know about."

"I wouldn't count on it. Everybody snoops on everybody else; even on allies. East and West do it. You know that."

Dalgleish shrugged for answer. He didn't seem to care. He fell silent for a couple of miles.

"Anyway," he carried on after a while, "I found myself in Turkey. I was met as arranged, and taken across the border to Tbilisi. Again, I felt uneasy about the way it was being conducted. They had supplied me with genuine identity papers, travel permits, work permits . . . they had done everything. I was beginning to feel more and more certain I'd been suckered into a trap; but what for, I could not begin to guess. I thought of all sorts of possibilities, even that we had someone they badly wanted exchanged. In the event, the simplest fact was the true one: Windshear did exist. You cannot even begin to imagine what it felt like to be working with members of the KGB and GRU, being totally dependent upon their goodwill, deep within Soviet territory.

"I learned a few things that destroyed a lot of myths we cherish here in the West. Do you know there are whole regiments of soldiers who would down tools in the event of a war between the blocs? The only trouble is, the authorities know it too, so there are other regiments, Guards regiments, whose specific job is to see that it never happens. Those soldiers who turn from battle will walk straight into the guns of the Guards regiments. What a choice. If the other side doesn't kill you, your own will."

"So why doesn't every regiment down tools? There can't be enough of the Guards to stop everybody."

Dalgleish gave a grim smile. "If that ever happened, it would precipitate the very war we're all afraid of. That's what the Windshear Group know. That's why they want to carry out their changes from within. It will cost them a lot of blood when the time comes; but they're prepared for it. Rather that than the wholesale destruction of their homeland.

"They moved me from military district to military district, partly to keep me from any interested eyes, and partly to let me gauge the temper of the people: to listen to what they were saying when they felt the KGB was not sniffing around. This took several months, during which time my various contacts fed me information about all sorts of things, even down to who was being made commander of a District, who was being demoted, who got drunk and was sent to a penal battalion . . . things you would consider not worth reporting, but which together gave a very substantial picture. We ourselves listen in to world communications traffic for the same reasons.

"It's the whole pattern that matters, and how single items affect it. Each time I was moved, I was given a new identity. Jesus. They were so efficient, you wouldn't believe it. I suppose that, working from inside the system, they could bend it to suit their purposes. Monolithic bureaucracies tend to be prone to that sort of doctoring; and believe me, they don't come more monolithic. The system feeds on itself, spawns itself. It's like a vast network of veins pumping life into the society it has created. To kill it, you've practically got to kill the society itself. Windshear believe their way may achieve the aim without too high a casualty rate."

The road began to hug the coast along Lub Score. Gallagher kept the *quattro* going at the same leisurely pace; but he never relaxed his scrutiny of the mirrors, which kept giving him the all-clear. Dalgleish's story was slowly congealing his blood. Somehow, somewhere, the Windshear Group had been compromised. The KGB, with the scent in its nostrils, was not going to give up. Gallagher did not want to be in the firing line. He was not into that kind of game any more. Why the hell didn't people leave him alone?

He felt a rush of resentment towards Dalgleish; less so than he did for the Department. He had told the Department to stuff it. It was harder to say that to Dalgleish. *Bloody hell, Uffa!* he thought angrily.

Dalgleish was looking at him. "I know what you're thinking. You're wishing you hadn't come."

"Is it that obvious?"

"You're looking a bit po-faced."

"I thought you needed a little help, perhaps to make peace with the Department so that they could cover you instead of trying to do you in. After what you've said, there is no way I can see the KGB giving up on you. How did you get away in the first place?"

"I'm coming to that. Do you want to hear more?"

"I'm here, am I not? Why waste the opportunity?" Bitterly.

"You don't have to sound so happy about it."

"Well, Christ! What do you expect?"

They drove on wordlessly through Duntulm and the road, the A855 since Uig, began curving back across the tip of Trotternish towards Staffin. The *quattro* hummed to itself.

"Everyone knows," Dalgleish said into their silence, "that Andropov is dying. When he goes, there's going to be a considerable period of flux, even after they've chosen a replacement. There are, at the moment, twelve possible candidates known to the outside world: eight Russians, two Ukrainians, one Azeri, one Kazakh. Of that lot, only four are 'youngsters', and only two of those are below sixty. They are both Russian. What makes you think there are not others, not necessarily Russian, who would like a taste of power?"

"I'm not thinking anything. I'm just listening."

"Well, there are," Dalgleish continued, undeflected. "A lot of people who would like to see young, radical blood calling the tune for a change. There is too much senility in the high offices of the world they feel."

"Younger blood would be more sensible, would it?"

"I was as sceptical as you are. But I've met some of those people."

"And now you've got a ticket to a KGB tea-dance that they're eager to collect."

Dalgleish fell silent again. The atmosphere in the car had become charged with something indefinable. It was not simply because Gallagher was annoyed by the fact that he'd been pitched headlong into Dalgleish's and the Department's mess. He felt very strongly that Dalgleish was holding something back, and still would be when the story supposedly came to an end.

Gallagher did not voice his thoughts.

Dalgleish said, "After Andropov, things are going to get colder; much colder. Inside the Soviet Union, there's going to be all sorts of jockeying for position. A few people are going to disappear, I think. Windshear intend to make sure none of those are theirs."

He appeared to swallow before going on, "The real breakthrough came when I was passed a film that had been taken, I was assured, some months before; even before that

time in Sharjah. I haven't seen what's on it—
not properly, that is—but I was told. It made my
blood freeze."

"You believed them?"

"The film, which I still have, will destroy
itself if the cassette is opened in the wrong sequence; but I was shown a strip copy with ten
exposures. It has since been destroyed. There
was an aircraft on it. It was eight-millimeter
film, so I used a magnifying lamp which they
had supplied for the occasion. The aircraft looks
like a cross between the *Backfire* and the *Blackjack*. Windshear have assured me that *Blackjack* is a red herring. The real baby is this new
aircraft, the Tu-22P—call it *Blackfire*—and it's
radar-immune. Totally."

"Good Christ!" Gallagher whispered.

"Exactly what I thought. There's your pre-
emptive strike. The West always thinks the opposition are way behind in technology, and that
their equipment spends most of its time falling
apart. That, in actual fact, is true in most cases.
Take the Mig-25. Fast as hell . . . in a straight
line. It can't turn; not in a dogfight. Hit it, and
bingo. But there's the new two-seat *Foxhound*
with brand-new radar and advanced performance. The point I'm making is that while it is
true they've got equipment problems, they also
have a knack for making pretty good stuff and
keeping it secret. What do they care if we know
their gear comes to pieces? As long as they can
keep the real goodies secret, that's all that matters; and believe me, they do."

"Until now."

Dalgleish nodded. "Until now."

"No wonder they're after your blood. You were going to tell me how you got away."

Dalgleish did not look round. "Yes. I am."

Gallagher waited as the road climbed out of Kendram. To his left, beyond the cliffs, was the darkened expanse of the upper reaches of the Sound of Raasay. He was not in the mood to wonder at the majesty of nature. He was thinking about the last ferry back and not wanting to miss it. He was thinking about a radar-immune aircraft. He was thinking about being caught in the KGB's and the GRU's hunt for Dalgleish; caught in the bloody middle. He was thinking, and wishing he were somewhere else.

"I still don't know exactly how it happened," Dalgleish was saying. "I was blown in Kopeysk. Instead of my contact, two bonafide KGB men came for me. I couldn't believe it. Everything had been working so smoothly. I suppose I should have expected it." Wryly. "A period of relative ease had made me complacent. Oddly, the KGB didn't get rough with me, which made me very wary indeed. I'd braced myself for a session in one of their psychiatric hospitals or even the big number itself in Kropotkinsky Street. But nothing like that happened."

There was still a sense of wonder in Dalgleish's voice. "I cannot even begin to tell you how relieved I was. The nightmares I had expecting all sorts of horrors! In a way, that was a form of torture. They were playing with me. They did not question me for three months. Can you believe it? Three bloody months while my mind did its own havoc on me. When they finally came, it soon became apparent they did not know I was with Windshear. By that time, of course, I had not yet been given the film, thank God.

"They didn't know why I had come. They had me as a spy, but what had been my purpose? It exercised them for a long time. They gave me another month with my thoughts. It was unnerving. Not a single hint of we-have-ways-of-making-you-talk. Yet, the all-pervading atmosphere was constantly present. They were working on me in a very subtle way. There was also the unspoken suggestion that I was in for ever. Then one day, out of the blue, when I was being transported to an unknown destination, the car was ambushed in isolated countryside. Windshear had struck. They killed everybody: KGB escort, the driver, and all of the guards in the back of the car that was taking me except one—he was Windshear.

"To avoid suspicion, they took all the bodies away, disposed of them miles apart. That way, the investigators would be unable to point at any one member of the escort party as a dissident. The man who was not killed is of course finished with public life. To all intents and purposes, he is as dead as his other comrades. Two burnt-out cars was all the evidence they left."

"So your friendly guard leaked the route."

"Seemed like it."

"Seemed?"

"I thought it might have been an elaborate KGB trick to get me to lead them to Windshear.

The price of the deaths was nothing compared with the actual prize."

"The thought had crossed my mind," Gallagher said.

"But, again, I had underestimated Windshear," Dalgleish said. "Never once had they tried to let me know they were doing something to get me out. It simply happened. But the KGB had been doing their own stirring. While I was in custody, they fed stuff out about my having been turned. It was pretty conclusive, and very believable. The Department believed. Kingston-Wyatt believed." Dalgleish's words had almost become a snarl. "The bastard."

"You sound as if you wanted to kill him."

"Wouldn't you?" Dalgleish countered.

Yes, I would, Gallagher said to himself. *Not so long ago, I wanted to.*

He said, quietly, "I can understand. But now, the Department's after you as well. We left the evidence back in that wood."

Dalgleish gave a brief, sour laugh. "The KGB's got its revenge."

"I think they wanted you to run, Uffa. They expected someone to break you out. It just went wrong on them. Windshear was a step ahead. They obviously couldn't have known that."

Dalgleish said nothing for a while, as if considering that aspect of the matter, then, "Perhaps. But there's more. The KGB and the GRU are on a joint operation in Western Europe."

"Aren't they always? Perhaps not together, but. . . ."

"No. No. This is something special, and directly linked to the Tu-22P. It concerns cruise and Pershing."

"This stew gets lovelier by the minute," Gallagher said drily. "When you jump in, you really make a meal of it, don't you?"

"That's what scaring the pants off Windshear," Dalgleish went on, unperturbed. "It should be scaring the pants off everybody. The KGB and the GRU—I think the idea first floated itself in the GRU, and as far as I know they're still playing it close to their chests. That lot wouldn't give each other a biscuit if the other were dying of hunger. Anyway, for convenience, they're both working on this. They seem to have the idea that the cruise missiles at Greenham Common are dummies, and that the real babies are being sited up here. . . ."

"Here on Skye?" Gallagher interrupted disbelievingly. "There's nowhere to hide them."

"Oh, I don't know. With a bit of ingenuity, you could hide a lot of things here. But no, not Skye. The mainland. While everyone's enjoying the comedy theater at Newbury, the hot birds are being sited up in the highlands. That's what the opposition think; that's why they've got a bunch of Spetsnaz prowling about up here. Think about the implications. As soon as they've pinpointed the new sites, down they go into their tactical plans. Imagine fleet upon fleet of Tu-22Ps. And don't say they can't build them without our knowing it. They can. After all, the Americans built the SR-71s in complete secrecy. They're not the only ones who can do it."

"Good Christ," Gallagher said slowly,

wondering if he'd heard correctly. "Windshear told you all this?"

"Yes. And I believe them, despite the fact it could still be an elaborate KGB hoax."

"It could be, you know. We both know they can take years to mount an operation. They're past masters of the double, triple and quadruple bluff. They—"

"No! I've seen them, don't forget. They're twitchy about something. If they're planning a deal as complex as a massive build-up of radar-immune aircraft to plaster Western missile sites in a pre-emptive strike, they can't afford to have the slightest sniff of the news coming out of there. To say that Windshear is making them jittery would be a raving understatement. It's one thing pitting wits with the West; it's something else again when you're doing it with people within your own organization, who know all the labyrinthine back alleys of in-fighting, who came through the same fire as you, who *think* like Russians because they *are* Russians. . . . Oh, yes. It's something else."

They passed Flodigarry, cruising now at 55. Gallagher looked briefly at the digital timer. It was 4:15. He had just over an hour to make it to the last ferry from Kyleakin.

"How far is it to the ferry?" he asked Dalgleish.

"From here? Oh, I'd say about fifty or so miles, give or take a mile."

"The last ferry leaves at five-thirty. I've got an hour and fifteen minutes."

"You'll do it in this machine. Easily."

"Perhaps you haven't noticed but it's dark

now, and I don't know the roads. That's not even counting sudden mist." Gallagher had perceptibly increased speed. The read-out was on 65.

"You'll make it," Dalgleish repeated. "What I've got to say won't take long. You can drop me off in Staffin. I'll make my way back to my hidey-hole."

"You're going to walk around the town with that bloody rifle?"

"I'll manage." Dalgleish was unworried by the prospect. "I'd like you to do something for me."

"You mean there's more?"

Dalgleish ignored the sarcasm. "The camera Lucinda gave you."

"What about it?"

"I'd like you to do a little hunting with it. It's got an infra-red selector by the thumbwheel adjuster. Use it to take photographs of some people for me. It's already loaded with infra-red film."

Gallagher did not like the sound of it. "What people, Uffa?"

Dalgleish passed him a piece of paper. "There's an address on it. You'll know what to do when you see the place."

Gallagher stared briefly at his companion before returning his attention to the road. "Are you perhaps trying to tell me you want me to take photographs of GRU operatives who may be at this address you've given me? And what are they going to do about it? Pose for me?"

"Don't say no, please, Gordon. I need those photos as proof for the Department. I need to

prove that I haven't turned. I can hardly go
across to do it myself."

"You need better resolution than an infra-
red shot."

"That little machine will give all the resolution I need."

"Your friends in the KGB gave it to you?"

"Yes."

"It's a good-looking piece of kit."

Dalgleish smiled briefly in the gloom of the
car. "They know how to build when they get
everything right. They have with the Tu-22P.
Believe me."

"What about the film of the aircraft? I
thought I was supposed to pick it up."

"Not yet. It's my insurance."

"It could also mean your death if they
catch up with you."

Dalgleish said, reflectively: "It will be,
whether I've got it or not, if I'm stupid enough
to let that happen. Right. We're in Staffin. Stop
. . . just . . . here. That's it." He freed his belt,
picked up the Dragunov. "Right. I'll be off."

Gallagher stared at him. "That's it? Do you
expect me to return here with the camera, take
it to the Department, or what?"

"Return with it," Dalgleish said, and was
quickly out of the car.

Gallagher watched him lope off, the Dragunov hidden beneath his jacket, barrel pointing
downwards; then he was gone out of the light of
the headlights.

"Shit!" Gallagher said exasperatedly, putting the *quattro* into gear.

He drove furiously, sometimes doing 100

mph where most cars would have balked at 60. Bends meant for 30 mph were taken at twice that speed. The *quattro* never let him down. Soon he began to enjoy the drive, pitting himself and the car against the unknown roads and the unpredictable weather. He slowed briefly for Portree, but put his foot down again as soon as he was out of the island capital.

The route to Sligachan had gentle bends. The car ate up the miles. The sweeping curve at the top of the loch was taken in stride, then it was on to Sconser, curving round the base of the basaltic ramparts of Glamaig, putting the power on. Tight bends at the top of Loch Ainort came at him. He hurled the *quattro* at them. It stayed on the road. Once, twice, he had to stop to allow an oncoming vehicle to pass. Nothing hostile. He drove on, savoring the feel, the urge of the powerful motor.

He made it to Kyleakin with ten minutes to spare. The same ferryman was there to greet him.

"You made it, then," the man said.

"Yes." Gallagher spoke easily, cheerfully.

"Saw the lights coming. Fast, is it?" The man nodded at the *quattro*.

"A bit."

"It looks it. And what do you think of Skye, then?"

"A beautiful place. I'll come back."

The talkative man smiled. "You love Skye or you hate it. If you love it, it holds on to you."

For ever, Gallagher didn't say, remembering the dead men he'd left behind. He wondered who would be the first to question the ferryman when the time came.

It didn't matter. By the time that occasion arose, he'd be well out of it. He hoped.

The ferry began to move. There were just two other cars on it. Gallagher had expected more, it being the last ferry. He stared at them, but there was nothing to arouse suspicion.

He relaxed as the ferry took him across the darkened waters.

Fowler looked up as the door to his office opened after a discreet knock. Delphine Arundel.

He smiled at her. "Still here? I've taken up all of your Sunday." She did not return his smile, so he frowned at the sheet of paper she held towards him. "Trouble?"

"Trouble," she said. "I think this was meant for Sir John and I thought you ought to see it."

"That should please him," Fowler said drily, taking the message from her. He read it, leaned forward on an elbow and placed his head in the palm of his hand. "Oh, my God!" he said slowly, softly; then he sat up, stared at her. "Where is he?" he asked tightly.

"At home."

"Get the bastard on the scrambler. Never mind. I'll do it from here."

"Right." At the door, she paused. "What are you going to do?"

"Do? Do? What I'd like to do is run the little runt over with a bloody tank!"

Delphine Arundel went out quietly.

Winterbourne was on the phone, listening to Fowler's barrage.

"You gave me your word, Sir John!" Fowler said with cold fury. "You were supposed to clear it with me first."

"I don't have to clear anything with you, Fowler!" Winterbourne was almost squeaking in his outrage. "It's the other way round! And you have no right whatsoever to read messages meant for me! I shall have strong words with Mrs. Arundel and—"

"Sir John," Fowler interrupted rudely, "you activated Rogues without my knowledge. Now, according to their controller, nothing has been heard from them for over two hours after they should have reported. You are aware, I trust, of what that means?"

"Fowler, I will not have you speaking to me—"

"It means they are dead, Sir John," Fowler again interrupted, this time with brutal relish. "Dalgleish got them, just as I warned. And as Gallagher *is* up there with him, you can make that an absolute certainty. Why didn't you leave well alone, Sir John?"

"Fowler . . . !" Winterbourne began to shout.

Fowler hung up on him and buzzed Delphine Arundel.

"Yes?"

"Arundel, Sir John will be coming back on the phone steaming from all orifices. Nature calls me urgently."

"Understood," she said. There was a hint of amusement in her voice.

Fowler cut transmission and stared about him sighing. "At times like these," he told himself mildly, "I'm glad I don't smoke."

Gallagher pulled up before the little hotel. In the lights of the car, he saw a big, dark-colored BMW coupé. It had Alpina side-flashes, which meant it was highly tuned. Gallagher knew what it was; a B9 and very fast, faster than an ordinary *quattro,* but not as fast as his.

He checked himself ruefully. There was nothing to indicate the car as hostile, and already he was comparing performances. But he continued to stare at the other car as he shut down and turned off the lights. He paused. British number plates, but left-hand drive. It didn't necessarily mean anything. His own car was left-hand drive, with British plates.

Still.

He climbed out of the *quattro* cautiously and got his bag out of the trunk. He locked the car. No one came at him. He walked the short distance to the hotel entrance, ready for anything.

Nothing happened. He entered.

The big American was a beacon that drew his eyes like ants after a picnic sandwich; but he resisted the temptation to give the man more than a cursory glance. Needles of anticipation danced on his spine as he walked to the reception desk. The same girl was still there. Either she was having a long day of it or she was just about to go off.

She greeted him with a big smile of welcome. "Ah, Mr. Thompson! Did you enjoy Skye?"

It took him a brief second to remember the name Lucinda had picked for him.

"A really quite fantastic place," he enthused. "Must go back."

She had spoken loudly enough for the American to have overheard. He wondered if the man had quizzed her about his whereabouts. Then he reasoned that the man would have asked for Gallagher, not Thompson . . . unless a description had also been supplied by the questioner.

Gallagher stopped himself. The American could simply be a tourist; but his instincts doubted it. You could always tell. Some of them would never change; a special breed whose entire presence was like a uniform.

The same savage U.S. marine haircut; the same type of suit that could only have been cut on the other side of the Atlantic; the same type of body that had played the strange game called college football.

The brief glance had showed Gallagher a tall man with a face like granite and a jaw that would frighten a brick shithouse. A clean-shaven face; a face that believed whatever job it did was elevated to being the equivalent of an evangelical mission. Gallagher knew the type. Dangerous, hard bastards for all their obviousness. But there were others too; those who did not look so obvious, who were even better at their jobs. They were rare, but they were twice as dangerous.

The big man, Gallagher felt, would have a

partner. They always worked with partners, that type. Gallagher wondered where the other was lurking. How had the Americans found him? He was sure now that was their reason for being here. The hotel was not their style.

"I knew you'd say that," the girl was saying; then her face clouded over. "Isn't it a shame about that poor woman?"

"What woman?" Gallagher queried, wondering what she was on about.

"Oh. I forgot, You wouldn't know, seeing you left your papers." She reached down, came up with the papers he'd ordered. "I kept them for you."

The face that stared up at him from the front page jolted him.

Oh, dear God, he thought, and muted his reaction for the benefit of the American. He was sure the man was staring at him.

"Terrible, isn't it?" the girl went on. "I used to watch her a lot when I was a wee bairn. London's not safe these days. I'd never go to live there."

Nowhere's safe, he didn't tell her, remembering his violent afternoon on Skye.

"Terrible," he agreed.

"Hooligans, these muggers," she said, her voice full of a mixture of sympathy for the dead woman and outrage at the people who had killed her. "They should put them in the army. Teach them some discipline."

Having a good idea of the identity of the culprits, Gallagher could only stifle the bitter, ironic words he could feel wanting to be spoken.

Instead, he told her, "I hope they catch them."

"So do I! Hanging's too good!"

Gallagher smiled wryly, remembering the Rogues lying in the misty wood. He wondered if they had been responsible. He hoped so.

"The dining-room's open if you want anything," she continued. "Sorry, but the bar's not open yet."

"That's all right. The dining-room will be fine."

In truth, he wanted neither a drink nor to eat. The callous murder of his friendly, lonely neighbor had robbed him of his appetite; but he would have to go through with it. He smiled his thanks at the receptionist and went into the dining-room feeling guilty about the cup of coffee he'd never found the time to share.

He did not look at the big American as he went out, but as soon as he'd entered the dining-room, he saw the other one, shorter, stockier, with a different haircut, and looking every inch a heavy. This one had very dark, shiny hair cropped close so that the spikes radiated from his crown. Reptilian eyes surveyed Gallagher swiftly, efficiently, before pretending to be interested only in the food on the table at which he sat.

Gallagher took a table in as far a corner as he could, put his bag close to hand and began to scrutinize a menu. A waitress came up. When she'd left with his order, he picked up a paper and began to read.

Moments later, someone was at his table.

He put the paper down slowly and looked up. It was the big American.

"I'm Winemaster," the man said. "Mind if I join you?" Winemaster began to pull back a chair.

Gallagher looked at him coldly. "Yes."

But Winemaster had already sat down. "Thank you."

"I don't think you heard me," Gallagher said flatly.

"Didn't I? How about that."

Gallagher deliberately picked up his paper again, began to read.

"That's not very polite," Winemaster said. An edge had crept into his voice.

"It's not polite to sit at tables uninvited," Gallagher said without looking up.

"Then I'll come to the point. The girl back there called you Thompson, but we both know differently, don't we, Mr. Gallagher?"

Gallagher put down the paper slowly. "Winemaster, or whatever your name is, piss off." He picked up the paper once more.

Winemaster seemed as immovable as one of the basaltic columns of Skye. "We had a man on the island. He hasn't reported for quite a while now."

Gallagher wondered if that had been the motorcyclist. His face registered nothing. He said nothing.

"I said . . ." Winemaster began.

"I'm quite capable of hearing. I think you've got your wires crossed, Winemaster. I don't know what you're on about." Gallagher pointedly continued to read his paper.

"Don't flim-flam me, Gallagher." Winemaster was beginning to sound angry. "I know all about you. I know all about the Tanner girl and what you did. I know about Fowler, and Kingston-Wyatt, and Winterbourne, *and* Dalgleish. Want me to go on?"

"They tell me it's still a free country. People can still say what they like. I just wish you'd go and do it elsewhere." Gallagher could feel his own anger beginning to tick. Had Winemaster's people been responsible for the death of that poor woman, after all? Had they been the ones following him in the white Mercedes?

The waitress returned just then with his order. He smiled at her as she set it down. "Thank you."

"Thank you, sir." She had a rich highland accent. She turned to Winemaster. "Will you be eating here, sir, or with the other American gentleman?"

Winemaster looked put out. Gallagher wanted to smile. Blown by a waitress.

"No . . ." Winemaster began, then: ". . . er, I'll have some coffee here, but I'll eat at the other table."

"Right you are, sir." She left to get the coffee.

Gallagher put his paper to one side, began to eat.

Winemaster said, "He was on a motorcycle; a big red motorcycle."

"Who was?"

Winemaster gave a loud intake of breath that was one of sharp irritation. "Gallagher, you'd hate it if I got angry with you."

Gallagher looked up then, hazel eyes freezing. "You'd like it even less if I got angry with *you*," he said quietly. "Don't you dare threaten me."

Winemaster was momentarily startled by what he saw in Gallagher's eyes. It threw him off his stroke for a brief second; then he recovered. He was the hard Winemaster again.

"Get this straight, Gallagher. Don't try to come up against us. Kroski over there can be a mean sonofabitch when he wants to be. There are more like him."

"Bully for Kroski. Bully for the others like him. Now can I get on with my dinner in peace?"

"Peace is the one thing you're not going to get, buddy, until you tell me what you and that psycho over on the island have done with my operative."

Gallagher sighed. "You obviously don't respect other people's privacy, even at meal times." He put down his knife and fork. "Habit dies hard, I suppose. That's what comes from a lifetime of snooping on others. But I can see you love it."

The waitress came with the coffee. Winemaster did not acknowledge her. She went away again after giving him a dirty look.

Winemaster said, "We know you came up here to see Dalgleish. Would you like to know how we found out?"

"Not really," Gallagher lied with heavy weariness, "but I'm sure you're going to tell me."

"Co-operation," Winemaster said. "Co-

operation between allies. Or perhaps you've fo-
gotten. We're supposed to be allies."

"What do you mean *'we'*? I'm not your ally,
Winemaster. Whatever business you're in, I'm
not in it. So we can't be allies, can we?"

"Oh, but you are, buddy. Deep in it. Right
up to your neck. The police are carrying out
infra-red surveillance trials on a stretch of
highway in Hertfordshire." He pronounced it
the American way. "And also, just on the Scottish border. The TV reads license plates, the
computer makes the connection, and the information is available to the right department. A
right-thinking head of department lets his allies have answers to certain questions."
Winemaster paused.

Winterbourne, Gallagher thought dis-
gustedly.

It would never have been Fowler. Winterbourne would have sent the Rogues. Of that,
Gallagher was now quite certain. Winterbourne would have requested police assistance.
Winterbourne would have wanted to under-
mine Fowler, and Winterbourne would have
blabbed to the Americans. The little bastard.

Gallagher thought about what Winemaster had said about the infra-red TV. It was the
first he'd heard of it. Things were getting more
and more like the KGB. The day couldn't be far
off when all the intelligence services saved
themselves a lot of trouble, clubbed together
and ran the world for profit. Perhaps they already did.

He smiled at his own cynicsm. He was
being unfair to people like Fowler, who, for all

their deviousness, actually held some principles; though how they lived with the contradictions of their job was something else. He himself had got out. But there were others; those upon whom he would turn his back with extreme wariness. Winemaster was one of those.

"I made a joke?" Winemaster said.

"You wouldn't understand."

Winemaster tried conciliation, "You've got a goddam fine record, Gallagher." Flattery too. "The boys in the black hats don't know about you. Hell, we only got to know about you some time last year."

Gallagher groaned inwardly. The boys in the black hats. Goodies and baddies. Christ.

Winemaster was saying, "You did pretty well when you went after the people who killed Lauren Tanner. . . ."

"Put a sock in it, Winemaster. I don't want to hear more. She's dead. Finished. Leave it." The pain was still there.

Winemaster's lifeless eyes stared at him, square jaw immobile. Finally, Winemaster said, "We know what happened still hurts."

Winemaster trying to be sympathetic was grotesque to listen to, but Gallagher remained silent.

"We know also," the American went on, "that because of the way you used to be in the field—still are, I'm positive—you're the best candidate Dalgleish has. You were college buddies, someone said."

Someone. Bloody Winterbourne.

Gallagher was scandalized. He had not expected it, even of Winterbourne, allies or no allies. He was quite certain that, in a similar case, the Americans would not have been so forthcoming. Winterbourne was on the grease.

"Dalgleish is way out on a limb," Winemaster said. "He can't handle all of us, *and* the Soviets. What we don't know is why the Soviets want him so badly."

Gallagher heaved a mental sigh of relief. At least Winterbourne had balked at giving everything away. Some modicum of loyalty must have stopped him.

"Find out for us," Winemaster continued into Gallagher's silence, "and we'll be prepared to forget you totalled our man. What the hell. The guy was in the field. The field is risky. We all know that."

Winemaster was now trying for trust. Gallagher watched these psychological contortions with an inward amusement. He would give more trust to an enraged scorpion.

He said, "I haven't seen anybody, and I have no information. I know nothing about your supposed man. You could be making all this up for reasons of your own."

"You think I'm up here for my health?" Winemaster snapped.

"Who knows what people do for amusement?"

Winemaster looked as if his jaw would burst off its hinges to slam Gallagher in the face. "I could have the cops on you."

"For what?"

"Speeding, to begin with."

Gallagher tried not to laugh. "You control

the British police now, do you? Had to happen, I suppose."

"We don't control, Gallagher," Winemaster said tightly. "We get co-operation."

"Same thing. The Russians get co-operation from their satellites."

Winemaster stood up abruptly. "You're making a mistake, Gallagher. It is better to need our help than to have us against you. If the Soviets are up here, you might have cause to regret your stubbornness. We know you were on the island. Our man reported seeing you. He reported following you at speed; then nothing. Not a squeak. There's a lot we can get you for. You've got dirt on your clothes. Think about that." Winemaster left to join Kroski, his coffee untouched.

Gallagher looked down at his plate. The food was cold. He hadn't wanted to eat, anyway. He stood up. The waitress appeared as if by magic.

"Didn't you like it, sir?" Her voice said it would be an affront to Scottish cooking if he said no.

"I enjoyed it," he said. "What little I was allowed to."

She glanced deliberately at Winemaster and Kroski. "I know what you mean. It's like that in hotels sometimes." She spoke loudly. "People you don't want to talk to coming to your table." She grimaced at the undrunk coffee. "Didn't even drink the coffee he made me get him. Who's going to pay for it?"

"He is," Gallagher said with some malice. She liked that. "I'll make sure."

Gallagher picked up his bag and his papers. "Sorry about the food."

"Come back later," she suggested helpfully. "I'm sure we can arrange something. The manager will be only too glad to help. We won't put this one on your bill. The manager will see to it. Your being a friend of Miss MacAusland."

Gallagher looked at her. "You know Miss MacAusland?" he asked quietly.

"We all do. She always stops here on her way home."

"I see. And where's home?"

"The family home? Big place up near Loch Carron."

It was amazing, Gallagher thought, what you could pick up through hotel gossip. He wondered whether Winemaster had done his routine with the staff. It seemed unlikely. Winemaster had already created a hostile reaction. It was doubtful whether the staff would have responded sympathetically. Besides, Winemaster probably wanted to keep as much of a lid on this as possible.

Gallagher gave the gossipy waitress another brief smile, thanking her for her fund of unwanted information, and went up to his room. He did not look in Winemaster's and Kroski's direction as he left. He hoped they had not heard mention of Lucinda MacAusland's name. It wouldn't do at all if they had.

It was 19:30 hours. Two hours later, after a hot bath and a change of shirt, he went back down to the dining-room. Winemaster and Kroski were nowhere to be seen. It didn't mean they were not somewhere in the hotel.

The same waitress came up to his table.

"You've got some peace now," she said cheerfully.

"Oh, yes?" The place was quite empty.

"Those Americans, they've gone. They paid their bill and left." She grimaced. "I'm not sorry. Pair of slaughters."

"Slaughters?"

"Horrible," she explained.

Gallagher smiled. It was a unique way to describe them. He waited, knowing she'd tell him more.

"Took off in their big car," she went on, "going north, I think. Whatever hotel they've gone to is welcome to them."

Gallagher wasn't sure he liked the direction they'd taken, if indeed they had gone north. While in his room, he had looked at the slip of paper Dalgleish had given him. It had been more of a location than an address. It was also north of Loch Alsh.

The waitress said, "Will you want the same again? You can order anything else you'd like, if you wish. The first order will not be put on your bill. The manager said."

"Thank you," Gallagher said. This time, he was hungry. He ordered a generous meal.

She smiled at him. "You are hungry. Anything to drink?"

He thought, what the hell, he was not going to drive tonight. "This is the land of Scotch," he said. "What do you recommend?"

"I'll bring it. Then you can tell me." She gave him a parting smile.

He watched the friendly waitress leave.

His mind left her almost immediately, as he remembered the time he had spent in his room familiarizing himself with the binocular camera. It was indeed, a neat piece of equipment. In addition to the thumbwheel adjuster, it had a push-button next to it on the right, for zoom control. The button on the left controlled the infra-red mode. There was a motor drive to power everything from shutter sequence to zoom.

He had tested the sighting on Skye. It had been remarkable. Kyleakin had come right up to his nose glowing with infra-red emanations, and in stark clarity. The shutter speed went up to 1/5000th of a second, which would give very high-resolution photos while virtually eliminating vibrations if the work had to be done in some haste.

Like dodging a bullet, he thought sourly.

The camera had been designed for ease of operation. The mode and operating push-buttons—four—fell easily to thumbs and middle fingers. The top buttons—trigger on the right, shutter-speed selector on the left—protruded slightly from the body while the lower ones blended smoothly with its contours. The shutter speed would come into view for a brief glowing moment to advise the user of what had been selected. This was simply done by pressing the selector while the camera counted upwards until the limit was reached. It would start all over again if the operator continued to press the button.

Gallagher wondered whether the Spetsnaz members Dalgleish had claimed were in

Scotland had such cameras with them, hoping for evidence of secret cruise sites.

A clandestine photographer after clandestine photographers. He smiled wryly. At least he would be doing his real job for a change.

The waitress returned with a generous measure of a darkly-golden liquid in a solid-looking glass.

"You'll not be wanting ice in it?" Her voice said, *Don't you dare.*

"I wouldn't dream of it."

She looked approvingly at him. "It's good to see a man who knows how to treat his whisky. Your order will be along soon."

As she went off, Gallagher wondered whether Winemaster had committed the sacrilege of asking for ice. Winemaster, he thought on reflection, was probably the kind who didn't touch the stuff and would make someone like Gallagher, who imbibed only sparingly, look like a raving drunkard. Winemaster had come across like that.

Gallagher tasted his drink. The mouthful went down his throat like warm silk. It was beautiful. He thought again of Winemaster. A dangerous individual; not one who would brook being thwarted. He took another swallow of the golden whisky, and thought of Lucinda MacAusland.

Why hadn't she told him she usually called at the hotel, and that her family home was in the general area? Perhaps, he decided, Dalgleish had wanted to keep as many things secret as possible. He could understand that. Dalgleish, as had transpired, could not have been totally sure of Gallagher's loyalty, even though he had cried out for help. Dalgleish had been feeling the chill wind of solitary exposure. He still was.

The waitress returned with the first course of his order.

"What do you think?" she asked, glancing at the whisky.

"Beautiful," he announced. "Never tasted anyting like it."

"We don't give that to the tourists," she said as she went away.

Gallagher felt privileged. It helped take the unpleasantness of Winemaster's shadow temporarily away.

He enjoyed his meal in blissful solitude. The gossipy waitress did not disturb him. For all her friendliness, he was glad of that. He wanted to think about Winemaster whom he was quite certain had not left Loch Alsh; and of the elusive Spetsnaz he was supposed to take pictures of. The problem was to do so without arousing Winemaster's interest, as well as the infinitely more lethal one of the GRU men.

Some hope. Dalgleish was crazy. I'm *bloody crazy,* Gallagher thought, going along with this.

But he couldn't bring himself to desert Dalgleish, despite the fact that he was still certain Dalgleish was holding out on him.

"Shit!" he said softly. It wasn't fair.

He finished his meal and stood up. The Scotch was a warm glow in his stomach. The food had been excellent and without frills.

The waitress came to clear. She had a plain face, but was so genuinely pleasant, she looked pretty. He was certain it wasn't the whisky. He wasn't that drunk, despite the potency of the liquor.

"A very nice meal," he told her. "Thank you."

"We aim to please," she said, giving him a teasing wink.

He left the dining-room, feeling good. The feeling evaporated as he approached the door to his room. He stopped and stared at it. The lock had been forced. He didn't move, thinking of the camera. If the intruder had been and gone, then it was goodbye to it, and any hope of getting Dalgleish's proof. If whoever had forced his way in were still around. . . .

Gallagher inched himself backwards until he was flattened against the wall. He looked about him, ears attuned, identifying and discarding unimportant sounds. Nothing came out of his room.

He was standing in a short, narrow corridor which was blocked at one end by one of the hotel's outside walls. At the other end, three steps that tended to creak led down to a landing from which two short flights of stairs led down in opposite directions. One went to the dining-room, the other to the reception area.

Gallagher listened for a good five minutes. No one came up the stairs, and no one moved in his room. He would have to go in. He didn't relish the idea. Despite what movies showed, he had not known anyone who liked bursting into rooms. Anything and anyone could be waiting to turn you into so much dead meat. But there were ways to minimize the risk if it had to be taken.

Cursing his oversight for leaving the camera, he gave himself another five minutes. The corridor remained empty. His room remained silent.

Without warning, he launched himself low, heaving the door open just sufficiently to give him entry, cutting down the light silhouetting him from outside as much as possible. He went in with a rolling motion that took him swiftly into the darkness of the room, lay still, waiting. The door swung itself shut. He'd made very little noise.

Gallagher stilled his breathing. Nothing moved. No gun roared in the gloom. He waited, drew breath slowly, quietly; and listened.

Five minutes, he judged. Ten. Absolutely nothing.

He began to move, crawling slowly, checking out the room like a prowling animal as his eyes absorbed the available light, enabling him to see. He had known in the instant of his entry that if any intruder had intended to shoot, the first shot would have come almost immediately, while he'd still been silhouetted. His low entry would have spoiled his unseen adversary's aim while giving him a clear indication of the person's position. His initial roll had taken him to cover behind the bed. He'd had the plan of the room firmly fixed in his mind.

It took him another five minutes to satisfy himself there was no one else in the room. He stood up and switched on the light. The place seemed undisturbed. He did not check his bag first. If the camera was gone, checking first would not bring it back. Instead, he did a care-

ful survey of the room, searching for bugs and
booby traps. It was clean. He at last checked his
bag. The camera was there. The bag had not
been disturbed.

It occurred to him that he had returned
inconveniently. Whoever had forced the door
had not had time to enter.

Gallagher paused suddenly, listening. The
three steps at the end of the corridor had
creaked. He went swiftly to the door and pulled
it open in a quick motion.

The corridor was empty.

He closed the door slowly, knowing what
had happened. His intruder had been hiding in
one of the other rooms, waiting for a moment to
make his escape. At this time of the year, there
were plenty of empty rooms.

Gallagher sat down on the bed, staring at
his bag with the camera peeping out of it. He
wondered who the person had been and how
come no one in the hotel had noticed his presence. Either the intruder was a guest, or he
knew the hotel well enough to be able to avoid
detection.

One of Winemaster's people, more of Winterbourne's Rogues, or perhaps even one of the
Russians Dalgleish had spoken about?

Gallagher did not put much credence in the
possiblility that it might have been one of the
GRU men. Even a deep-cover field man would
not have risked it; assuming he even knew
where to look. Dalgleish would have said if the
GRU knew about him.

Gallagher paused. Would Dalgleish not
also have kept that knowledge to himself? Dal-

gleish wanted nothing to jeopardize those pictures being taken.

Gallagher continued to stare at the bag and the offending camera. Bloody Dalgleish.

At last, he got up and balanced the two chairs in the room one on top of the other near the door, so that they'd form a first line of defense. They would crash to the floor with more than enough noise to alert him, should anyone try another entry. He surveyed the twin panes of the double-glazed window, taking care to do so with the lights out. Breaking them would be too clumsy, and cutting through would give him enough warning.

Satisfied, he went to bed. He had a perfectly undisturbed night.

Monday

Moscow, 0700 hours.

Ulvanov watched neutrally as Skoryatin entered the room.

"You do not mind, Comrade, that I have called our meeting so early?" he queried mildly, putting the right amount of regret in his voice.

Skoryatin took his usual seat. Ulvanov did not fool him. He knew his colleague and rival was as regretful as someone who pulled wings off flies.

"I like an early beginning to the day, Comrade," Skoryatin said, equally midly. "Moscow is bracing this morning."

Ulvanov permitted himself a smile and waved a hand at the silver samovar. "As you can see, I have your tea ready for you."

"And today, Comrade," Skoryatin got in quickly, "I shall serve."

Ulvanov looked at him neutrally. "How kind of you, Vladimir Mikhailovich."

"A pleasure, Dmitry Vasil'evich. A pleasure."

After Skoryatin had carried out his insincere ritual, they got down to business.

Ulvanov said, "It appears that Dalgleish has drawn more blood, this time British and American."

Skoryatin smiled with satisfaction. "I have seen the report." He had to get that in. It wouldn't do for Ulvanov to think his fingers were not right there on the pulse. "It will give your very efficient disinformation even more credence." After the gentle slap, some flattery would go down well. "They must now be quite confused about him."

Ulvanov, unsure of how to react, chose a roundabout way to respond. "He has, however, sufaced dangerously close and has brought both the Americans and the British with him."

"They are after Dalgleish, Comrade. Not after us. If we do nothing to excite them. They will be none the wiser. Dalgleish has clearly been unable to communicate with them. My team have instructions to eliminate him only when they are certain they will leave no trace of themselves. That includes bodies. The affair near Nottingham will not be repeated." It was almost an admission of failure, but Skoryatin felt he could live with it. Ulvanov would feed on it, though he would not be so crude as to do so obviously; which suited Skoryatin perfectly.

To gloat, even mildly, would be a display of weakness. Ulvanov would not want to appear weak. He would have to enjoy his little titbit privately.

Ulvanov briefly looked like someone who had been given a juicy-looking morsel only to find when he'd bitten into it that it had tasted sour.

"Perhaps we should wake the sleeper." Ulvanov suggested. He looked unblinkingly at Skoryatin.

"With respect, Comrade, I would strongly advise against it." Skoryatin knew he was on solid ground and could be as unyielding as he liked. The sleeper had been placed for one purpose and one purpose only. "The sleeper is linked beyond recall to the Tu-22P strategy. The Comrade is aware of this and that the sleeper, in position, is vital."

"A mere suggestion, Comrade," Ulvanov said, retreating unblushingly. "I am well aware that you have personal responsibility for the sleeper. I also appreciate the importance of the strategy. My suggestion was simply an expression of my concern that everything must be done to ensure lack of failure." Ulvanov smiled fleetingly, as if at a secret joke. "You will notice I did not say success. Lack of failure sounds more positive, more absolute. Would you not agree, Comrade?"

Skoryatin was not put out by this oblique reference to the possibility that his teams might fail in Western Europe. He knew all about Ulvanov's conversational tricks.

Skoryatin said, "My people will achieve what they have set out to. I shall naturally expect no less from the KGB."

It was not an out-and-out challenge; more of a warning that Ulvanov should not step too far out of his own territory.

"The KGB will be quite dependable," Ulvanov said smoothly. "Can we expect to see the proposals for crew training soon? At your convenience, of course."

Skoryatin poured himself another cup of tea before saying, "The schedules are being finalized." He spoke easily and, though not taken in by Ulvanov's patently false "at your convenience," knew he was well within schedule. Ulvanov's sly probes would find no weaknesses in his armor. "You will be able to see them soon enough. We shall be authorizing one more flight of the Tu-22P with Kakunin in command. On that occasion, it will be carrying the new air-launched weapon with the fourteen independently-targeted warheads. Thereafter, he is to be moved to take command of crew training. He will be promoted, of course."

Ulvanov nodded. "A very proficient officer," he said approvingly. He gave another jerk of his lips. It was meant to be an amused smile. "Though," he went on, "it has been said that politically he is. . . ." He moved his hands expressively to denote ambivalence.

Skoryatin said, "You do not, Dmitry Vasil'evich, doubt Kakunin's patriotism?"

"May the God that I do not believe in forbid," Ulvanov said with heavy-handed cheeriness. "I would not dare."

Skoryatin did not smile. "But you chose to mention his supposedly uncertain loyalty to the Party."

"A mere aside, Vladimir Mikhailovich. A small joke."

"There are to be no more such jokes,

Dmitry Vasil'evich." Skoryatin's eyes were suddenly hard.

Ulvanov's own eyes became hooded. "Understood, Comrade. There will be no more such comments." He paused for a sip of tea. "What about Winemaster?"

"He will give us no trouble. He is to be left alone unless he gets in the way. He knows nothing. It would be clumsy to take out the Americans unnecessarily. Also counter-productive at this stage. Besides . . ." here Skoryatin permitted himself a smile of genuine amusement, "Dalgleish will probably do some more decimation for us, before we, the Americans *or* the British get him."

Ulvanov gave an exaggerated sigh. "Winemaster. Sometimes, these God-fearing patriots frighten me."

Skoryatin looked sceptical. A frightened Ulvanov was as unthinkable as the fright of a tiger facing a tethered goat.

Ulvanov raised his cup. "To a lack of failure."

Skoryatin raised his own cup and drank silently. Neither of them had spoken of the matter that occupied their minds most urgently: the concerted and continuing efforts that were being made to identify those responsible for Dalgleish's escape. It was a race against time, and each knew that more, much more than their respective careers was at stake.

They continued to sip at their tea with mutual wariness born of the years-long distrust of each other's organization.

* * *

London, 0900 hours.

Sir John Winterbourne came through the outer office with a face like thunder. He strode to the coat stand, removed his navy blue military-style coat from Gieves of Saville Row and hung it up.

"Mrs. Arundel," he began, not looking round at her, "is Mr. Fowler in?"

"He was here all night, Sir John. He's having a rest."

"I want him in my office immediately." Winterbourne strode out, still not looking at her.

"Yes, sir," she said contemptuously at the closed door.

In the windowless annex to his office where there was a surprisingly comfortable bunk, Fowler picked up the phone.

"Yes, Arundel," he said wearily. "Don't tell me. He's in." He made a face as he listened. "All right. I was getting up anyway. Thanks." He hung up.

He had been lying down fully dressed, save for his jacket. He stood up and went to the small washbasin with a mirror above it, the only other furnishings in the small room. He moved carefully to avoid his glasses which he'd removed and placed on the floor near the head of the bunk. Gratefully he sluiced his face in cold water. He felt his chin. There was a good growth of stubble. He grimaced a second time, patted his face with a towel hanging from a bracing strut beneath the washbasin, then replaced the towel carefully.

He went back to the bunk, picked up his

glasses and put them on before going into his office. He went to his desk, sat down and pulled at a drawer. He took out a battery-powered shaver and began to work on his stubble. He took his time about it. By the time he was finished and had put on his jacket, he did not look like a man who had spent the entire night on duty. His mind was sharp and ready for battle. Many a colleague had wondered with envy where in his lean frame Fowler got his energy from.

He left his office a good twenty minutes after Winterbourne had asked for him. He took nothing with him.

Winterbourne said as soon as he'd entered, "Twenty minutes, Fowler! I asked that you come to see me immediately!"

"I was making myself presentable, Sir John," Fowler explained mildly. "I did not think it right that I should be seen coming in a rumpled state to your office by any staff who might have been wandering about. Bad for discipline."

Winterbourne stared at Fowler as if expecting to see a smile that he could term insubordinate. There was no such smile on Fowler's lips. Winterbourne knew there was nothing he could do.

"Try to be quicker in future," he remarked sourly, reluctant to concede the point. "What I really want to talk to you about," he went on, "is yesterday's little business. I do not like to keep reminding you that *I* am in command here! I made several attempts to contact you. Each time, you were unavailable. You—"

"Sir John," Fowler interrupted calmly, causing Winterbourne's eyes to widen with outrage, "we had a crisis here. We still have, and I've been up all night trying to repair the damage. We now know," he continued inexorably into an attempt by Winterbourne to do his own interrupting, "that the three Rogues are dead. A helicopter was sent to their last known positions with night sights and infra-red monitors. They were found. One had a broken neck and was lying at the base of a rock face. Another was shot clean through the head and the third. . . ." Fowler paused. Winterbourne stared at him as if mesmerized. "And the third appeared to have had his throat ripped open. He too was shot, no doubt to put the poor devil out of his misery."

Winterbourne's mouth opened and closed slowly, like a fish taking its last gasp. Fowler placed his hands behind his back, paced a few times, stopped and faced Winterbourne once more.

"The Dragunov they had with them is gone. We suspect it was used at least once." Fowler made a sound of disgust. "Their own weapon used against them. As for the one with the torn throat, I suspect either Gallagher or Dalgleish improvised. My money's on Gallagher. He was always good at that sort of thing."

"Are we . . ." Winterbourne began, "are we going to let them get away with this?"

Fowler looked at him with open pity. "As if that were not enough," he said, ignoring

Winterbourne's question, "we now have an *American* missing. He'll be dead too."

"Fowler. . . ."

"With respect, Sir John, yes, we are going to let them get away with it. The Rogues were out to *kill* them! Those men would still have been alive if *you* had not decided to act independently. To make matters worse, you informed the Americans! My God! This Department always works as a team. How am I to keep abreast of the situation if these developments take me by surprise?

"The information we had about Gallagher's trip north was not for sharing with *anyone.* Now, with this appalling mess, God knows what the Russians will do; friendlies and unfriendlies. How can the people who've been making the overtures believe in our ability to keep control of such an enormously complex matter. . . ."

"We are still not certain the whole thing is not a KGB game."

"Whether we are or not, Sir John, is immaterial at this stage. The important thing is that we stay in control, no matter what the real purpose may be. Dalgleish may be genuine, in which case we are risking the most important coup the West has ever had in years. If he is not, such actions will be seen as panic on our part, and will play us right into their hands. It would mean that their game *is* succeeding. We're chasing all over the place while the real meat is being stolen elsewhere.

"I propose that, from now on, everything be done low-key. There will simply be discreet surveillance; nothing more for the time being. There are to be no more Rogues, and no more passing of information to the Americans until this is over; and perhaps not even then. That is my proposal, Sir John. If you have objections, my resignation will be on your desk by this afternoon."

Fowler turned and walked out without another word. Winterbourne stared after him in disbelief, completely thrown off balance.

Back in his own office, Fowler sat at his desk, picked up a phone and spoke into it quite calmly. It was as if he had never been in Winterbourne's office.

He finished his call and sat back in his chair. He still could not understand why Kingston-Wyatt had killed himself.

In the hotel dining-room, Gallagher had the surprise of his life. He looked up to see Lucinda MacAusland walking towards his table. She was wearing exactly the same clothes she'd had on when he had last seen her. It was ten o'clock.

He stood up as she reached him. "Lucinda! You're the last person I expected to see up here."

She smiled as if very pleased to see him; but he thought the smile a little strained. There were shadows beneath her eyes, as if she badly needed sleep.

She noted his scrutiny, gave another smile, more obviously weary. "I know I look a mess," she said as she sat down.

He regained his seat, still looking at her. He didn't think she'd ever look a mess, no matter how tired she was. He didn't say so and waited to hear her reasons for being in Scotland.

"You'd look a mess," she continued, "if you'd just driven most of a day and all night in a car that was determined to make life difficult for you. I've had my mini for years and it works like a dream; usually. During the course of the day and last night, it broke down three times. Take a tip. Never break down on a motorway, at night, and on a Sunday." She sounded as if she'd had it up to there.

"God," Gallagher began sympathetically. "How bloody awful." Ironic. While she was busy breaking down, both he and Dalgleish had been occupied with killing people. He wondered what she would say now if she knew. "Is the car all right now?"

She nodded, absently he thought. "It had better be. I've paid a fortune to the breakdown people."

"Look. How about breakfast? You look as if you could use it. Shall I order? There's still time." He paused. "But I don't have to tell you that. You know these people."

As if on cue, the waitress who had served him the night before appeared. "Miss MacAusland! What a nice surprise. Shall I get you your usual breakfast?"

Lucinda gave a weak smile. "Thank you no, Moira. But I will have some of that lovely coffee."

The waitress called Moira peered closely at her. "There's nothing wrong, is there, Miss? At home, I mean."

"No, Moira. Nothing wrong." Again the weak smile.

Moira the waitress went away, unconvinced.

Gallagher said, "She's right though, isn't she? Something is wrong."

Again, Lucinda nodded. She bit at her lower lip. "It's my father. He's very ill. He might die."

Gallagher took this in silence. "I am sorry," he then said quietly. As if she did not have enough trouble with Dalgleish's problem. He continued to look at her. What could one ever say to such news?

"Oh, I've always known," she said briskly. Her eyes were defiantly dry. "He hasn't been well for some time. We both pretended not to notice. He used to be a robust, fit man. He hated admitting he wasn't any more and I, remembering what he used to be, went along with the pretense . . . for my sake as well as his." The blue eyes stared puzzledly. "Does that make sense?"

"It does to you. That's all that matters." Gallagher could remember his own relationship with his father. Most of the time, it hadn't made sense; but he had loved that old man. Now Liam was gone for good. He could understand how Lucinda was feeling.

She smiled at him suddenly. "You understand, don't you?"

He nodded. "I had a strange relationship with my father for a long time, but we had a strong love for each other. It took a while before either of us realized just how much."

"He's dead, isn't he," she told him softly. It was not a question.

"Yes."

She reached out, as if without realizing it, to touch his hand. She left her own hand on his for long moments. It was as if she were giving him warmth, as well as taking it. It was a strange feeling. Then with a gentle sigh, she withdrew the hand.

"I got the message yesterday and came up right away." She gave a wry smile. "Mini willing. I thought I'd look in to see if you were still here." She lowered her voice. "Did you see him?" She was talking about Dalgleish.

"Yes."

"How is he?" The eyes were concerned.

"He's all right. Got himself sorted out. What I mean is, he's safe for the time being." What a bloody lie.

The eyes were looking into him now. "Are you telling me everything?"

"No," he said.

"Thank you for that, at least. I'd have hated it if you'd treated me like a fool."

He gave her a wry smile of his own. "I wouldn't dare."

Her answering smile was the first relaxed one she'd given since her arrival. "Just keep remembering that."

Moira came with the coffee. She fussed about Lucinda like a mother hen. "You look more cheerful now. That's better."

Lucinda said, "It's the long drive, Moira."

"Change that wee thing you call a car.

That's my advice to you." Moira went off unrepentantly.

Gallagher said, "She speaks her mind when she feels like it."

"She always has. I like Moira." Lucinda poured herself a steaming cup of coffee, looking thoughtful. She took it black, without sugar. "This will keep me awake for the rest of the journey." Her brow furrowed briefly. "Have you had a chance to use the camera?"

"No. He's given me a location. I've got to get there first."

"Is it far?"

He stared at her, saying nothing.

She moved her hands about, searching, it seemed, for the best way to present what she wanted to say.

"Look. Perhaps I can help."

"If Uffa wanted you put in danger, he would have done so by now. He probably feels he already has. I'm not going to compound it." He didn't want her near him. God knew how many more Rogues were sniffing around; and there was Winemaster, not forgetting the Russians. It was a lovely soup. "I'm not that crazy." He was thinking of his lonely neighbor. He didn't want what had happened to her to be Lucinda's fate.

"Besides," he went on, "you're up here to be with your father, not chasing about the countryside dodging people who may kill you as soon as look at you." Give it to her brutally. That should scare her.

"You don't have to try to frighten me. I've

been frightened, deep down, ever since Uffa came back."

"Then what was that brave show back in Nottingham all about?"

She shrugged. "Bravado?"

Bravado. Christ.

He said, "It's not a game, Lucinda. People kill people for expediency's sake."

"Look," she repeated, ignoring what he'd just said. "Wherever it is, I could find it more quickly than you ever could. What will you do? Waste time looking at maps? What if people are still following you?"

If only she knew.

"You can't afford the time," she was saying. "This is my part of Scotland. I've known it from childhood. I know all the back roads. We could—"

"We? What's this we? You're supposed to have a father at death's door."

Her eyes were pleading with him. "I want to help. Can't you see? I can't do anything to help my father. If he doesn't die today or tomorrow, it won't be far off. I can try and save Uffa. I'll . . . I'll keep out of the way."

Keep out of the way? How could she keep out of the way? Winemaster, the Rogues or the Russians would steamroller right over her. How naive could she get?

Gallagher paused in his thoughts. He was being unfair as usual. He was a lone wolf, and liked it that way; ever since O'Keefe. Even with what little she knew about Dalgleish's line of work, she could not possibly begin to imagine what it was really like; the savagery, the deceit. . . .

There are times when you need local help. Don't be afraid to use it. It could save you valuable time, time that could save your life. On other occasions, it could be fatal. You must learn to recognize the right occasion. It's a mistake you'll make only once. You foller, sir?

O'Keefe.

Gallagher considered what Lucinda had said. It was certainly true she knew the place better than he did. Any local would; but she was no ordinary local. Yet. . . .

She would hold him back, make him vulnerable.

As if sensing his hesitation, she pressed home what she thought was her advantage. "You know I'm right."

"I've been in far more unfamiliar territory than this."

"And have you never had contacts?"

He smiled. *"Touché."*

"Does that mean you'll let me help?"

What the hell, he thought. Perhaps she was right. Besides, Winemaster would be even more unfamiliar with the area than he was. Having Lucinda as a guide could well turn out to be a plus. It would certainly give him an edge over Winemaster if the American tried to follow.

But he still didn't like it.

"All right," he at last said reluctantly.

She brightened immediately, looking eager.

Christ, he thought. She should go back to

her business in Nottingham, or stay at her father's bedside.

"We'll go in my car," he said. "Leave the mini here. You can pick it up later. I'll take you home so that you can check up on your father. Then we'll see."

It was as much as he was prepared give for the time being.

The blue eyes studied him. "That was dragged out of you. But I understand, and accept the conditions."

"You don't know them yet."

"I accept whatever they may be."

"As long as you know. Now that's out of the way," Gallagher went on, "are you sure you won't have breakfast?"

She shook her head slowly. "I couldn't. Not until I know how my father's doing. The coffee was enough."

"Well, at least you won't have to drive. You can relax for the rest of the journey. I've got my bag with me, so we'll leave as soon as you're ready." After what had happened, the bag would go everywhere with him from now on.

"I'm ready," she said.

They left the dining-room.

As Gallagher handed in his key at the desk, the receptionist said, "Will you be staying another night with us, Mr. Thompson?"

"Yes, I will." He wondered if anyone would check.

"That's fine. See you later then, Mr. Thompson. Enjoy yourself. Hope to see you again soon, Miss MacAusland. 'Bye now."

" 'Bye."

They went out into the car park.

Lucinda took her small weekend bag out of the battered mini and locked the car. Gallagher kept the trunk of the *quattro* open for her while he looked about him casually. There was no sign of the BMW.

So who had tried to invade his room last night?

Lucinda dropped her bag into the trunk. Gallagher shut it, pausing briefly for another scanning glance. Still nothing. That was no reason to feel good. The bastards could be anywhere.

"It's open," he said to Lucinda. He got in behind the wheel.

"Mmm!" she said as she took her seat. "Very nice." She looked about her appreciatively, clipping on her belt. "Makes my poor old mini look like an apology on wheels."

"Don't knock it. It got you here."

"Oh, I love my mini," she said as if talking about a favored pet, "for all its faults. We go back a long way. My first and only car. But if I'd had *this* yesterday. Ah, well!" She smiled at him. The blue eyes sparkled, momentarily forgetting her seriously ill father.

Gallagher liked the way her right cheek dimpled when she smiled. He found he was actually beginning to like her presence in the car. He switched on. The instrument panel glowed briefly with a galaxy of digital read-outs. The speedometer showed 188 mph before converting itself to kilometers to read 288 km/h, then everything settled down to the standard display. The speedometer went back to a big zero

in miles per hour. The engine burst into growling life, its power insinuating itself throughout
the car.

Lucinda stared at him, said, "Oh, God. This
is nice. Does it really do 188?"

"No. But it's only about twenty off."

"You're not serious."

For answer, he smiled at her and put the
car into gear. The digits began to dance slowly
upwards. He checked all mirrors. No one appeared to have pulled out behind him. Early
days yet.

Lucinda noted his scrutiny. "Expecting
company?"

"I'd be very surprised if we didn't have any.
Which way?"

"Back along the A87, to Auchtertyre.
We're going left from there to Stromeferry. The
roads are good enough for you to show me what
this thing can do."

"This is not a thing," Gallagher said
lightly. "This is Lauren."

Her eyes widened in surprise. "Why
Lauren?"

"Ah," he said, and would not tell her more.

"I see," she said. She spoke with a sudden
quietness in her voice.

"No, you don't. When this is over, I'll tell
you. That's a promise."

"I'll hold you to that."

"You can." He checked his mirrors, and
there it was. The big BMW. In daylight, he
could now see it was a dark gray, its shark-like
prow giving it the look of a hunting predator. A

gray nurse was on his tail. "They couldn't wait."

She turned round to peer. "That big gray car?"

"That's the one."

"Who are they?"

"Americans." So where were the Rogues and the Russians? Waiting, that was where.

She said, "Americans. That's all right then."

Oh, the innocence. He said nothing.

She said, "Does that silence mean you don't consider them friendly?"

"I consider no one who follows me friendly. Outside Uffa and yourself, I trust no one as far as this business is concerned." *And I'm not too sure about Uffa,* he didn't say.

She leaned towards him to peer into the passenger mirror. "Still there."

"Until we lose them. This is where I find out whether you really do know the roads around here."

They were now clear of Kyle of Lochalsh and he put his foot down suddenly. The fat wheels of the *quattro* bit into the road, hurling the machine forward as the turbo power came on in a sudden rush that pinned them to their seats. The digital speed read-out began its maniacal counting act. In the mirrors, the BMW appeared to streak backwards. Ahead, the road turned into a streaming conveyor belt that fed itself beneath the front wheels.

Lucinda said, *"Wooo!* I don't believe it. I don't believe it!" She giggled, a little nervously, he thought. "My God!"

"They'll be coming up again once they've worked out what has happened to them," he said. The acceleration was still pinning them to their seats. He changed into fourth, the read-out gave him a glowing one partnered by two zeros that stared at him balefully.

She noted the figure. "Are we really doing a hundred?" Her voice said she did not believe it.

"Yes."

"Already? My God," she repeated.

They were no longer doing that speed. The numerals had gone up to 110. Gallagher checked the mirrors. The BMW was coming up, but it was still far behind. It cut dangerously in front of three cars in its attempt to make up the lost ground. Gallagher could imagine the sounds of irate horns.

He checked the mirrors once more. It would not do to gain the attention of a police patrol.

"What are the police like up here?" The *quattro* loped along in fifth, continuing to eat up the asphalt ribbon.

"That depends."

"On what?"

"On how they're feeling."

Just like anywhere else. He'd have to hope they were otherwise occupied. In a contest with them against Winemaster, he'd lose out; for the time being. They'd find the camera too.

He said, "Keep your eyes open for police. I'll handle the BMW."

"All right," she said.

He glanced at her. She was smiling at him.

"Afraid?"

"Of your driving?"

He nodded. The BMW had grown appreciably bigger. Plenty of time.

"No," she said. "Of everything else to do with whatever Uffa's involved in . . . yes. I think I'm beginning to be, now."

So she should. He said nothing. At least her awareness might make her less of a hindrance. He still wasn't sure whether he'd allow her to continue to accompany him after he'd taken her home.

A fine drizzle had begun to spray down. The *quattro* roared unworriedly along the dampening road. Gallagher watched the rain clouds building above the peaks with satisfaction. *Quattro* weather was coming. *Let's see how you handle this, Winemaster.* To their right, the waters of Loch Alsh appeared misty in the fine rain.

Gallagher put the wipers on intermittent and slowed for a line of four cars ahead. The BMW tucked itself in a good six vehicles behind.

Gallagher watched the oncoming traffic. There would soon be a break; not much room, but the *quattro* could handle it.

The gap came. He dropped gear into third and floored the *quattro* so it hurtled out of its place in the line of cars, surged past them in what seemed like a scorching leap and was back in and streaking ahead before the BMW knew what was happening. Winemaster was balked, for the gap had closed.

Lucinda was looking round. "He's still there!" she chortled. "That was brilliant!"

"I have my moments," Gallagher said lightly; but his thoughts were grim. Winemaster was not going to like that one little bit. Sod him.

They came to Auchtertyre soon after and turned on to the A890 for Stromeferry. The BMW had still not caught up. There were no police patrols to spoil the fun either. Gallagher wondered where the Rogues or the Russians would make their play. He kept a constantly watchful eye on the mirrors. He saw nothing as yet to excite his interest.

"Where is this place Uffa told you about?" Lucinda asked after a while. There was a strange glow to her face.

Instead of replying, he said, "You look as if you're blushing."

"I'm not blushing. This turns me on."

"What does? The car, the speed, or the fact that the Americans are chasing us?"

"The car and the speed. Not the Americans chasing us."

"I see." He could understand. The *quattro* did that to you.

She said, "But you're not going to answer me, are you?" And when he'd said nothing to that, went on, "How can I tell you how to get there if I don't know where you want to go?"

"It's not absolute that you'll be coming with me. Not yet."

"I see," she said again.

"No, you don't."

They traveled in silence for a while, the

powerful background throb of the *quattro* a potent counterpoint to the hiss of its tires on the wet road surface. Every so often, Gallagher made a visual sweep of his mirrors: left external, interior, right external.

The BMW had still not managed to close the gap; but it was visible now. Not good enough. Winemaster had to be lost, dispensed with.

Gallagher said, "Right. Do your stuff. I'm going to pull us out of sight, then I want some back roads. This is supposed to be your neck of the woods. Show me."

She glanced at him appraisingly, studying his control of the hurtling machine.

"It's part of you, isn't it?"

"What is?" He didn't glance at her. Instead, he gave the interior mirror another brief scrutiny. The BMW was hanging on, but not gaining.

"This car," she said.

He said nothing.

"Who is Lauren?"

He didn't answer.

She said, "If you can lose him within the next two miles, we can get off this road."

A few degrees of chill appeared to have crept into her voice, but perhaps he was mistaken. He took the *quattro* to 120 and began to draw perceptibly away from the distant BMW. Winemaster or whoever was driving was clearly unsure of how to use the massive power of the big coupé on the wet and unfamiliar road. The rain was falling strongly now; which pleased Gallagher. The *quattro* towed a high plume of spray as it increased the distance between it and its pursuer.

Lucinda said, "In about a mile or so, there'll be a road to our left. That's the one we want." She leaned forward a little to peer through the windshield at the rain. She had to shift her body gently before the inertia belt would allow her movement. "That's it!"

"Right. I've got it."

Gallagher stabbed at the brakes briefly. The car halted its headlong rush without drama. He turned sweepingly on to the narrow road that had been threading itself through the A890 for the past few miles. A sign pointed the way to somewhere called Braeintra.

They came upon the village soon after. As he slowed, Gallagher checked the mirrors. No BMW. A Landrover had pulled out from behind a building, but turned off the road almost immediately. False alarm. Still no BMW.

"They didn't see us," Lucinda said.

"Doesn't seem like it. But they'll be backtracking soon enough. They'll have seen this road."

"They can't be sure we're not ahead of them, and they'll lose time if they double back."

"Which is good news for us." *Unless they've radioed ahead to watch the side roads,* Gallagher didn't add. No point in putting a blanket on her obvious pleasure at the thought of having lost Winemaster. Winemaster could well have a fleet of cars saturating the general area; not counting any interested Rogues or Russians.

She guided him through the scattered village. If he'd had the time or inclination, he would have enjoyed the contrast of the high ground to his left rising almost straight off the narrow undulating road, and the rushing waters of Allt Cadh an Eas to his right. But he wasn't thinking of scenery. He was thinking of Winemaster, of Fowler, of Winterbourne, of Dalgleish, and of an unsuspecting, lonely woman who had been murdered outside his home. Somebody, he thought, ought to pay for that; at the very least.

Lucinda said into his thoughts, "If we stay on this road, it will eventually take us to Plockton." She spoke in such a way that it was actually a question. "It's got an airstrip."

"We're not going to Plockton."

"Then take the next right. That will take us through Achmore and back to the main road." She paused. "They may be waiting."

Gallagher mentally conceded the point. "Are there other roads?"

"Plenty of tracks in the woods near Plockton, and on the other side of the main road. You could lose them easily, if the car can take it."

"It can. Can you take me across the main road and then into the woods on the other side while still keeping to our general direction?"

She nodded, glanced at him uncertainly. "Some of the tracks are . . . well . . . precarious. The car. . . ."

"Show us the tracks. We'll do the rest. The more precarious the better."

"Fine." She sounded as if she thought he'd taken leave of his senses. "When we get to Achmore, turn right after the school. I'll tell you when. That will put us back on the main road; then we'll turn right, going back the way we came for about quarter of a mile or so. A track branches off it and into the woods. I can take you on a route that will have us back on course." She sounded pleased with herself.

"You enjoyed that, didn't you?"

"Just proving my worth." She did not look at him, but he could sense her smiling to herself.

He said nothing, permitting himself a brief smile.

The rain was bucketing down when they got to Achmore. No BMW had appeared in the mirrors. Lucinda showed Gallagher where to turn and soon they had made it back to the main road. He followed her directions and got to the track on the other side.

"Shit!" he exclaimed suddenly.

A car had flashed past, going back towards Auchtertyre just as he'd reached the track. There was the sudden flaring of brake lights, a sharp fishtailing as the car came to a sliding halt; and even as he floored the *quattro* up the sharply climbing track, Gallagher retained in his mind's eye the frantic efforts of the car to turn on the wet road.

The BMW. A few seconds earlier or later in reaching the track and Winemaster would have been well away in the wrong direction.

"Shit!" Gallagher said again.

Lucinda stared at him. "The same people?"

"The bloody same. They must have gone on to Stromeferry and decided we had either turned off or gone back. Now they've found us again. Right, madam. Show me how to lose them."

"Go left here! There. That's it."

The track had forked on to another which continued, curving to the right. He turned the *quattro* on to the tight left-hand approach and put his foot down. The car hurled itself sure-footedly forward. The ground rose steeply to Gallagher's right, but dropped steeply to his left. Lovely place to go over. He wondered how Winemaster was doing. There was no sign as yet of the BMW. He hoped the bastard would plummet down into the trees.

The track took them back to the main road.

"We're back on the road! What. . . ."

"In a few hundred yards," she interrupted, "we'll be going off it again, this time back on the Stromeferry side. They didn't see where we turned, so they'll probably go right. They'll find themselves in the middle of nowhere; unless they'd like to walk up a mountain in this weather, in their suits."

He could hear the laughter in her voice. "You're really enjoying this." He found the new track and turned on to it.

"I know I shouldn't, with my father nearly at death's door. But I've been expecting it for so long now, it's not a shock any more." She looked at him. "Does that sound callous?"

"Just practical."

She looked away. "I wouldn't like you to think I am. Callous, I mean."

"I don't."

"Good. I'm glad."

Strange conversation. The blue eyes, he

knew, were surveying him once more. He concentrated on keeping the fast-moving car on the track. The rain had eased off and visibility in the woods was good, all things considered. Down away to his left, the Plockton railway line hugged the southern banks of Loch Carron.

Gallagher kept a constant vigil in his mirrors. No BMW. Then abruptly, the track ended. Great. The *quattro* hummed to itself waiting.

Lucinda did not seem worried. "There's another track," she said.

"Oh, yes? Where?"

"Down there. To your left."

From his seat, Gallagher looked out and down. He could just make it out. It began practically where the one they were on ended. The only trouble was, it was about fifty meters down the tree-studded slope.

"I can do that in a Landrover," Lucinda said, as if reading his thoughts. "I've done it many times."

Gallagher bit back a retort. The *quattro* was good, but it wasn't a bloody Landrover. A Landrover could hit a tree and get away with it.

"Isn't this the car that wins all those rallies?" she asked, rather too innocently, he thought.

"It is."

"Well, then. The more precarious, the better, you said."

"Me and my big mouth." He had no intention of bending his car for anyone, but something had to be done.

They could not remain up here all day, neither could they go back. It was possible that

Winemaster might have escaped his own track to nowhere. So down it had to be.

Gallagher stared at the terrain, working out a route that would take them unscathed through the trees. The *quattro* could handle the ground, he'd have to look after the vegetation.

"Right, Miss MacAusland, hang on to your belt. We're going down."

He had locked the center and rear differentials on first entering the woods by pulling the switch on the central console right out. The green operating lights had come on with faint warning squeaks as each had locked on. Now, he glanced at them. They glowed mutely back at him.

"This is where you do your stuff," he said to them, and turned the *quattro* off the track.

The car plunged downwards, slid for a short distance as gravity tried to pull it down faster than it wanted to go; then the fat wheels bit purposefully into the ground, gaining complete traction as Gallagher steered it through the trees, a growling metallic creature whose sound echoed throughout the wood.

The *quattro* bounced now and then on its downward journey, and Gallagher would brace himself as he waited to hear something nasty bang into the underside. But, mercifully, the path he had chosen was free of the kind of lurking obstruction that could do damage. At times, the car appeared to be about to stand on its nose. At others, it seemed to travel on only one front and one back wheel; but it hit no trees, and made its way quite safely to the lower track, which it took to eagerly as Gallagher put the power on.

"That was quite good," Lucinda said approvingly. "Faster than in the Landrover."

I won't do this to you again, Lauren, Gallagher vowed silently to the car. Aloud, he said, "This is the car that wins rallies. Remember?"

"Touché."

They glanced at each other, smiled. A bond had grown between them.

She leaned over to peer into her mirror.

Noticing, Gallagher said, "Somehow, I don't think that's where we'll see them . . . assuming they've found their way out." He said that with some pleasure.

"Even if they do and they know where to come, they won't risk taking their nice car down to this track."

"Not like me, you mean." But he smiled to himself.

He powered the *quattro* along the rough surface until, eventually, the track took them back to the main road near Ardnarff, north-east of Stromeferry. Here, the road itself was quite narrow. Gallagher pushed the differential switch home. The green lights winked out. He put his foot down. The speed climbed.

He glanced in the mirrors. Nothing to worry about.

"I think we can safely say we've lost them for the moment," he said. "One to you, Lucinda."

"Does that mean I've now earned my place on the team?"

It was difficult to decide whether she was

teasing or being serious. He chose to believe she was teasing.

"What team?"

"Going back on your word now, are you?"

"Going back? How can I go back on a word I haven't given? Besides, I thought you were frightened."

"I am." She didn't look it.

"Well, then."

"I just got you away from that BMW," she said with some justification. "They'll never guess which way you've taken; not unless they've got someone who knows this place as well as I do. You're in an area that is as strange to you as it is to them," she went on into his silence. "I don't know exactly what you did when you and Uffa worked together. . . ."

"We never worked together."

"You know what I mean. Don't cloud the issue." She sounded annoyed. "Whatever you did before, whoever you worked for or with, I'm certain they never sent you anywhere without first giving you some information about the place."

Want to bet? Gallagher thought sourly, remembering with a bitterness born of experience. People outside intelligence departments always thought everything was thoroughly worked through before personnel were committed to the field. That only happened in movies. Even the massive and monolithic KGB sometimes came up with appalling blunders. Had they now made one with Dalgleish? And what about the elusive, ethereal Windshear Group?

Fact, myth of bluff? Was the Department going to get its fingers well and truly burned?

Gallagher felt no sympathy for his former unit, particularly not for Winterbourne. He hoped the sod would get his balls chewed off; if he had any.

Lucinda was saying, "You'd still be towing that BMW if it hadn't been for me."

"You don't give up, do you?"

"No."

"Besides, this car will have the legs off that BMW any time of the day or night."

She said nothing.

The *quattro* hummed to itself as it sped along. Twice, Gallagher had to pull in to let a huge truck pass, going the other way. There were a few cars, but nothing that constituted heavy traffic. No one appeared to be following them.

At last, he said, "All right. Perhaps you can help me find the place quickly. But . . . you keep well out of trouble. I don't want you slowing me down."

She tried not to look triumphant, failed. "Anyway, I'm trying to help Uffa."

"The road to misery is paved with good intentions."

"Don't you mean the road to hell?"

"I thought I'd modify it a bit."

Winemaster stared at the dead end of yet another track and swore. It was the third one they had tried.

"Sonofabitch!" he said tightly.

Kroski said, "Now we know he's in this with Dalgleish."

"We don't *know* that, Kroski. All we know is that he's got away from us, and the Brits are not giving us anything now. Someone's sat on Winterbourne."

Kroski made a rasping sound that could have been a chuckle. "Brave. Whoever it is could catch something."

Winemaster stared at him. "You don't like that guy, do you?"

"Do *you?*"

Winemaster looked away. "The little shit."

"Who're you thinking of now?"

"The whole goddam bunch of them."

"What a way to talk about our allies."

Winemaster made a sound of disgust. "Jesus. I get more goddam help from the goddam KGB."

Kroski made another rasping sound and began to carefully maneuver the big car to point it back along the track.

"Watch it, Kroski, goddammit!" Winemaster snapped. "I don't want to go into those goddam trees down there."

Kroski whistled soundlessly.

"Gallagher must be working for the Brits," Winemaster muttered to himself as the BMW made its way gingerly back along the track. "The sneaky bastards."

"What about the woman we saw in the car with him?"

"How the hell am I to know about that, Kroski? We both saw her for the first time today. Maybe Gallagher's a fast worker with the women. She was not in the hotel last night. Maybe she's some local piece of ass that's taken his fancy. We've gone over that before. The Brits are saying they know nothing about any woman. The hell they don't."

Kroski decided to say nothing more. Winemaster was irritable. When Winemaster became irritable, people were liable to find themselves sent on asshole missions: like to Lebanon, or El Salvador, or even Grenada.

Come to think of it, Grenada would not be so bad. Kroski continued to whistle soundlessly as he tried to find his way out of the wood.

"Stop doing that, Kroski."

"Doing what?"

"Your goddam whistling."

Korski stopped doing it, surprised. He'd not been aware he'd been making any sound.

The road hugged the Plockton rail line as it headed for Strathcarron. The *quattro* had passed Attadale before Gallagher decided to tell Lucinda of the location Dalgleish had given him.

She was stunned.

"Kincarron Lodge!" she exclaimed. "But that's not possible!" There was a heavy layer of fear in her voice.

He glanced at her just as she looked towards him. The blue eyes mirrored the fear he thought he'd heard. The corners of her eyes were tight with a strange tension.

"What do you mean it's not possible?"

"I know it! It's not far from my home. Why

didn't he tell me?" The question had in it the
tones of someone who felt betrayed.

Gallagher said into his own surprise, "Perhaps to prevent exactly what's happening now.
He didn't want to frighten you." She had every
reason to be bloody frightened. A KGB-GRU
operation right on her doorstep, and her own
cousin the man they were hunting. . . .

Gallagher was not surprised Dalgleish had
not told her; only by the proximity of the Russian base. Dalgleish had played Lucinda well,
had used her to good effect. No wonder she felt
betrayed.

"He never told me," she said to herself. Her
voice had temporarily shut Gallagher out.

He's using me too, Gallagher thought
grimly. *When is it my turn for betrayal?*

And yet, Dalgleish needed his proof in
order to pacify the Department; needed someone to do so for him.

Me, Gallagher thought again, sourly.

It was too late to duck out. He'd been responsible for the death of one man, possibly
another, if he counted the motorcyclist. He had
helped Dalgleish. He was involved in four
deaths. The Department could find all sorts of
ways to make life very difficult. Behind all that
lot came Winemaster, and the Russians. There
was really no choice now.

Besides, there was still his lonely neighbor.
Her death ought to be paid for.

"What is Kincarron Lodge?" he asked.

She had become strangely quiet and took a
long time replying; so long in fact, he thought
she was not going to.

So he said, "Look. You don't have to show me. I can find it. Perhaps it's for the best. I've always been unhappy about involving you further. You know that."

"I'll show you," she said. She had spoken determinedly, quietly. "Kincarron is a hunting lodge. The people who own it live abroad, so it's rented out, usually to those with a lot of money. All sorts of people have used it over the years, for as long as I can remember; and all kinds of nationalities. There have been Germans, Americans, British, Arabs. . . ." She sighed. "God knows how many others. No one's ever taken much notice. The land is private so all those really wealthy people can have all the seclusion they want."

"And how big is this piece of land?"

"Quite a few acres."

Which up here would probably mean a few thousand, glens and forests included. Oh, it was perfect. The "Germans," "Americans" and "British" could easily have been deep-cover agents with accents, so perfect their own mothers wouldn't be able to tell. All sorts of Eastern-bloc allies would have been accommodated too.

"Did you ever see or meet any of these people?"

"No," she replied. "We never mixed with them. They kept to themselves. Understandable. If you pay a lot of money for your seclusion, the last thing you want is intrusion by the locals. I just heard about them. 'The rich tourists' they're called around here."

"But you know of no one who's actually *seen* them."

"Well, no . . . but. . . ." She stopped, turned her eyes on him. "You don't mean you think the Lodge owners are *Russian?*"

"Why not? The West has got its own 'Lodges' all over the world. Why can't the Russians?"

And in what better place? he didn't say. Slap bang in the middle of what had become a crucial piece in the NATO defense jigsaw puzzle. Credibility would have been built up over a long period of years, long before Holy Loch, Faslane and the Greenland-Iceland-U.K. gap—the lobster-pot for the Russian surface and submarine northern fleets—became fashionable in military thinking. And now they were plotting cruise-dispersal sites for future tactical operations. It would be one way to offset the bottleneck in the North Sea.

Lucinda said, almost in a whisper, "Why hasn't anyone even known about this?"

Gallagher smiled without humor. "Lucinda, like most people, you think intelligence services are omnipotent. If they were, there would be no spies in any country. The Russians are masters at deep cover."

"Deep cover? What is that exactly?"

"When you put someone into a country with a complete identity and leave him or her for years until required, that's deep cover. The person, to all intents and purposes, fits perfectly into the landscape. It could be your local grocer, postmaster, even. . . ."

"Lodge owner?"

"Precisely. It's even better when the per-

son is known but never seen. A good cover story
sees to that, killing any suspicions."

"You know a lot about it."

"I used to be in it . . . once, after all, as you
now know."

"Yes," she said in her quiet voice. "Yes. I
know."

"I meant what I said about your not taking
me to Kincarron. In fact, I'd prefer it. . . ."

"No. I said I'd do it. I will."

"Plenty of time to change your mind between now and when we get to your house."

"I won't change my mind."

Gallagher said nothing. They journeyed
on in silence, Lucinda retreating into her
thoughts. The *quattro* hummed.

Just after Achintee the road curved sweepingly left to cross the river Carron that had
come down from the glen to empty itself into
the loch. It had cut through a valley floor that
was a mile wide at that point, and Gallagher
again found himself wishing he had the time
to linger and marvel at the beauty of the
landscape.

He said, "Are the lodge owners British?"

She answered almost immediately. "Apparently, but not Scots. The gossip has it that
they're from the south. Home counties. They
made their money in the City, went abroad to
escape the grubby hands of the taxman."

"Better and better."

"What do you mean?"

"I'd lay odds that if anyone bothered to
check, they'd find a cast-iron background. Ev-

erything would fit nicely, even down to club membership."

She thought about that for a while, then: "You mean they could be *Russian?*" The blue eyes stared at him.

He kept his own eyes on the road, on the mirrors. Nothing.

"Why not? This sort of thing has been done before. I could give you a couple of well-known examples. The identity given is usually that of a real person, someone with no relatives who died a long time ago. By the time anyone interested enough to check has eventually done so, the operation will be over."

"But for how long can they keep this up?"

"Years. As much as twenty sometimes; even more in very special cases. God knows how many sleepers they've got planted in the West. For every one uncovered, you can count on three or four that have gone undetected. Some people will argue that the ratio is even higher."

"I can't believe it!"

"Believe it."

"But what about all the wonderful machinery, fancy computers and such, that we're supposed to have?"

Gallagher's smile was that of someone who knew better. "For every weapon, there's a counter-weapon. True, there are many sophisticated detection and surveillance systems; but there are equally sophisticated *deception* systems. So the spiral continues. It is move and counter-move . . . all the time; with nobody really getting anywhere, except perhaps nearer the big bang."

"Is that why you left? Uffa said you had special reasons."

"That was one of them."

He told her no more. The road formed itself into a T-junction once it had crossed the top of the loch. Lucinda directed him left on to the A896 and the *quattro* headed west along the opposite shore, towards the town of Lochcarron. But they did not go all the way. Just under two miles later, they reached Kirkton and, on Lucinda's instruction, Gallagher took a turning off the road, to the right. It was a narrow pebbled track that led across country for about another half-mile, climbing gently through an archway of slender trees, intertwined branches in sparse autumn foliage forming an effective screen. It was like driving through a tunnel. There was no sign of the MacAusland home.

Then suddenly, after a sharp bend, there overlooking a vast garden was the huge building, an imposingly spread mansion that seemed to dominate even the mountains that rose a mile away behind it. It was not, however, a beautiful structure. A lot of ideas had gone wrong. Still, it had presence. A regiment of tall firs formed a thick crescent of bodyguards about it.

A circular drive took them to the front of the house. Gallagher stopped the car, but left the engine running. He could now see the blue-gray waters of the loch. The view was astounding. He could see all the way to Plockton. What a view to wake up to every morning. It more than made up for the ugliness of the house.

He said, "Amazing. I could live with this."

She smiled, the single dimple a tiny con-
cave in her cheek. "The view is great, but the
house is ugly."

"Well . . ." he began, searching for something diplomatic to say about it.

But she gave a little laugh, interrupting
him. "Don't try to say something nice. I've seen
more friends embarrassed than you'd believe.
That house has been a family joke for over two
hundred years. Legend has it that the MacAusland who had it built—or rather commenced its
building, since it took two generations—did so
between bouts of clan fighting. Progress and
design depended upon how well the battle went.
I never believed it, of course; but it was a good
story to tell a young girl." As if the memory of
her childhood had suddenly reminded her of
the reason for her being there, the cheerfulness
went out of her features. "I'd better go and see
how my father's doing."

"Right," he said. "I'll get your things from
the trunk. If you can tell me where I can find a
simple hotel, I'll spend the day there, out of
circulation till night. I'll come for you then, if
you still feel up to it after you've checked on
your father."

He climbed out, opened the trunk, took out
her things then pushed the heavy be-spoiled
lid shut. He looked about him. The place had an
expectant stillness about it. Not surprising, he
thought, with the old man about to pop off.

Lucinda had climbed out. "Why do you
need to find anywhere to stay? There's plenty of
room here."

"Oh, come on. You can't expect me to do

that. I'm a stranger. I'd be intruding. This is a very personal family sadness. No. Thanks for the offer, but I can't accept. It wouldn't be right. It will be bad enough taking you with me tonight."

"I don't feel you're a stranger," she countered. "It's as if I've known you for years. Besides, there's a practical reason. The BMW doesn't know where you've gone. I can't think of a better place to be in the circumstances. We're very secluded. Those men will never find you unless they know where to look. If you go back to the main road, you might run into them, just like the last time."

She stopped, her eyes defying him to find fault with her reasoning.

"You can hide here all day," she went on, pressing home her point, "in perfect safety. You can take your time preparing yourself for tonight without worrying about someone popping in on you unexpectedly."

It was an argument that was hard to counter. The idea was highly attractive.

As if she had never doubted she would win, Lucinda continued, "You'll be left to your own devices, I'm afraid, because of my father. You probably won't see me all day; but I'm sure you'd prefer it that way."

"I wish you hadn't put it quite like that."

She gave him a tiny smile. The eyes were enigmatic. Whatever she had been about to say was disturbed by the approach of a short, weather-hardened man, dressed like a gamekeeper.

"That's Jamie," she said. "Our sort of man

about. He's been with us since before I was
born."

The man she'd called Jamie came up quietly, walking like someone who had stalked animals all his life. He stopped and gave Lucinda
a tight smile.

"Miss Lucinda." He stared at Gallagher
blankly.

Very talkative, Gallagher thought drily.
He half expected Jamie to magic a shotgun out
of thin air and point it at him. Jamie, Gallagher
felt, did not like seeing him with a MacAusland
woman.

"Jamie," Lucinda was saying, "this is Gordon Gallagher, a very good friend. He very
kindly drove me up."

Not strictly true, but Gallagher let it pass.

"He will be staying with us," Lucinda
continued.

Jamie's eyes were neutral. "Very good,
Miss."

"How is my father?"

Jamie's face at last showed some anima-
tion. He clearly thought very highly of the
dying MacAusland. "As well as can be expected.
It could be any time. Well, I'll be off." He began
to move away.

Talkative. They watched him depart.

"We'd better go in," Lucinda said, her voice
heavy. "If you'll get your things, I'll show you
to your room; then I must leave you. I'll warn
the staff."

"He didn't exactly like me, did he?"

"Jamie? Oh, don't mind him. He's like that
with every man I bring here. He sees himself as

my second father. All my men must first have
his approval. But of course, it's different with
you."

"Oh?"

"Unless you're intending to be my lover."

The boldness of it took him completely by
surprise. "Even for a MacAusland," he said,
"that was. . . ."

Her brief smile challenged him. "I did tell
you about us." She began to walk away from
him.

He had no choice but to take his bag out of
the car, lock it, and follow her.

Fowler read the most recent report and smiled.
The Americans were not happy. Their continuing happiness was not his concern. What mattered was that he had stopped, or rather
frightened Winterbourne into behaving himself. But for how long Winterbourne would resist taking matters into his own hands once
again was anybody's guess. What was important was that Gallagher had apparently
managed to elude everyone and had gone to
ground. Winterbourne was stumped.

Fowler smiled for a second time. Gallagher
was like a ferret. Put him down a hole and all
sorts of things would begin to happen; even
when he did not realize he had been put down
the hole in the first place.

Gallagher could not believe the room he had
been given. Like the other parts of the interior
of the house he had so far seen, its opulence was
as stunning as it had been unexpected. The ugly

building held within it a surprise of warmth and color that belied its forbidding exterior.

That was what she loved about it, Lucinda had said. The place was called Duncarron.

The room was large and painted all over in a pale cream. The sun, which had managed to shine briefly through the overcast, had bathed it in a golden light that had come in through two large windows. There was a huge four-poster bed with its own pelmet that matched those of the windows. A chaise-longue reclined at the foot of the bed. There was a dressing-table, an armchair, two lattice-backed chairs, and a tall swivel mirror set within a frame on castors. All the upholstery was a matching herbal pattern on a cream background, and the furniture, bed-posts and pelmets were marked out in black and gold. The curtains and bed hangings were of palest gray swagged silk with gold borders.

It was a room fit for a king. Gallagher felt as if he would be committing sacrilege just by lying on that elegant bed. But he had lain on it for over an hour now since Lucinda had left him. The house was absolutely quiet, and it was not too difficult for him to imagine himself alone in the entire building. There was a phone on a small table nearby.

He had left the room just once to put the *quattro* out of sight in one of the six adjoining garages that Lucinda had shown him. Three of the garages had been empty. No one had disturbed him since. His quiet hour had done him good. He had lain, tuning himself as he'd always done prior to going out on a job.

*Take the tension out of your body. No point
going in half-cocked. You might end up without
any. At least you won't know about it; and what
you don't know about, I suppose you won't miss,
if you'll excuse the liberty, sir.*

O'Keefe.

Gallagher smiled at the memory, raised
himself to a sitting position. He had kept his
booted feet hanging over the edge of the bed.
The mirror faced him from between the two
windows. He stared at himself dispassionately.
Hazel eyes in a honey-bronze face stared right
back at him from beneath a crop of soft brown
curls that grew down to the back of his neck. He
had his father's sharp nose, with a slight flare
to the nostrils. That had come from his mother.
The corners of his mouth turned up very
slightly. His mother again. It was a mouth that
performed the impossible feat of being at once
firm yet generous. Those meeting him for the
first time as an adversary had misread that
mouth to their cost, mistaking it as evidence of
softness. It was a psychological weapon he had
used more than once without compunction.

He stared at his chin. He had never been
happy about that chin. He would have liked it
to have been just a shade firmer.

Oh, vanity, he chided himself.

Lauren had loved him. It still surprised
him. She could have had her pick.

He sighed, stood up. No point going back
into old memories. Lauren was dead; months
dead. Life went on.

He was a tall man, sinewy rather than
muscle-bound. At nearly thirty-four, his stom-

ach was still flat and hard. He didn't jog nor take exercises. He ate as he pleased. He didn't smoke.

Smoking can kill you in all sorts of nasty ways. The nastiest is by the bullet that comes at you from the night because you were stupid enough to give a sniper a beacon. I've seen many a man give his last gasp for a gasper.

O'Keefe again.

Gallagher was not sure that everyone on the intense training course had believed all of O'Keefe's homilies, but he was positive no one forgot them.

He reached down for his bag, took out the camera and sat down on the bed once more. He put the camera to his eyes. It was on standard mode. The other shore of Loch Carron jumped at him. He increased resolution until he could see the occupants of passing cars on the A890. None was the BMW. He had not really expected to see it. That was too long a shot. Winemaster would hardly have been patrolling up and down the same stretch of road.

He switched to infra-red and directed his attention to the woods in the vicinity of the house. Heat radiations fluctuated redly in the glasses. Small birds, perhaps. Were there rabbits or hares around in this area? Maybe wildcats.

He swung the camera, scanning casually. There was a big fluctuation, about a quarter of a mile away, from a small clearing. He held the camera on the spot and waited, expecting deer. What he eventually saw was Jamie; with a shotgun. Gallagher continued to watch. Jamie seemed to be stalking something.

Gallagher swung the camera away, trying to gauge the position of Jamie's game. Nothing. He went back to Jamie. Lucinda's "sort of man about" seemed to be waiting now. The shotgun was at the port, ready for instant use.

He scanned once more, searching for whatever had excited Jamie's attention. It took him a good two minutes before the sudden blooming of infra-red radiation appeared in the lenses. Whatever it was, was big. Gallagher increased resolution. The target patch of wood came smoothly closer. He halted the zoom. Masses of radiation, but no image.

Moving along an imaginary line, he swung back to Jamie. The tough little man was looking in a totally wrong direction. Perhaps he did not even know.

Gallagher felt his spine tingle suddenly. What then had he found? He retraced his imaginary line quickly. The infra-red target was gone. Pulses beginning to slowly increase in frequency. He knew it as a sign that something hostile was out there. When he'd found the source again seconds later, he knew his instincts were correct. The fluctuations had moved to a position *behind* Jamie. No ordinary animal this.

Gallagher waited, still hoping for an image. At last, he got it. A man had appeared; a man with a sniper's rifle.

Gallagher felt himself go cold as he continued to watch. There was nothing he could do for Jamie. He got as good a close-up as he could and took a picture. He switched to standard mode, to get a better look. It was no one he recognized. It could be anybody.

The man suddenly disappeared.

Gallagher switched back to infra-red immediately to pick up the body-heat radiations. The source was moving closer to Jamie.

"Get out of there!" Gallagher muttered to the distant guardian of Duncarron. "Get out, for God's sake!" He tried to will his message across; but he could only watch helplessly at what was soon to happen.

He got another clear view of the sniper; watching as the man set himself up on target. He took the camera away from his eyes. He didn't have to look. Jamie was as good as dead. The unknown sniper was using a telescopic sight, but no infra-red. It would help when the time came to hunt him out.

Gallagher knew he would have to go out there. What was a sniper doing in the woods near Duncarron? How could anyone possibly have followed him here? Was Dalgleish playing a double game, after all? But Dalgleish could not possibly have known Lucinda would be coming up. Hadn't he kept the secret of the lodge from her?

Gallagher was positive Lucinda knew nothing about what was happening. She would not have been a party to having Jamie murdered.

Which means, Gallagher thought bitterly, *I must have led them here. Shit.*

But how? And who were they? Winemaster's people? Rogues? The Russians? Questions, questions.

He had not heard the report of the rifle, had not expected to. The sound would have been muted by the woods and the distance; and besides, the windows were double-glazed. But someone outside might have heard.

Taking the camera with him, he decided to do a little hunting of his own. This time he hoped to make the sniper talk—if the man were still around. What if he had friends? Gallagher drove the thought out of his mind. He would meet each problem as it came.

He opened the door and looked into Lucinda's eyes. Her hand was raised, as if about to knock.

She gave a sheepish smile. "Have you any idea how stupid it makes one feel to be caught with a hand in the air like this? I nearly fell forward as you opened the door." She looked at the camera. "And here I am, thinking we're telepathic. I thought I'd pop round to see how you were. I feel guilty about leaving you so isolated." She seemed as relaxed as someone with a father waiting to die could be expected to be.

"Don't worry about it. I'm fine. How's your father doing?"

"Holding on . . . which isn't news any more. Dr. Murchan thought this was finally it, but my father seems to have fooled him again."

"This has happened before?"

"Oh, yes. Twice. Each time, I hurried up. Each time, a false alarm. Now I'm afraid not to come up just in case that would be the time he actually would die. I have this nightmare that he's going to sneak out on me one day." The eyes were pleading it seemed, to something unknown and omnipotent. Suddenly she gave another of her sheepish smiles. "We have a strange relationship, my father and I." She glanced at the camera again. "Where were you off to?"

"Oh, I thought I'd have a look round the woods," Gallagher replied, "and get myself familiarized with this thing." He waited, secretly watching for a reaction.

Nothing. Not even a flicker. No strange dancing in the eyes.

"Well, don't stay too long. I'm having something prepared for us to eat. Do you like your room?" The smile was now mischievous.

So she didn't know about Jamie. Couldn't. Hadn't anyone heard the shot?

He said, "I couldn't believe it. But it's fantastic. I like it."

"Yes," she said. "It's very sensual." Her eyes were fathomless. "It's my favorite room."

"Your room? But. . . ."

She took him lightly by the arm. "Don't say anything. I have more than enough to choose from here. Come. I'll walk out with you."

"How's your mother . . . sorry, stepmother taking it?" he asked.

"She hasn't been here for some time."

Lucinda's voice had a hard edge to it that made Gallagher decide to ask no more. There was clearly no love lost between Lucinda and her stepmother. An old and all too familiar story. MacAusland was going to die without his dearly beloved wife by his side.

And it's none of my business, Gallagher

thought, distancing himself from it. The real business was waiting out there in the woods.

As they walked through the house, he could hear faint movements and voices, but saw no one. There was a hush in the place that seemed to forbid anyone to speak or move loudly.

Lucinda took him round the back of the building. "There you are," she said, indicating the great expanse of woodland. "All yours. Don't let the wildcats frighten you. They're shy creatures, really." She was teasing.

"Oh, I believe you."

A wildcat with a rifle.

He gave her a casual wave, and set off. As he made for the woods, he was aware of a strange, gentle smile on her lips. He knew she was still looking at him.

He reached the edge of the wood and turned back: She was still there. He waved again. She raised a hand slightly, seemed to leave it hanging in the air before lowering it slowly. He entered the wood, and she was lost to sight.

Immediately he entered he felt his entire being switch into a new mode, senses finely tuned, sniffing out his surroundings. Out in the open, he had been acutely aware of the fact that the sniper could have had him in his sights. He had forced himself to remain unperturbed for Lucinda's benefit. Now, he could become his true self. He would turn this place into his hunting ground.

He moved silently, on the balls of his feet, taking his time. Now and then, he stopped for an infra-red scan with the camera. He found Jamie's body after fifteen minutes. It's residual warmth had pinpointed it. Jamie's last mark on Earth.

The body was lying face down on the damp ground. The high-speed bullet had neatly punctured the back of the neck, traveling upwards, blowing the forehead away as it exited. The sniper would have been lying hidden, perhaps against a low mound, while Jamie had walked on higher ground. The little man would have seen and heard nothing. He had been stalked by the most dangerous of all animals.

"At least you wouldn't have felt anything," Gallagher muttered to the body. He wondered how Lucinda would take it when she found out. He decided not to tell her. She had enough on her plate.

Jamie had looked like the sort of man who had come and gone as he pleased. She would not think it amiss if he were absent for some time.

Gallagher had been inspecting the body from a safe distance. No point giving the sniper another easy target. The unknown hunter might well be waiting to see who would come across the kill.

Gallagher now moved back deeper into cover. As far as he was concerned, the whole area was hostile, the entire wood. He used the camera again, taking care not to move any vegetation suddenly. There were no heat traces big enough; only plenty of woodland animals.

He moved from his position and continued his hunt, again stopping every so often for a scan. An hour later, he found his target. The sniper had moved closer to the house!

Gallagher's route had taken him in a wide circle. Obviously, his adversary had not seen him enter the wood and still believed him to be inside the building. The man was thoroughly ruthless and would kill anyone who got in his way. The dead Jamie was proof of that. Jamie must have unwittingly disturbed him and had paid for the mistake. Gallagher began to worry about Lucinda.

He moved quickly but unhurriedly. To be spotted now would be disastrous. He took no chances. He was going up, weaponless, against someone who was a complete pro. Why, he wondered as he made his way towards the target, were they now trying to take him out? What had caused the decision to be taken? They would know by now, if Winemaster could be believed, about the man on Skye. Was this merely crude revenge? By the Americans? The Rogues? The Russians?

More bloody questions. No answers.

Gallagher paused to take a sighting with the camera. The heat source had moved closer to the house, but not as far forward as Gallagher had expected. He smiled grimly. The sniper was taking no chances; he was taking his time about it. The man, Gallagher knew, could take all day if he felt like it, becoming one with the woodland so that the creatures that lived there would come to accept him and do nothing to betray his presence.

Jamie's years of experience as a woodsman had been less easy to deceive; but even Jamie had become a victim. The sniper could safely expect no one else of such experience and could concentrate on getting at his intended target.

Conscious all the while of the impending danger to Lucinda and her grievously ill father, and God knew how many staff who would get in the way of the implacable man ahead, Gallagher closed the distance as swiftly as he dared, using all the skills he had learned years before. There was no time to fashion a weapon. It would have to be a straight attack against an unknown well-armed opponent. It was not something he was looking forward to.

Another fifteen minutes brought him almost on a parallel course with the sniper who had now moved laterally. The man, he was sure, would select a vantage point after first making a circuit of the building. He would then wait, and watch, and wait, and watch; for hours, if necessary. Gallagher knew that was what would happen because it was how he himself would have gone about it. The trick was to get at the unknown gunman before the circuit was begun; before he had settled down to wait; before he had achieved the stillness of being that would make the woodland floor a very extension of his senses, warning him of any breaks in the pattern. Gallagher did not feel he was overestimating his man. Only an exceptionally good operative could have surprised an old veteran like Jamie. It was far better to weight the odds a little. The explosion of action, when it came, would be far more irresistible, more devastating.

But I want him alive, Gallagher thought

with some annoyance. *I want the bastard alive.
I want to know who sent the shit.* It would not
be easy.

Gallagher had now moved to a position behind the sniper, continuing to close in, still undetected. He was now quite certain he was
dealing with a loner. Well, it made life less
hard. The new move cost him another fifteen
minutes.

He himself had now achieved partial one-
ness with his surroundings. Even the force of
the fall of reluctant droplets that had collected
on the trees after the last rain had become dis-
tinguishable. Each fall had its signature. He
could not see the vast structure of Lucinda's
family home from where he now lay, but it registered as a massive heat source which came in
on the lenses through the screen of the undergrowth. He knew where the sniper was too. The
sniper, fortunately, did not have an infra-red
aid. The strange man would have to expose himself a little from time to time to take his bearings. There was no reason for him to think he
was being tracked by infra-red. Gallagher continued to make his way closer. Ten minutes
later, he could actually see his man. He gave
another grim smile. Not bad. Not bad at all.
Even O'Keefe would have been pleased with his
performance.

The man was sitting with his back resting
against the bole of a tree and his rifle across his
knees, but held in such a way that it would take
an infinitesimal part of a second to bring it to
bear on a target. His head was tipped backwards, resting on the trunk. His eyes were

closed. But Gallagher was not fooled. The man was not asleep.

Something fluttered overhead. The man did not move. This convinced Gallagher even more. The man had become so attuned to what was around him that he ignored the overhead flutter, knowing it to be nothing inimical to him.

Gallagher's eyes surveyed the immediate area about the gunman. The tree, a silver fir, was a tall specimen—a good fifty meters—and Gallagher judged its girth at about six meters. Though it appeared isolated, there was plenty of cover close by for a rapid exit, should the man decide the occasion warranted such action.

Gallagher watched him for some minutes, taking care not to move suddenly. The man's eyes remained closed. Gallagher memorized his own position, then placed the camera in a hiding place in the undergrowth. He marked it with an unobtrusive dried twig planted in position just in front of the screened mouth of the hide he'd made for it.

He paused. The man was about thirty meters away; about a hundred feet, give or take a couple of feet. The question was how to disable him enough to get him to talk without becoming a casualty in the interim.

First get your man, sir.

Thank you, Mr. O'Keefe. I'm well aware of that.

Just making the point, sir.

How, how? Bloody well how!

Gallagher's thoughts halted abruptly and spiraled back into his childhood.

When very young, he had been taken to the Caribbean to meet his mother's relatives in Jamaica. He had been surprised to find that they had ranged in color from white to black. He had still been too young to make the intellectual leap to understand that, since she was also descended from transplanted Scots, that was how it should have been. In Jamaica, he had become friends with a local boy. Together, they had gone lizard hunting, using the thin stalk of a reed the boy had called lizard grass.

The "lizard grass" stalk was about eighteen inches long, and for half of its lower length it was brittle. The upper half, however, which bore clusters of pinhead-sized yellow blossoms, was very flexible. The boy had shown him how, by cleaning off the blossoms between forefinger and thumb, the bared upper stalk could be fashioned into a sliding loop. They would then creep behind one of the small yellow lizards sunning themselves on hot rocks, pass the loop slowly over the unsuspecting reptile's head, then pull suddenly. The startled animal, in leaping forward to avoid danger, would only succeed in trapping itself.

Gallagher could still remember the sudden flash of the silver-gray belly as the frightened animal was yanked off its comfortable perch. They had never killed them, but had set them free to scuttle swiftly away from further unwelcome attention. The boy had said that was why the stalk was called lizard grass. The lizards were mesmerized by it. To this day, Gallagher still wondered about that. He also wondered what the boy—who, he remembered, had been called Winston—had become.

The Winston of his childhood had given him an idea.

He poked his hand into the hide and pulled out the camera. It had a three-piece strap. Two ends were attached to the body, while the long, adjustable center-piece was completely removable. This section had a buckle at one end. Gallagher removed the center-piece, put the camera back into its hide and again marked the place with the twig. He then slid the arrowed end of the strap through the buckle. He put his hand through the loop thus made and pulled; the noose slid tight. He put the fingers of his other hand between the strap and his wrist to try to free the hand. The tongue in the buckle jammed against the leather, keeping the noose tight. It could only be slackened by freeing the buckle.

Gallagher freed his hand, pleased with himself. He had his weapon. He had his lizard grass. The strap was long enough for the job; but no lizard he had come across was a trained killer with a high-powered rifle for company. Makeshift garrotte versus rifle. Some odds. Still. . . .

Knew you'd think of something, sir. You're the best improviser to have passed through this school. Nice one about the lizard grass. Now show the rest of the team.

O'Keefe.

Gallagher wondered what his childhood friend Winston would say if he knew that his innocent little game with lizards had been incorporated into a clandestine training system.

Gallagher made a wry face as he began the most dangerous part of the hunt. Not even childhood things were incorruptible.

He made a circuit of the man's position, pausing frequently to listen for movement. He moved with infinite caution so as not to disturb the woodland community and thus gave his quarry a warning; yet he moved swiftly. Within ten minutes, he was in position. The man had not moved. The rifle was still held across his knees. Gallagher was a mere twelve feet away, and still undetected. It might as well be twelve miles if he did this wrongly.

The man's head was still resting on the large tree trunk. The head needed to be free to enable the loop to be slid over it. Gallagher had picked up a fist-sized stone on the way for the purpose. He was about to make his only deliberate noise. After the quiet, it would take a very remarkable person indeed to avoid reacting. Gallagher hoped this was not one such. He prepared himself and then lobbed the stone like a grenade. No point waiting any longer.

The stone described a beautiful parabola as it arched through the trees to slam against a distant trunk. The sound it made was so sudden and exaggeratedly loud that the waiting man could not have helped himself. He was up with rifle pointing almost in one motion; but Gallagher had also moved, on the instant of his having lobbed the stone.

He had already covered the distance before the man suddenly became aware of his immediate danger. Gallagher heard the sharp hiss of surprise just before he slid the noose over and pulled, moving away and round the trunk as it tightened.

The man dropped his rifle to claw at the strap at his throat. Gallagher sensed him panic momentarily before training took over. Instead of trying to get away and thus tighten the noose further, he tried to back round the trunk towards Gallagher and thus gain some slack. But Gallagher was ready for that move and constantly retained tension on the strap by going round the trunk himself.

The two of them performed their macabre dance about the tree, strange worshippers of an indifferent totem. The woods silently observed with omnipotent impartiality. It was a long five minutes before the man at last began to weaken. By then, his face had become darkened by his vital need for air. His struggles weakened, his steps faltered. Gallagher continued to tow him round the tree.

At last, the man fell. Gallagher kept tension on the strap. He was not going to be fooled by any corny possum trick. The rifle was nearby. He gave the man a full thirty seconds before releasing the strap to swiftly pick up the gun. He pointed it at the fallen man.

"Right. Get up!"

The man did not move.

Gallagher stepped back. He knew only too well the dangers of being too close to a supposedly vanquished adversary. He had once, in a small country, seen someone take a knife in the gut from an apparently dead soldier. Both he and O'Keefe had been sent in to get a cap-

tured man out and were being helped by anti-
government forces. The eager anti-government
man had leaned over to rob the "dead" soldier
of a digital watch and had collected a knife for
his troubles. To keep the noise down, O'Keefe
had finished off the reincarnated soldier with
his own knife. The anti-government man had
died with the watch in his hand. Some people
would throw their lives away for anything.

Gallagher was not prepared to throw his.
He stared at the man on the ground.

"I'm not going to fall for that. On your
bloody feet! You can't hold your breath for
ever."

Gallagher looked hard at the leather noose.
It was tight, but did not appear to be unduly so.
Once he had let go of the strap, there would
have been some give in the noose itself. Perhaps
the man had blacked out.

Then he saw the bluing of the lips. Shit.
Cyanide. The bastard was dead.

Still not taking chances, Gallagher moved
forward cautiously and prodded the body with
the rifle. Nothing. Using the muzzle, he pushed
it over. The body flopped. There was little doubt
now.

"Shit!" Gallagher said exasperatedly. All
that effort for nothing.

He continued to stare at the man, who was
dressed almost like the Rogues on Skye. But he
knew that this man was no Rogue. Most people
did not realize it, but some agents did still go in
for the cyanide capsule bit. As far as he knew,
no one with the Department went in for such

theatrics. Those who got found out usually went down fighting.

No, they didn't. Dalgleish was still alive. Gallagher felt an uncomfortable shiver as he thought about that; then he put it out of his mind. Department people were not suicidal either. Dalgleish had survived. Dalgleish was a noted survivor.

Still holding on to the rifle, Gallagher lowered himself on one knee and searched the body swiftly. Nothing. Naturally. But he found a nasty-looking knife which he kept. He removed the strap.

He stood up. The rifle was a long-barrelled, semi-automatic job of American manufacture. The dead man was not American. He was sure of that. An American would have tried to argue his way out. Allies and all that shit.

That left the Russians. Gallagher did not like that thought at all. Who had told the Russians where to find him? Who had told them *about* him, for that matter? It could not have been Dalgleish. Dalgleish wanted pictures. Why would Dalgleish then set him up? Besides, unless Dalgleish were himself clairvoyant, there was no way he could have known Lucinda would be coming up from Nottingham.

Winemaster's revenge? Would Winemaster, with his marked inability to win friends and influence people, have gone that far?

Gallagher looked about him. He had remained in this place long enough. Even if the dead man had been operating alone, it did not mean some of his friends would not come to join him. Gallagher stooped to grab the body and

dragged it into some bushes. He threw the shed-
dings of the trees about the area and stepped
back to scrutinize his handiwork. Even on close
inspection, it was impossible to tell that a body
had been dragged through. If the man's friends
came looking, it would take them a long time to
find the body, if at all, without dogs. He picked
up the rifle once more.

He went back to where he'd left the camera, retrieved it and pushed the rifle deep in, in
its place. He covered the entrance to the hide
with casually dispersed material from the
woodland floor. They'd have to hunt for that
too. He was glad he had kept the knife. You
never knew.

He moved away, turned to look; there was
no way of telling anything had been disturbed.
The springy woodland floor had even
obliterated his footprints. It was as if he had
never been. He fitted the strap back on the camera and turned away to return to the house.

His mind was now full of even more questions. Answers were continuing to prove elusive. The whole affair had taken three hours.

He ran into Lucinda on the way back to his
room. She brightened when she saw him.

"I was just coming to see if you were back."
She stared at his clothes. "What have you been
doing?"

He had brushed them down, but some
marks had remained. He said, easily: "Practis-
ing for tonight. I lay down on a wet patch of
ground while I was scanning for animal heat
traces." He smiled sheepishly.

"I can have those cleaned for you."

"No need. Besides, I didn't bring much with me. No changes as such."

"I'm sure I can find something that will fit. It won't take long."

"It's really quite all right. I'll just sponge the marks off."

The blue eyes seemed disappointed. "If that's what you want. Are you ready to eat?"

He nodded. "I'm sorry I was away so long."

"You don't have to be. You're not holding anyone up. I decided I'd wait for you."

"In that case I'll put the camera away, sponge those marks, and be right with you."

"Can I come in and wait?"

"Of course."

There was a bathroom *en suite* and he went in there after he'd put the camera back in his bag. He left the door open so they could speak without shouting.

"I really do love this room," he said. He could hear her moving around, studying it.

"Did you enjoy yourself in the woods?"

"Yes." That was one way of putting it, even if it was the only answer he could give her.

"Any wildcats?"

"Not one." But two bodies, he didn't add.

"I told you, didn't I? They're shy creatures."

"It would seem like it."

"Jamie likes the woods. Sometimes he's gone all day. I've even known him to stay out there for a whole week."

Gallagher felt relief. It would be all over before she started worrying about Jamie.

"At this time of the year?" he queried.

"Oh, the weather holds no terrors for Jamie."

The weather. No. Not the weather. There were other terrors, and Jamie had succumbed.

Gallagher was glad to have the bathroom as a shield. He would not have enjoyed seeing her while she spoke about Jamie. He hated keeping the awful knowledge from her; but there was nothing for it.

"There," he said. "All finished. I'm ready to eat. Lead me to the table."

He came out of the bathroom. She was sitting on the bed. Her eyes were like dark pools as she looked at him. She did belong to this golden and black room. He felt a sudden warmth coming over him; then she stood up and broke the spell.

She came close to him. "Let's go," she said.

As they left the room, Gallagher was not quite sure whether he'd seen a secret smile that had briefly touched her lips.

Winterbourne summoned Fowler to his office.

"I'm having trouble with the Americans," Winterbourne began as soon as Fowler had entered.

"Trouble, Sir John?"

"Yes." Testily. "They are not happy with the change in arrangements. The Minister. . . ."

"With respect, Sir John. There would have been no . . . trouble, as you put it, if they had not been contacted in the first place."

"But dammit, man! They're our allies. We're expected to consult them!"

"In everything, Sir John?" Fowler spoke

mildly. "The way they consult us?" Fowler placed his hands behind his back and paced briefly. "Let me see. Consult, you said, Sir John. Let me think of the occasions when we were consulted. Grenada, El Salvador, Nicaragua . . . no, not those. . . ."

"Don't play games with me, Fowler!"

Fowler's eyes gleamed behind his glasses. "I do not play games, Sir John." The mild voice had suddenly become harder than Winterbourne would have thought possible. "This affair is too important to the security of this nation, to the Western Alliance itself, quite possibly, for me to allow *anything* to jeopardize it. When we are quite certain of what is happening, *then* . . . will the Americans be told. The security of this nation comes first, above all else . . . including allies. I think you will find the Americans feel the same way about themselves."

The two men locked eyes. Finally, Winterbourne looked away.

"Will that be all, Sir John?"

"Yes, Fowler." Reluctantly. "Yes. That is all."

Fowler gave a little nod and made his way out.

When he had reached the door, Winterbourne fired a parting shot. "Perhaps if you could find out why Kingston-Wyatt shot himself we might just have the answers we need."

Fowler did not pause, but shut the door quietly behind him. This had far more impact than if he had slammed it.

Winterbourne stared at the closed door, his mouth stiff with impotent anger.

It was 1900 hours when Gallagher got the *quattro* out for the drive to Kincarron Lodge. The rain had held off, but the night felt heavy with the promise of its return. Gallagher hoped he would have finished what he was setting out to do before that happened.

Lucinda joined him in the car. She had dressed for the occasion. The Lucinda of the daytime now wore waterproof overtrousers, stout walking boots, with a duvet jacket over a thick woolen shirt and sweater. Over that lot, she wore an anorak. On her head was a woolen hat. She had tucked her rich hair beneath it.

Gallagher stared at her.

"I've got thermal long-johns too," she said. In the courtesy light, he saw her smile before the shutting of the door plunged the interior of the car into gloom.

He said, "Can you move in all that? You'll roast in here."

"Perhaps; but once we get out. . . ."

"What do you mean '*we*'? You . . . are staying with the car, to warn me with the horn, if anyone comes near it. I've shown you how to drive it. It's quite easy. All you've got to do is watch the power. Treat it gently, or it will run away with you. I'll make my own way back. We've talked about it already and we're not changing anything. Is that clear?" She couldn't know that they would by now have worked out that something had happened to their man and would probably be crawling all over the woods by the Lodge, just as a precaution.

She chose to ignore the question. "How are you going to find the Lodge if I don't take you there?"

"Direct me as close as possible with the car. I'll walk."

"But it's still a long way from where we'll stop. You could spend all night looking."

"You're forgetting something," he said. "The camera. I'll just follow the heat traces. The Lodge will be illuminated as if by searchlights." He started the car. The powerful engine growled, eager to get going. The digital dashboard went into its act. "I want your word on this, or I'll leave you here and do it on my own. It may take more time, but I won't have to worry about you playing hide-and-seek in the dark with men so dangerous you wouldn't want to meet them in broad daylight." He looked at her. "Do I get that promise?"

She nodded.

"Good. I feel bad enough as it is, with your father lying up there. You should be with the rest of the family." He had met two aunts, severe-looking women but pleasant enough. They didn't know she had left the house but had been told by Lucinda—to explain the car—that he was taking a night drive.

"I've told you not to worry about it."

"What about your nightmare about not being with him?"

She appeared to shrug. "If it happens, it was meant to."

The *quattro* began to move down the drive.

Gallagher drove away quietly, on low beams. When they were a long way into the tunnel of trees, he went on to full beams.

"Didn't your aunts want to know why I wanted to drive tonight?"

"I told them you were so crazy about your car you simply liked driving it just for the fun of it. It's a most natural story to believe. That was mild compared to some of the stories I've had to give them in my time."

He smiled to himself. He could well imagine.

They reached the main road and turned left. Gallagher cruised at 60. Traffic was sparse. The road surface was still wet. He checked all mirrors.

Lucinda noted his actions. "Do you think the BMW might still be around?"

"I'd be very surprised, but you never know." He hoped Winemaster was well away from the area by now; perhaps on the way to Aberdeen, with luck.

They joined the A890 for the run to Glen Carron. No car took up station behind them. Gallagher wondered when would be the best time to tell her about Jamie; not that there ever was a best time for such news. He decided he would tell her after their return from Kincarron Lodge. She would have to be made aware of the danger. Hopefully, after he'd seen Dalgleish once more, everything could be turned over to the Department. They'd be able to clean up this affair quickly, and protect her while they were doing it.

Then he remembered his neighbor. What protection? Christ, what a mess.

"Did you say something?" Lucinda was looking at him.

He stared at the black ribbon of road unfolding in the swathe of his lights. Had he spoken?

"Not that I know of."

"You made a sort of noise."

He made a joke of it. "Thinking aloud perhaps."

"Ah." There was silence for a while in the car, then, "You're worried about me."

"You could say that. Yes."

"Well, you don't have to be. I'll do as you say."

She'd better. He couldn't think of an easier way for her to get her throat cut than if she left the car.

The road, with imposing peaks looming in the dark to their left and the Carron valley to their right, took them on to Achnashellach. About two miles later, she directed him off the road to the right and on to a track. The track crossed the railway line which bordered the road, turned left and continued close to the railway line for another half mile. Here it turned right on to the first of two bridges.

"We're crossing the Carron," Lucinda said. She giggled a little nervously. "In this darkness, let's hope it's not Charon taking us across." The track had taken them into woodland.

"You have a nice line in light conversation."

She giggled even more. "If that was meant to be a joke it was terrible!"

"Yours wasn't so hot either." He smiled in the gloom of the car.

The black *quattro* slid through the darkness.

They did not cross the second bridge. The road branched off to the left, just before it, its main strand continuing over the bridge and into the mysterious dark. Lucinda directed him left.

"The second bridge crosses the Chonais," she said. "It feeds the Carron. This track will take us close to it." She paused for a good minute before going on; "I think I'm really beginning to feel frightened." It was said quietly.

Gallagher glanced at her. She was staring straight ahead, the back glow of his dimmed lights showing no expression on her face. He had dimmed the lights deliberately and drove the car as slowly and as quietly as was practical. No point in advertising their presence.

"How far to go?" he asked.

"The track will be forking soon. We'll take the right fork. A mile later, it comes to an end. You'll have to walk for another mile."

Two miles, at least. Would they have guards this far out?

He said, "There must be a track that leads directly to the Lodge."

"There is. It branches off from the right fork. You'll be going across country from where we'll stop. Isn't that what you wanted?"

"It is exactly what I wanted. You've done a great job."

"You see? You did need me." Her voice sounded livelier.

"Yes. I needed you. I still need you . . . to remain in the car and not go out there to get yourself into trouble."

"I promise to keep my promise." She gave another sudden giggle. "Sorry. I must be nervous."

In her place, he'd be terrified.

They came to the fork. Gallagher took the right. He said, "You really know it around here, don't you?"

"Jamie used to take us."

"Us?"

"I sometimes brought friends. Sometimes I came alone with Jamie. He must have decided to stay out tonight. He wasn't back when we left."

Jamie. "Does he have a wife?"

"Oh, yes. She's a lovely old soul. They have a lodge on the estate. Not tenanted. My father gave it to them in perpetuity, years ago. I always like seeing her. Now that my father's so ill, she spends most of her time at the house. You haven't seen her because she spends most of the time with my father."

"Doesn't Jamie mind?"

"Jamie?" She gave a brief chuckle that spoke of her fondness for the hard little man. "I've told you. He sees himself as the guardian of Duncarron and all that's in it. He would expect no less from her."

Gallagher felt even worse about Jamie. But he couldn't tell her just yet. He didn't want her to freeze out on him.

The track came to an end. He turned the car round, stopped, and turned off the lights and the engine. As the cooling fan whirred softly to itself, he could hear the sound of running water above it. He unclipped his belt.

"That's the Chonais we can hear," she said.

Gallagher let his eyes grow accustomed to the dark. Soon he could see clearly defined shapes. No matter what anyone said, light always came from somewhere. He looked about him. He wondered if they'd have mobile patrols. He listened. He heard no sounds of motors.

He reached behind for his bag which he'd put on the back seat. He took out the camera and turned round once more.

"Did Uffa ever come here with you?"

"No." She sounded surprised. "Why do you ask?"

"Oh, just wondering." He made light of it.

"You're wondering about *Uffa?*"

"Would I be here if I weren't sure about him?"

"No. No, I suppose not."

Which grades me as some kind of nut, he thought sourly, *because I am wondering about him.*

Aloud, he said, "Right. When I get out, you climb into my seat. Be ready to take off in an instant. Anyone who approaches who's not me, you don't think about it. *Don't think!* You start up and you *go.* If I come running, it's ditto. I'll take over when we're out of immediate danger. Got that?"

She seemed to swallow. "Yes."

"Good. Keep a good lookout, particularly

behind. Your eyes will have become accustomed to the dark . . . but you know all that. Jamie would have given you some woodlore."

She nodded. Her eyes, he thought, were wide as they looked at him. He turned the key in the ignition lock to give him power to operate the driver's window. He lowered it slightly. The rushing sound of the river came in at a suddenly increased volume. Cold air sneaked gleefully into the car. He switched off.

"There," he said. "You should be able to hear anything moving if you allow your ears to tune themselves. Jamie would have told you about that too."

Again, she nodded.

"Right, then. I'll be off. It shouldn't take long. I'll be back before you know it. All those clothes you're wearing will be of some use, after all. Even with the window open, you won't feel the cold and you won't have to start the engine to keep warm." He had spoken lightheartedly to cheer her up. It wouldn't be fun waiting here alone in the darkened forest.

She leaned across suddenly to kiss him lightly on the lips. "Be very careful, Gordon."

She should talk. He was more worried about her safety. But he said, "I'm always careful."

"Just like the MacAuslands?"

He knew she was smiling. "Like the MacAuslands, the Gallaghers are careful folk too."

He opened the door. The courtesy light seemed blinding. He got out quickly and shut the door softly. The click the lock made sounded abnormally loud. The cold air seemed to claw at him for a brief savage moment, then his body began to protect him. He still wore the same clothes, but the sweater Lucinda had given him in Bleasby was efficient enough for the job in hand. He didn't want to be encumbered by too many clothes. His gloves were warm enough and light enough not to impair dexterity.

The *quattro* rocked momentarily as she moved into the seat he had vacated. The shape that was her head moved and he knew she was looking up at him. He raised a hand briefly, turned off the track and moved into the deeper inkiness of the wood.

The ground rose steeply and soon he had forgotten about being cold. At least, no arctic wind was howling through the trees. It was, in fact, a strangely calm night.

As he climbed, Gallagher again wondered about mobile patrols. The other track, off which the access to Kincarron Lodge branched, was fifty meters above him and a quarter of a mile away through the thick wood. It would not be difficult to hear engines. The ground leveled off suddenly and he made good progress. He was careful not to blunder into vegetation and he moved unhurriedly so as not to startle the nocturnal travelers of the forest. Even so, there were many scuttlings. He paused now and then to listen; but nothing gave him cause for alarm. Quick scans with the camera showed no large heat sources.

He went on, wondering how Lucinda was coping with her solitude.

He was perhaps a hundred yards from the

track when he heard engines. He immediately went to ground. Here the terrain again sloped steeply so that the track was almost perpendicularly above him. The sounds appeared to be coming from the direction of the Lodge, but unless he changed position it would be impossible for him to tell what those motors belonged to.

He was reluctant to move, but there was no other choice. He had to see.

Taking a chance that because the part of the wood he'd traveled through had proved empty of any patrols he could afford to be less cautious—at least up to the track—he scrambled upwards, using the trunks of saplings and anything that didn't come away in his grasp, to give him leverage. He made it close enough, just as the first of the approaching vehicles came round a bend through the trees that bordered the access track leading to Kincarron Lodge. It was traveling at speed, more speed than was safe for the conditions.

Gallagher did not need the binocular camera to see it was a four-wheel-drive vehicle: a patrol-type vehicle, based on the cut-down body of a Landrover. The sweep of its lights as it joined the main track caused him to duck, so he did not see how many people were in it. By the time he'd raised his head once more, its lights were flitting, bouncing will-o'-the-wisps through the trees, and fast receding.

The second vehicle came much more slowly, virtually curbcrawling. Gallagher kept his head well down.

"Is all this activity for little old me?" he muttered to himself.

They must have finally decided their man was never going to return. But why the sudden patrol? They could not possibly know he was here. And what about the first vehicle? Was it heading for Duncarron or was it going to check the lower track? Had they heard the *quattro*, after all, despite the care he had taken?

Sweet Jesus. Lucinda was trapped down there, if that was what the high-speed rush had been about.

He felt an impotent anger that was directed at himself. He should never have gone against his better judgement. He should never have brought her. One extra thing to worry about. The anger turned to rebuke. There was little point in anger. He could do nothing to help her in time. The situation could not be changed. He had to get on with what he had come to do. Time enough to worry about other threats later.

He froze.

The second vehicle had come on to the track and had stopped. From his hiding place beneath the lip of the rough road, Gallagher saw the lights go out. Shit. Soon, they'd be cutting the engine, to listen.

They did.

No one spoke. It was eerie. The creatures of the night, frightened into immobility by the sudden raucous noises of the engines, held their own silence. The darkness waited. Gallagher wondered how many men there were. The stillness had amplified sound so much, he could hear the cooling ticks of the motor, the slight creak of itchy bums on seats; the sigh of metal touching metal. Someone not being careful with his weapon.

Gallagher found his ears still listening for the sounds of the first patrol vehicle. He heard it, faintly now, but with a continuing surge of sound. He felt relief. At least, they were not checking the bottom track; not yet. But they would. He hoped they were first going to check where their man had left his own transport. That would mean a journey all the way to Kirkton and back. Time enough to take some photographs and get the hell out. Perhaps.

But first there was the little matter of the silent vehicle waiting just a few feet away.

Seconds seemed like hours, minutes like days.

Someone began to speak quietly and was quickly, imperiously hushed.

Impatient. That was good. Gallagher did not need to be a linguist to recognize those few, abruptly cut-off syllables. It was Russian. That did not necessarily mean the speakers were in fact Russian. Russians in the field spoke perfectly good English—better, in many cases, than the natives. The same applied vice versa. Dalgleish was a case in point. He had fooled the KGB for two years. Still. . . .

The engine was started; but they did not move off right away. They lingered for what seemed an excruciatingly long time before, at last, the vehicle began to move. At a crawl.

It passed directly over Gallagher's steep hiding place, then the lights came on. Gallagher inched himself cautiously upwards. He might get a picture if they kept to that speed.

He reached the edge of the track and propped himself precariously on his elbows, feet resting on small plants growing at right angles from the face of the incline. He put the camera to his eyes. The vehicle jumped at him in a blaze of red. It was another cut-down job.

There were four men in it, clothed against the cold. The three passengers were carrying rifles with scopes. Nightscopes. Tricky, tricky stuff. He'd better get out of here fast.

He got good shots of the passengers, who were turning their heads this way and that, searching either side of the track. One of them was using a mounted searchlight and didn't think to swing it behind them; for which Gallagher was grateful. Something nagged, teasing at his memory. He'd get some good profile shots. When Dalgleish passed those on to the Department, they'd be able to check with their records. He paused. He'd recognized a face. The teased memory had responded. A long time ago, in East Berlin, the face had been above a Russian uniform. Army. GRU? It was Fowler's problem.

Time to return to the car. He had done enough. Dalgleish could not have wished for better proof. Armed men in a patrol vehicle in the Scottish Highlands, one an identifiable Russian. Dalgleish would be in the clear.

Gallagher began cautiously to lower himself back down. Lucinda would be terrified out of her wits after having heard those vehicles. He'd have to get back to her as quickly as possible.

Pity he had not taken a shot of the man who had killed Jamie; but that could not be

helped now. He would tell Dalgleish about the
body. The Department could then take it from
there.

His thoughts screeched to a halt.

Someone below. Close. Very close.

Even as the realization hit him, Gallagher
knew what had happened. When the patrol
Landrover had stopped, one of the men had got
off. So there had been five. *Shit, shit, shit!* That
had been the slight metallic sound he had
heard. The man getting off, catching his
weapon briefly. It had been careless.

*Didn't do me much bloody good though, did
it!* Gallagher thought with sour chagrin. *I
should have picked up on it.* Now here he was,
hanging neatly trapped, with a nightscope looking up his backside.

While these thoughts were churning
through his brain, Gallagher had not paused in
his movements. Nothing must warn the other
that his presence had been detected. Gallagher
hoped the man was either hoping to take him
alive or had not yet set himself up properly for
the shot.

Gallagher let go.

He fell, tucking himself into a ball, holding
on to the camera, which was slung from his
neck by its strap. The man below, taken completely by surprise, instead of shooting, instinctively tried to get out of the way. Gallagher
collided with him with great force, hands now
grabbing for the rifle. He found it and held on
as they tumbled.

In your place, I'd have shot, you bastard,
Gallagher thought grimly as they fought each

other and gravity, grateful for the man's over-riding instinct for self-preservation. A dead man would not have been fighting to take the rifle.

Bushes scraped at them as they fell. Boles of trees slammed painfully; but still they held on to the weapon. The ground began to level out. Their momentum decreased; then a single shot barked out of the rifle. It echoed through the darkness. That would bring the others running, Gallagher knew. He did not have the time for a long-winded rough-house job. This had to be sorted out quickly.

They found themselves in a shallow trough which prevented them from rolling further. They grunted like animals as they fought to gain possession of the weapon. Gallagher knew what he had to do.

Tied to his middle by its sheath with twine he had asked Lucinda to get him was the knife he had taken from the dead sniper in Duncarron wood. Lucinda knew nothing of the knife. He stopped struggling suddenly, confusing his unseen adversary. It was all the time he needed.

His left hand was still on the rifle as he unzipped his jacket with his right and pulled out the knife in one fluid motion. He knew, even in the dark, where the point of impact would be. The knife went in just below the sternum, plunging through the layers of clothing as if they were non-existent. Letting go of the rifle the man screamed with the shock and sudden-ness of it. Gallagher moved the knife upwards, hating what he had to do even as he understood that the man would have done the same to him. He could not feel it as yet, but he knew the blood was pouring out of the man.

Gallagher pulled the knife out and threw it away from him. The man was still screaming. Gallagher found the rifle by the glow of its nightscope, stood up, sighted on the thrashing man and, seeing a ghostly distorted face, shifted aim and pulled the trigger. Another bark echoed through the night. On the heels of that, he heard a racing engine.

He turned to hurry down the gentler slope towards where he'd left the *quattro*. He felt sick. He'd left all this behind. Why didn't they leave him alone? *Why,* dammit?

The Landrover was hurtling along the upper track. Gallagher felt pleased. It gave him more time to make it back to the *quattro*. He hurried, now and then brushing roughly against indistinct trees.

Ruining my bloody jacket, he thought inconsequentially.

He ran on. Up above and behind, the Landrover had arrived at the point where it had first stopped to drop off the now-dead man. Gallagher knew more men would be dropping down into the wood, to hunt the source of the shots. Almost immediately, the Landrover was moving again. It had turned and was heading back down the track.

Gallagher made it to the *quattro*. Lucinda was standing next to it.

"Gordon! I heard. . . ."

"I told you to stay inside! Get back in! Start

up and turn on the lights!" He removed the camera from about his neck and slung it in.

She did as she was told and lowered a window. "What. . . ."

"Time for that later! Drive carefully, and slowly forward. That's all."

She raised the window, giving up on trying to talk to him. The *quattro* lunged forward as its awesome power got the better of her, then it jerked to a stop. The engine stalled.

"Oh, Christ!" Gallagher muttered as he watched. The Landrover would be ploughing up the track soon.

The lights flickered barely perceptibly as she started the car once more. This time, she was more in control. It moved cautiously forward. Gallagher heaved a sigh of relief, ran on and past it, carrying the rifle. The weapon was another American model, an M16 adapted to take the fat, electron-tube nightsight.

He ran along the track until he was well away from the car; then he ducked into the wood, continuing to work his way towards where the tracks forked. The slow-moving *quattro*, with its lights full on, was bait. As he neared the fork, he could hear the Landrover pause at intervals. They had obviously dropped men along the other track.

He reached the fork and got into position just as the Landrover slowed to take the sharp corner that would put it on a collision course with the *quattro*. Even as the sight glowed greenly on the target, Gallagher's mind was filled with the vision of armed men pouring out of the wood and converging on the *quattro*, with a very frightened Lucinda in it. Reason told him they would not have had the time.

The green disc of the sight shifted to the gas tank. Gallagher fired a burst of five. The tank exploded in a thick ball of red-orange that flung the Landrover upwards and sideways off the track. A second explosion tore the vehicle to pieces. The glare lit up the surrounding trees, etching them out, somber flickering silhouettes against the background of the dark. There was the high smell of burnt fuel and scorched vegetation; and of something else too. There had been two men in it.

But Gallagher had not stopped to watch. Already he was running back along the track, waving to Lucinda to hurry. He watched the nose of the *quattro* rise as she stamped on the power. In seconds, it seemed as if she would run him down, then she was stamping on the brakes. The ABS prevented her from disappearing into the trees. That would not have been fun.

He hauled at the driver's door. "I'll take over! Put on your belt when you've got to your seat."

She moved quickly, squirming across to the passenger side. She was clipping on her belt as he put the rifle on the back seat, then took his place behind the wheel. He shut the door and had the car moving even as he clipped on his own belt. He urged the *quattro* forward. The engine roared, the nose thrust itself upward, the car hurled itself gleefully along the track.

"Were you worried about me or the car?" she asked.

"Both," he replied truthfully.

"In what order?"

He smiled to himself. If she could still say things like that, she couldn't be doing too badly; but it wasn't over yet. They had escaped the men on foot, but there was still the other Landrover.

They powered past the fork, heading for the two bridges. *The bridges.* Good place for an ambush; to be caught in one, or to mount one. Gallagher slowed down, cutting in the isolation switch that turned off his rear lights. He dimmed the heads.

Lucinda, who had been staring interestedly at the rifle on the back seat from time to time, now stared at him. "What's wrong?"

"I'm not sure." Thoughtfully.

They could have put men on the ground covering both bridges and blocked the one over the Carron with their vehicle. Gallagher stopped the car and turned off the lights. Lucinda was breathing quietly, tensely. He could imagine how she must be feeling, but she still wasn't having a fit of the screaming panics. A tough lady, all things considered. He warmed towards her.

"Do . . . do you think they're out there waiting for us?"

Someone had to put it into words.

"It's possible." No point lying to her. She had far worse information to receive. Before he'd turned off the lights the odometer had shown they'd traveled just over a mile. It was roughly two hundred yards to the first bridge from here, if he remembered correctly. Down away to his left, he could hear the Chonais as it rushed to empty itself into the Carron. He unclipped his belt and reached for the camera and the rifle. "I'm going to check it out. I won't be long."

"What about those men behind?"

"Unless they can come through those woods and run a mile with a weapon load within the next ten minutes, we'll be all right. I'm more worried about anyone being up ahead." He climbed out. "Won't be long," he repeated, and was gone.

He stopped a short distance from the car to take a scan with the camera. No heat traces worth bothering about. He continued at a trot, the rifle held across his body. He noted that the man he'd taken it off had favored the guerrilla practice of taping two magazines together. When one was in use, the other pointed downwards. Re-loading was simply a matter of switching ends; handy when time was at a premium. It also doubled your ammo capacity; a life-saver in certain circumstances. It was a habit Gallagher himself favored.

He had gone a hundred quiet yards, when the track curved. It was now a straight run to the bridges. He went to the edge of the wood silently, then used the camera again.

Four heat traces, two at each bridge. There was no sign of the other Landrover. He took a minute, scanning carefully. There was no residual trace. It must have stopped very briefly, only to let the men off. That meant it was on its way to Kirkton, possibly coming back already.

They would not have wasted time searching for their man.

Gallagher moved slowly forward. They would have nightsights, so he'd have to be bloody quick about it. All four would have to go; before any of them could take a shot. He took yet another scan, just to make sure. Definitely four.

In relation to each other, the bridges were so positioned that the spots chosen by the four men placed them in a staggered line from where Gallagher now waited, going from left to right. He memorized each position with absolute precision. If he started with the left-hand target, he'd merely have to shift his sighting to the right after each shot, and the next target would be on-line; if he did it quickly. They weren't going to stay in place to be shot at. The one on the far right would be the most difficult. He would have the most time to get out of the way.

Gallagher settled down. Three minutes had gone. Seven minutes remaining by his own reckoning, in which to clear the bridge and return to the *quattro*. *Damn*. He should have told Lucinda to take the wheel again. It would have saved time. Too bad. He would just have to do it within the limits he had set himself.

They would have heard the *quattro*, heard it stop. They would also have heard the shooting and the explosion, and seen its glare. But they hadn't moved. They would not move until the ambush was sprung or they were told there would be no ambush. Trained men who would not panic.

Gallagher lay flat on the ground, the glow of his own scope screened by trackside bushes. He moved the rifle in a slow arc. It was working, at least in the sight. What would happen after the first shot was anybody's guess. Both pairs of men were looking up the track. One raised his rifle for a practice sighting. Gallagher brought his own rifle down, ducking behind his screen.

Nothing whistled past him. He hadn't been seen. He gave it thirty long seconds before cautiously peering into his sight again. The one who had raised his weapon was now talking to his partner in sign language. There seemed to be no urgency. He was the third in line, and was "talking" to the fourth.

Abruptly, Gallagher knew exactly how he was going to do it.

He sighted on the first man, who was now also looking at the third. They would have radios but probably would not use them for fear of noise. Gallagher knew the time was now.

He fired, shifted to the second man, fired again. He shifted swiftly past the third man, catching a glimpse of an open disbelieving mouth, to sight on the fourth man who was already diving for cover. Gallagher nailed him in mid-flight, switched to the confused third man, fired again. It was all done. The four shots had sounded like a measured burst, with scarcely a pause in between.

Gallagher was up and running, saw with joy the *quattro* lights come on. *Well done, Lucinda.* He felt he could kiss her.

The car came up to him. He jumped in. It was again moving while he was still closing the door. He put the rifle and the camera back on the rear seat.

"You're wonderful!" he told her as he clipped on his belt. "Bloody wonderful!" He gave her a quick kiss on the cheek.

She flashed him a look of pleasure; but she appeared to be trembling. He was not sure whether this was due to excitement or fright. Probably a bit of both, he decided. They crossed the bridge over the Carron without pause, then just after the sharp left off it, Lucinda brought the car to a halt.

"You drive," she said. "I'm shaking too much."

"Right," he said. They changed places quickly and the *quattro* was soon moving again.

"What about the other Landrover?" she asked.

"If we can get back on the main road before. . . ."

But it was already too late. They saw distant lights swinging off the A890. It could only have been the other patrol. Someone must have used a radio, after all.

"Looks like we'll have to carry out our second ambush," Gallagher said grimly. He stopped the car and reversed back to the corner near the bridge. On the corner itself was a narrow slip road that led to a railway cutting. There was just enough room to get the *quattro* through. With Lucinda out to guide him, he reversed along it with main lights out, the only illumination being that of the reversing lights. It would be stupid to be caught pointing the wrong way. The *quattro* was far enough to be out of sight until the very last moment. By then, it would cease to matter.

Lucinda got back in to wait, this time in the passenger seat. Gallagher took the rifle and ran back to the track to lay his ambush. The corner by the bridge, he decided, would give maximum results. He positioned himself in bushes by the slip road, about fifty yards from the apex of the corner. Behind him, the Carron flowed indifferently.

The headlights came bouncing along the track. It was almost too easy. There was no need for those in the oncoming vehicle to expect an ambush at that point, for it became swiftly obvious that whatever the message that had brought them back, it had not been about the attack by the bridges. The Landrover barely slackened speed on the corner. It was therefore at its most unstable.

As the green image came into the sight, Gallagher emptied the magazine at it. The bullets chattered away, raking the speeding vehicle from stem to stern. It actually crossed over, then right between the two bridges, it exploded with a roar and a starburst of flame that sent the shattered pieces of its former self hurtling outwards in all directions. He waited with some trepidation for a chunk to fall on the *quattro*. Mercifully, none did, he had parked it sufficiently far away.

He heard something rolling back across the bridge. He got the sight on it quickly. A wheel, completely free, was making its way towards him. For one ridiculous moment, he thought the wheel knew exactly where to find him and was coming to exact retribution. The wheel went right past him, rolled down the bank and into the river below. Gallagher threw the rifle after it. He went back to the car and got in.

"Time we were well away from here," he said as he started the engine. He drove quickly away.

They were on the A890 heading back to Kirkton when she said, "What did you do with the rifle?"

"Threw it into the river."

They did not speak further for some miles.

It was Lucinda who eventually spoke, "Now I know why Uffa wanted you to help him. He told me you could be quite lethal when you got going."

"I was not always like that," he said quietly after a while.

"I think I understand." Softly; but she didn't sound quite sure.

How could she? he thought philosophically. How could she know or understand what was done in the name of Queen and country? She would never understand. He felt a sense of bitterness that was directed at no one and at everyone.

"I have something to tell you," he said. What the hell, this was as good a time, or as bad a time, depending on how you wanted to look at it.

She stared at him, warned by the hard edge to his voice.

He told her as quickly as possible, and without frills, about Jamie and the sniper. His voice came across much harsher than he'd expected.

After a sharp cry on hearing of Jamie's death, she held her face in her hands and said nothing for the remainder of the journey.

They put the car away in silence, went up to their rooms. "Goodnight" was all they said to each other. Neither felt like eating.

Gallagher thought she was in a state of shock. He could well understand it. He was in shock himself, he decided, he wished he could have got away from those people without having had to kill his way out. That they would have shot both Lucinda and himself without compunction, he well knew; and certainly, he would not have liked the two of them to have been captured. He had no illusions about what would have happened then. But it did not make him feel any better.

In his room, he had a long bath then fell gratefully into bed. Tomorrow he would go to Dalgleish, give him the camera with its exposed film and that would be it. He'd had it up to there. Dalgleish would have to cope from now on. A quick flit to Skye, then back to London. The limits of friendship had been pushed beyond reasonable bounds. No more could or should be expected of him.

With those thoughts in mind, he fell asleep.

His eyes snapped open. He didn't move.

Someone was in the room.

He allowed his breathing to retain its measured pace, as if he were still asleep. His eyes were accustomed to the dark, but whoever had entered was still by the door. He could not see unless he turned his head; which would give him away.

So they had come for their revenge. It would have been easy to break in. Such a big house with no security would have been child's play to them. What weapon would the intruder use? Gun? No. Too much noise.

Never heard of silencers? his mind queried of him sarcastically.

He wasn't thinking straight. With a gun the intruder would have little need to come close. A knife . . . now that would make things a little less difficult.

Gallagher poised himself to move, gauging the moment when he thought the person would shoot. He let his ears tell him what his eyes could not detect. He could hear shallow breathing, movement. The person coming close, tensing for the kill. The moment was approaching. It. . . .

"Gordon?" A soft call. Lucinda, fear still in her voice.

Gallagher let out his breath slowly. He felt his skin move with the relief of it.

"Gordon? Are you awake?" Hesitantly.

"Yes. I thought you were someone else."

"Someone from Kincarron?" Her voice shook. He could imagine her thoughts. "No. Don't switch on the light," she added quickly.

"Yes," he repeated. He did not switch on the light.

She came closer. Her shape was covered by something voluminous. Dressing-gown.

"And you were ready to attack?"

"Just about." *With plenty of luck,* he didn't
say.

She seemed to shiver. "I don't know who
frightens me most. Them or you." She sat down
at the foot of the bed.

"There's no need to be frightened of me."

"I don't suppose I really meant you . . . as
a person. It's . . . it's what I now know you can
do." Her voice faded absently, as if her mind
were really on other things.

A silence fell between them. He listened to
her breathing, waiting for her to go on.

"I . . . I couldn't sleep," she said at last.
"Everything. . . ." Her voice faded again.

He patted the bed. "Get in."

"I don't want. . . ."

"I didn't say I was going to make love to
you. Get in. I'll hug you to sleep. You can leave
in the morning with your virtue intact."

She hesitated some more, then she stood up
and slowly removed the dressing-gown. There
was something else underneath it; a thin nightdress. He made room for her to get in next to
him. She slid beneath the covers and brought
her body uncertainly close to his. He felt its
heat. There was charged air between them. She
came even closer, pressing herself against him.
He felt the softness of her fitting to him. She
trembled once.

He was naked. He always slept nude.

After a short while, she raised her head so
that he could pass an arm beneath it. She
tucked herself in.

"You can't get any closer," he told her
gently.

"Hold me," she said. "Please."

He put his other arm about her. They lay like that, unmoving, for a long while. Neither fell asleep. Presently, she kissed his chest softly.

"No hairs," she said. "I like that."

No further movement came from her for another long while. Then she was kissing him on the chest again, moving upwards. She reached his mouth. It wasn't long before the kissing became much more vigorous and the squirming began. Somehow, her nightdress had come off.

"Oh, God!" she said when he entered her. She was very eager and ready for him now. "Oh, God; oh, *God!*"

They fought pleasurably, locked to each other until their exertions made their bodies slippery with moisture. It went on for a long time. At last, her body heaved upwards and shuddered, stiffened and shuddered again. Gallagher felt an uncontrollable force overwhelm him. His arms tightened about her, almost squeezing the breath out of her. She gave a long ululating whimper; then their bodies relaxed.

She began to cry quietly. He held her close, not really understanding why; though he thought he did.

Sometime during the night, a violent rainstorm broke. She held on to him tightly. By morning, the storm was gone.

So was she.

Tuesday

0900 hours.

Gallagher was ready to leave for Skye. He had taken a nice hot bath and changed into the last clean shirt he had. The rest of his clothes looked battered, but that was hardly surprising. He'd brushed them down as best as he could. At least they weren't torn. He would have been annoyed if he had ripped his jacket. His bag was packed, the camera neatly stowed for delivery to Dalgleish.

He thought about Lucinda. Had she left before dawn because she'd felt self-conscious? Embarrassed because she had needed comfort and had come to him almost like a child afraid of the dark?

He sighed. You never knew with people.

He picked up his bag, went to the door and opened it. Lucinda was there, hand up, about to knock. She was dressed in jeans and sweater, her hair tied in a single bunch.

She gave a weak smile. "We ought to turn this into a double act." The blue eyes were red-rimmed. The corners of the mouth trembled. She went on, quietly, "He's dead. He died last night when we were. . . ."

"Lucinda, I—"

She put a hand gently to his mouth. "Shhh. You don't have to say anything." Her face was very pale. "Can I come in for a bit?"

He moved back. She entered. He shut the door after her. She came close, putting her arms about him tightly. Her body gave a slight tremor. He knew she was crying. He put down the bag so that he could embrace her. They stood there in the gold and black room, neither speaking.

At last, she released him and stepped away. "I'm . . . I'm sorry. I know this probably embarrasses you, seeing me make a spectacle of myself." She wiped her eyes with the back of a hand.

He stared at her. "No. It doesn't. Cry all you want to. I understand."

She gave him another weak smile. The dimple lived briefly. "Do you? I'll be all right in a minute," she went on, not waiting for nor expecting an answer. "I really came to tell you breakfast is ready. I'm afraid you'll have to eat alone. I don't . . . I can't. . . ." She paused uncertainly, not looking at him now. Her thoughts seemed far away.

"There was no need to have breakfast prepared for me. I could just as easily have eaten on the way."

The blue eyes were focused on him once more, but they still seemed far away. "Well, you'll have to eat it now, or I'll never forgive you. I prepared it myself." The mouth twitched, as if to smile.

"In that case, I will."

"There is . . . something else."

He waited.

"I'm coming with you to Skye. Don't try to stop me," she went on quickly as he was about to object. "After all that has happened, especially because of Jamie, Uffa owes me an explanation."

He owes me one too, Gallagher did not say.

". . . the man who killed Jamie . . ." Lucinda was saying.

"I told you," Gallagher interrupted. "He came for me."

"Or Uffa."

"Impossible. He's not been near here."

"He could have *said* he was coming here."

Gallagher stared at her. "To whom?"

She shrugged, gave a little sigh. "I don't know, I don't know." Wearily. "I've got to see him, and I want him to tell me the truth. It's the least I should expect."

He said nothing.

"If you don't take me," she said, "I'll only follow. One way or the other, I'm going across to Skye today." She sounded very determined and looked it. The face was still pale, eyes still red-rimmed; but there was now a stubborn set to her stance. The MacAuslands were coming down through the centuries on the warpath.

He knew she meant every word. He did not relish the idea of her being out on her own on the roads. The people at Kincarron might have cleared house because of what had happened

the previous night, taking their dead with
them. On the other hand, they might well have
left someone behind to take care of loose ends.
If they knew how to get to Duncarron, they
knew how to get at Lucinda. And there was still
Winemaster.

Gallagher said, "Your father. . . ."

"Jamie's wife was looking for him this
morning to tell him about my father's death.
Now she's worried, wondering why he stayed
out in last night's storm. She's afraid something
may have happened to him. I couldn't bring
myself to tell her. Not yet. That's another reason why I can't stay here today. I couldn't face
her. As for my father, he's all right now. Nothing can touch him any more."

It was an odd thing to say, and Gallagher
did not understand. She did not enlighten him.

He said, "All right."

She nodded once, satisfied she had proved
her point. "I'll get ready while you're eating."
She went to the door, paused, came back to
stand close, directly in front on him. The blue
eyes looked up into his. "You were very good to
me last night; good for me, too. It was. . . ." She
kissed him gently, lingeringly on the lips. "I'll
always remember it. Always. I don't have to tell
you what it did to me."

She went out without looking back.

He stared at the opened door. You never
knew with people. He picked up his bag once
more and went out to his solitary breakfast.

He did not close the door.

* * *

She came up to the *quattro* dressed in the same clothes she had worn the night before for the drive to Kincarron. She had a tiny nylon holdall with her.

"Did you enjoy your breakfast?" she asked as she climbed in. She clipped on her belt with a purposeful snap.

He started the car, watching the digital acrobatics detachedly. "Yes. Thank you." He looked at her to smile his appreciation. The entire house had settled into a hush; the hush of death. He had seen no one throughout his meal. "It was kind of you to make it."

"Therapeutic. I needed the distraction." She gave a quick apologetic smile as the car began to move. "I didn't mean it to sound quite like that. I did enjoy making it for you."

"You don't have to explain," he told her gently.

He drove down the pebbled drive, taking it easy. In the mirrors, the vast dimensions of Duncarron receded into the backdrop of the mountains until the bend into the tree tunnel eventually hid it from view. As the car entered it, he suddenly thought of Jamie's body lying out there in the wood.

"The Department will get the police up to take care of Jamie," he said to her. "I'll get Uffa to do it. On second thoughts, I'll contact the Department myself, just to make sure it's done."

She gave him a grateful smile, before turning to look back along the tunnel. "Jamie should be buried properly." She turned once more, eyes seeing private visions.

He glanced at her. "Yes," he said quietly.

The journey back to Kyle of Lochalsh was uneventful. They saw no sign of Winemaster's BMW. Constant scrutiny of the mirrors had disclosed no shadowers. Gallagher almost felt deprived. They caught the ferry to the island. Gallagher's friendly boatman was again on board.

"Back again, I see," the man said cheerfully. He stared at Lucinda. "Why, Miss MacAusland! If I'd known this young man was a special friend of yours I'd be taking him round Skye myself. Had a pleasant chat we did, when he first came aboard."

She smiled at him, though Gallagher knew she did not feel like smiling. "Then I thank you for that, Mr. Roberts."

"And your father, Miss MacAusland. Is he improving?"

Gallagher waited to see how she would handle that.

"The usual, Mr. Roberts," she answered with the right amount of philosophic acceptance in her voice.

The boatman was sympathetic. "Sad it is, Miss MacAusland. Very sad. I remember your father as a strong man. Sad."

Gallagher glanced anxiously at Lucinda. He knew the boatman meant well, but he didn't want her cracking up on him now beneath the onslaught of the man's solicitude.

But Murphy's Law was working overtime. The next question was inevitable.

"And that old wreck of a man, Jamie Cameron. Is he still pretending he is as young as the rest of us?" Roberts gave a gleeful laugh.

Lucinda handled it well. "When I last saw him, he was."

Roberts laughed again then mercifully went off to see to the boat. They had arrived.

Skye greeted them with a bright, dry morning. Gallagher drove at a leisurely pace. Dalgleish would not be going anywhere.

It was eleven o'clock.

Moscow, 1300 hours.

Ulvanov looked across the empty table at Skoryatin. "So, Comrade, today is the last of the present series of flights of the Tu-22P."

Skoryatin nodded. "And the last with Kakunin in command. It won't be his last flight, of course. As commander of crew training he will have an even greater workload."

"What of the others?"

"Narenko and Velensky? Good men. Excellent flyers."

"Should they not also go to the training command?"

Skoryatin smiled. "With respect, Comrade, I believe the Army to be the best judge of that."

"I would not presume to teach the Army how to handle its training schedules, Vladimir Mikhailovich," Ulvanov said smoothly, and insincerely.

Skoryatin held on to his smile. "You are not again suggesting, I hope, Comrade, that there may be reasons other than military to ground them?" He had deliberately retained the formal address, knowing it would needle Ulvanov.

Ulvanov's face was expressionless, barely succeeding in ignoring the slight. "You put words into my mouth, Vladimir Mikhailovich," he said, persisting with the familiar.

Skoryatin felt he could give a little. "Then I apologize, Dmitry Vasil'evich."

"Now that we are both satisfied," Ulvanov went on with a straight face, "is there news of Dalgleish?"

Skoryatin said, without flourish, "I believe we have found where he is hiding. The precise spot. This was unknown before. He was seen, and followed."

"That is very good! No. I will say more. It is excellent! And where is he?"

"On the island of Skye."

Ulvanov said, "If the British or the Americans have not succeeded in eliminating him by the time today's flight is over, we shall have to do it ourselves. *Your* operatives will have to carry it out. We cannot wait for much longer. The Comrades in the Directorate are becoming . . . shall we say . . . restive."

Ulvanov was of the Third Department of the First Chief Directorate, with responsibility for the United Kingdom, New Zealand, Australia and, oddly, Scandinavia. Skoryatin had always thought that a strange grouping. He would have thought putting Australia and New Zealand into the Asian/Oriental axis and covered by either the Sixth or Seventh Department would have been more logical. Perhaps the KGB, in following the old British imperial groupings, were perhaps themselves secretly imperialistic.

Skoryatin smiled inwardly at his heretical thoughts. Ulvanov's bluster did not worry him. He had control of the operation, and Ulvanov was well aware of it.

Skoryatin said, "The GRU will do what is expected of it."

"What is the time of the flight?" Ulvanov asked, changing tack abruptly.

Skoryatin took the change with ease. "2300 hours their time, 1800 our time. A mere five hours to go, Comrade. Then our first phase of the new strategy will have been successfully completed."

Ulvanov actually smiled. "Do you know what gives me the greatest pleasure about all this, Vladimir Mikhailovich?"

Skoryatin waited politely, knowing he would be told without his having to ask.

"What gives me pleasure," Ulvanov went on, "is the fact that the Americans are dragging themselves into a quicksand in Central America while all this is going on without their knowledge. They can laugh at us in Afghanistan, and we laugh at them in Central America, in Beirut . . . but *we* still hold the high card. You do not gamble, do you, Vladimir Mikhailovich? But of course I know that. Gambles sometimes pay handsomely."

"They also cost handsomely, Dmitry Vasil'evich, if they are not carefully monitored," Skoryatin said with a guileless smile.

Ulvanov looked at him, wondering what to read into it.

* * *

Gallagher turned the car slowly off the road on the ridge of the Quiraing, stopped and switched off the engine. The *quattro* sighed to itself. The engine cooling fan hummed on, fanning the fevered metallic brow.

Gallagher said, peering upwards through the windshield, "This is where I stopped the last time. If he's here at all, he would have seen us coming a long time ago. We'll just have to wait till he shows." He looked at her. "Are you all right?"

She had been very quiet for most of the journey.

She nodded slowly. "Yes. I'm fine." The eyes were no longer red-rimmed, but they looked tired, as if all she wanted to do was lie down.

"Would you like some music?"

"That would be nice." She looked out at the Quiraing landscape. "This is so beautiful."

"When I was here last, you couldn't see anything. We were above cloud, but it was the most amazing thing I had ever seen. It was like being in another world." He went on to describe the strange mist to her as he selected a cassette.

"I would have liked to see that," she said when he'd finished.

"What would you like?" He showed her four cassettes. "Choice of jazz, heavy metal, electronic or classical. The classical is the Brandenburg Concertos."

"I'll take the Bach. I like the recording with Martin Galling on harpsichord. My favorites are the Third, Fourth and Fifth."

"Incredible! That's the cassette I've got."

She turned the blue eyes on him, smiled. "We have a lot in common. And I didn't look. Put it on."

Gallagher slotted the cassette into the Blaupunkt Toronto. The Fifth took up the whole of Side One. The strains of the First movement flooded through the four speakers. Gallagher balanced them until the rich music of two and a half centuries filled the interior of the car softly, but completely.

"It suits this place," she said, staring out at the dark peaks. "My father . . . my father used to like his Bach." She stopped, remembering. "Yes." Softly, to herself, "He used to like it."

Gallagher said nothing. From the way he'd parked the car, he had a good view of the approach road from Staffin. Nothing was coming.

He said, gently, "You listen in privacy. I'm going to have a quick look at the other side to see if anything's coming up from Uig."

She smiled her appreciation at him as he got out. He shut the door softly and walked away from the car. He glanced back. She was not looking at him but was immersed within the music and her memories. The car still gleamed but looked a bit grubby, he thought idly. He turned away, walked to the apex of the hairpin bend and listened.

The Brandenburg came softly to him. No sounds of climbing motors intruded. Where, he wondered, was Dalgleish? The *quattro* was unmistakable. He would have seen it coming from a long way off. Its sound was unmistakable too.

Come on, Uffa! Where the hell are you?

Gallagher wanted the whole matter off his hands. He had no desire to meet up with Winemaster again, nor to tangle with the enraged survivors of the last night's little firefight. That was the Department's job, and the Rogues, and the police, and the bloody kitchen sink. As long as he was out of it. Now and then, he would look back at the car. Lucinda appeared to be staring at nothing, deep in her music.

He stayed out of the car until the entire side of the cassette was played through. Dalgleish had still not put in an appearance. The day was still bright and pleasantly mild up there on the ridge; but though he would have liked to enjoy the incredible view, the nagging uncertainties of the affair spoilt his appreciation of it. He walked back to the car, opened the door and got in. He pulled the door to, but did not shut it.

He said, "Looks like we're in for a long wait. Would you like the other side?"

She nodded. "It was very kind of you to leave me to it. I went back into my childhood."

"Pleasant memories?"

The stereo unit clicked to itself. A tiny triangle winked out, another winked on. Side Two began to play.

Lucinda said, "Some were. Very much so."

"And the others?"

She shrugged dismissively. "Not really important."

He did not press her, and listened to the music instead.

At the end of the Third Concerto, she said, "Alice came here once."

"Alice?"

"Dodgson's little angel in Wonderland."

"Ah. That one."

"She was grown up then, and not at all like the person he had invented. People never are what we think them to be, sometimes."

"No." He was thinking of Dalgleish.

The Fourth Concerto began.

"This is my next favorite," she said. "Particularly the second movement."

They listened to Bach doing his stuff and, by the end of it, Dalgleish still hadn't put in an appearance.

"Do you think he's here?"

Gallagher punched out the cassette. "Yes. He's watching us from somewhere, checking to see if we've been followed. He'll take his time about it. But I hope he doesn't make it overlong. I want to be away before dark. More music?"

She shook her head. "No. That was fine, thanks. I don't want to spoil it."

"OK." He put the cassette away and switched off the stereo.

"I've brought some food," she said. "Are you hungry?"

"Food! Now you've mentioned it, I am a little. But I'd like to wait for a while. What did you bring?"

"Made some sandwiches. Brought a couple of cans of orange juice too."

"You got it all into that excuse for a bag?" The bag was one of those cylindrical jobs in shiny material that could be bought from any camping store. This one was a foot long with a shoulder strap attached to it at each end. A zip ran along the top from end to end. It was olive green in color.

"Don't be rude about my bag," she said without rancor, "or you'll get nothing."

"I think it's the most beautiful bag in the world," he said with alacrity.

"Liar."

They smiled at each other. She reached out to touch his hand briefly, looking up at the track that led into the Quiraing itself.

"What do you think those people at Kincarron will do?"

"Most will get out," he answered. "They'll also have informed their Rezident. . . ."

"Rezident? What's that?" The eyes stared confusedly at him.

"Local controller, responsible for operations in this country. He could be anywhere, but most likely in London. His job will be to let them know back home what has happened. I don't think he'll do so just yet."

"Why not?"

"It's a failure that will carry a lot of stink with it for a start. But the most likely reason is the transmission window; that's the best time they can transmit in order to escape the hordes of listening centers and snoop satellites."

"And this goes on all the time? This communications snooping?"

"Round the bloody clock."

"So how does anyone get anything out?"

"There are all sorts of ways. Nothing is impregnable."

"It's all a big joke, isn't it?" she said after a while, thoughtfully. She stared up at the track once more.

"If people didn't get killed, I'd agree with you. It's a sick bloody joke that will run and run, I'm afraid; and a lot of not very nice people will keep it going."

They fell silent. The peaks of the Quiraing looked down upon them in dark majesty.

"Gordon." She did not look at him.

"Yes?"

"Last night . . . last night was lovely. I want you to . . . I wish . . . oh, this is impossible. It doesn't matter, anyway." She sounded annoyed with herself.

He looked at her, puzzled. "What's wrong, Lucinda?"

She sighed, shook her head determinedly. "Nothing you can help. . . ."

"Try me. You never can tell. . . ."

"No! Look. I'm . . . I'm sorry. I didn't mean to shout." She sighed. "It's the whole thing. It's Jamie, my father, Uffa. It's just getting me down, that's all. I'm sorry," she repeated. "I'll be all right in a minute."

He reached out to touch her shoulder gently. She flinched involuntarily before relaxing again.

"You are jumpy," he said kindly. "You shouldn't have come and I shouldn't have let you. It was crazy of me to agree."

"I had to. I couldn't have stayed in the house." Her voice shook, her body began to tremble.

"Hey, hey," he said softly. "Come here." He put an arm about her.

She leaned across, resting her head on him. She didn't cry.

"Tell you what," he said. "Let's go for a walk. Being cooped up in here isn't helping. We'll go up into the Quiraing. I'll take my bag with the camera, you bring the food. We'll find a spot to picnic. If Uffa's around, he'll see us and know we got fed-up with waiting down here. That will probably bring him. What do you say?"

She nodded against him.

"Right," he said. "Let's do it before we change our minds. The weather's perfect for it."

They got out with their bags. He locked the car, and they took to the track, working their way upwards. After a while they paused, looking down on the car.

"Will it be all right?" she asked.

"Yes." There was always a chance that someone could come and play around with it while they were in the Quiraing, but he didn't tell her that. "Besides, I'll check it when we get back. I always do."

They went on, taking their time. If Dalgleish were indeed watching from somewhere, hurrying would not make him show himself any earlier. Gallagher wondered if Dalgleish had them in the sights of the Dragunov even now. He felt his skin crawl, but continued without pause as if no such thing troubled his mind. Then he laughed at himself in his mind. Dalgleish would not be so mad as to shoot his own cousin, no matter how jumpy he might be.

They trekked for well over a mile, clambering up and down bracken and boulder-strewn slopes; pausing now and then to admire the jagged spires that stood like forbidding sentries guarding this fortress of mystery. No wonder Dalgleish had chosen this place. There was a distinct primeval air about it and Gallagher felt it would not take much to imagine it inhabited by all sorts of awesome beings.

Their journey took them to a place Lucinda said was called the Prison; then she showed him a spire of rock she said was the Needle; but it was the flat expanse of ground high up in this rocky fastness that stirred his imagination. She called that the Table.

From its edges, the land sloped steeply, in some places it was a sheer drop. Going over would be a one-way trip. It was the view, however, that took his breath away. Standing on the Table gave one the impression of being suspended in space for in the distance and far, far below stretched before him a toyland of undulating shapes. Splashes of water stained the landscape and toyland houses dotted it.

Lucinda came up to him. "That's Loch Fada closest to us. Over there is Digg." She pointed, then moved her arm to the right. "That's Glashvin. . . ." She went on to point out the distant communities.

"I'd like to come back here when this is all over," he said when she'd finished. "I'd like you to show me around. Properly."

She gave him a little smile, took his hand. "Let's eat."

They sat down in the middle of the Table to

eat their sandwiches and drink their orange juice. Gallagher found that the walk had made him quite hungry. Lucinda had made a varied selection and had brought a fair amount. Looking at her as she heaped them on paper napkins that had been neatly unfolded, he wondered how she'd managed to get them all into her bag.

"You're a gem," he said as he bit into one. "Mmm. Good."

"Of course," she said. "How could they not be?" The laughter in her eyes was marred by a deep layer of preoccupation.

They ate in silence after that. Every so often, they would look at each other. Once, she reached out to touch him briefly. Above them, the Quiraing sky remained clear.

When he'd finished, Gallagher lay back to stare up at the empty sky. The ground on the Table felt as if rain had not touched it for weeks. Lucinda was about to say something when a thunderous roar cut across her intended words.

Gallagher sat up immediately to look. Flying low, a pair of RAF Tornadoes screamed above them on swept wings, heading towards Lewis. They were tucked in close to each other, holding a tight formation. He watched as their shapes swiftly turned to mere dots in seconds.

Lucinda said, "You wish you were with them, don't you." It was more of a statement.

"Not a chance. I gave that up a long time ago."

"I suppose you'll eventually believe it if you say it often enough."

"Oh, come on. Besides, I never flew Tornadoes."

She was unconvinced. "I can see your eyes. You can't."

By three o'clock, Dalgleish was still nowhere to be seen.

At 2300 hours precisely, the Tu-22P lifted itself off the darkened arctic runway and tore upwards into the cold, inky night. It hurtled for its operational ceiling where it performed its magic of vanishing off the monitoring screens. It streaked northwards, eventually to describe a wide sweeping curve to the west and south. It was heading for the GIUK gap, its engines shrouded from infra-red and acoustic detection. It the central recess in its belly, it carried the new multiple-targeted weapon.

In the right-hand seat, Velensky felt surreptitiously for a stowage panel set into a switch console on his right between the seat and the cockpit wall. The lid in the panel opened inwards. He put his hand through, making quite certain neither Kakunin nor Narenko could see what he was doing. The hand stopped. He gave a low grunt of satisfaction.

The pistol was there.

Kakunin's voice came on his headphones. "Did you say something?"

Valensky froze, but recovered quickly. "No, Comrade Colonel," he answered in his usual Party manner. "A sigh, perhaps." His hand remained where it was.

"A sigh from you, Velensky? Don't tell me

you're pining for that gymnastic young thing I have been hearing about."

"There is no gymnastic young woman, Comrade," Velensky said stiffly.

Kakunin gave the sigh of a man who had been brought close to despair. "Try to live a little, Yuri. It really isn't so bad. There is more to life than flying."

"Yes, Comrade Colonel."

Kakunin gave another sigh and got on with the job of piloting his awesome aircraft towards its designated area. Behind them Narenko tried not to laugh at Velensky.

Velensky slowly withdrew his hand from the panel. He had not been seen. He had found a note in his flight suit simply telling him the goods had been delivered. Who had placed the note and who had secreted the pistol was a complete mystery to him. It was not in his interest to even think about finding out. Weeks before, another note had told him where to look. That had been all. Previous to that, the very first note had told him what was to be done.

He relaxed in his seat, glancing at the digital counter of the elapsed flight time. Long way to go yet.

At the pilot's station, Kakunin surveyed the three main CRTs—arranged in T-form—that gave him all major flight information. The same display was repeated at the co-pilot's station and again on Narenko's systems operations panel.

Kakunin said, "I'll be sorry to leave the ship. She's a great old bird."

"Just think," Narenko began, "you'll be

able to fly every one that comes out to the training base."

Kakunin snorted derisively. "Probably
have my neck broken by some eager virgin on
his first flight."

"Wish I were coming with you," Narenko
said wistfully.

"So do I, Alexei. So do I."

Valensky said, "Are you in favor of person-
ality cults, Comrades?"

That succeeded in killing all conversation.

In the Quiraing on Skye, it was just after four
o'clock. Gallagher stood, looking to the north-
west. The sun had just set, but there was still
plenty of twilight. On the distant horizon, was
an ominous dark patch. A light breeze had
sprung up, taking a couple of degrees of temper-
ature with it.

Gallagher said, "I don't like the looks of
that out there. I think it's coming this way. I
hope to hell Uffa finally gets himself sorted out
and makes it before that bloody storm does. I
don't fancy being caught in this place. Do you?"

"Not if I can help it," she said. "Oh, we'll
find shelter, but sleeping in the Quiraing is not
my idea of fun." She had come close to him,
looking into his face. The breeze teased at her
hair gently.

He said, "May I kiss you, madam?"

Her smile was strangely hesitant. "You
may, sir. You may."

"Then I shall."

He kissed her softly, slowly.

"Oh, very romantic!" a voice called.

They broke apart, startled, and whirled in surprise. Dalgleish was coming towards them. He was carrying the Dragunov.

"Very romantic," he repeated into their consternation as he reached them. "Well, Gordon old son. It seems my rather sexy cousin has nobbled you. Dangerous that, you know. Gets the old guard down. I've had a bead on you for some time now."

Gallagher was sure of it. At times, during their long wait, he had felt an uncomfortable tingling along his spine. He had said nothing about it to Lucinda. There seemed to be a feral gleam in Dalgleish's eyes, but he was not sure. It could have been the twilight.

Dalgleish was looking at Lucinda. "And so, sweet cousin, what a surprise to see you here. Worried about me?"

There was something about Dalgleish's whole stance, his look, his voice that sent warning shivers through Gallagher's body. What the hell was going on now? And Dalgleish had the Dragunov.

Lucinda said, "Jamie Cameron's dead, Uffa. Someone shot him in Duncarron wood."

"The old gamekeeper? Don't look at me, old girl. I've not been off this island."

Gallagher looked from him to Lucinda. Surely, she did not think Dalgleish had had anything to do with Jamie's death?

Dalgleish noted the look. "You seem confused, Gordon." What might have been a smile twitched his features. "Did you bring the camera?"

"Yes."

"Managed any pictures?"

"Yes." Gallagher repeated.

"Wonderful. I always knew I could rely on you. Trouble?"

"A little."

"Ah-ha. I know what that means in real terms. Since you're still alive, I assume you must have given a good account of yourself."

Gallagher briefly told him what had happened.

Though it had now got appreciably darker, Gallagher could see that Dalgleish was definitely smiling.

"A bloody one-man army this lad, when he get's going," Dalgleish said to Lucinda. "And you were there to see it all. You two have really got yourselves involved. Well, I suppose I shouldn't be surprised. You really are quite sexy, Lucinda. And as for Gordon well. . . . Women have been known to find him attractive."

Not knowing what game Dalgleish was playing and not really caring, Gallagher said, "I'll get the camera."

As he turned to go, the snout of the Dragunov followed him. He paused, stared at Dalgleish.

"What the fuck are you doing, Uffa?"

"Bring back nothing but the camera, will you? There's a good lad."

Gallagher said, wearily, "You're back on that old tack again, are you? Do you think I've got a gun in there?"

"After last night, who knows?"

"Well, for God's sake, go and get it yourself

then!" Gallagher said exasperatedly. "We've been waiting here for hours while you've been skulking about the place—for what, only you know—and all *I* want to do is get the bloody hell out of here before that storm breaks."

The wind had grown perceptibly stronger.

"You get it," Dalgleish said mildly. "I do hope there's no gun in there, for your sake."

"Christ!" Gallagher said in disgust and went towards where had left his bag.

Lucinda had neatly cleared up and now had her own bag slung from her shoulder. As he walked, Gallagher glanced up at the sky. There was still some light left up there, and the columns and spires and cliff faces of the Quiraing were pasted like dark battlements against it. Beyond the edge of the Table, the land had disappeared.

He picked up his bag and took it back. "You open it," he said to Dalgleish. "You can see for yourself there's no bloody gun."

Still holding the rifle alertly, Dalgleish lowered himself to unzip the bag. He took out the camera, felt around inside the bag, made a slight noise of satisfaction. He stood up again, leaving the camera on the ground.

"All right," he began mildly, "there is no gun."

"Well, put your artillery away. We're leaving. You've got your pictures, and I've had it. I've got to take Lucinda back. Her father's dead."

"Is he, now? The old boy has been due for a long time anyway."

Which, Gallagher thought, was a curiously

unfeeling way to talk about a relative. As he watched, Dalgleish put the rifle on the ground. But then he did something else, even more disturbing.

Dalgleish had swiftly pulled out the big automatic and was now pointing it at Gallagher and Lucinda. "You two must think I'm stupid."

"Jesus Christ!" Gallagher shouted. "Are you bloody mad? What has Lucinda to do with this?"

Dalgleish laughed into the oncoming darkness. The ramparts of the Quiraing took the laughter and bounced it off its basaltic surfaces, laughing with him.

"Oh, quite a lot, old son. Quite a lot."

Gallagher was dumbfounded. Why would Dalgleish want to point a gun at his own cousin?

"She's not," Gallagher began with sudden insight, "with the Department, is she?" He wouldn't put it past that lot.

Dalgleish laughed again. "Oh, the innocence! Gordon, Gordon! There must be a guardian angel that protects you sometimes. Lucinda with the Department. Oh, that's a good one." His voice dissolved into laughter for a third time and, again, the Quiraing laughed with him. The cold wind, coming down from Iceland, was beginning to tug at them tentatively.

"My dear Gordon," Dalgleish continued, "I would like you to meet Irina Alieva, Major, KGB, with whom you've no doubt been quite intimate, to judge by appearances."

Gallagher felt the ground rock beneath him, and a sudden pulverizing in his stomach.

But the ground had not moved, and no one had hit him.

"I don't believe you," he said at last, quietly.

"You don't have to, old son. Ask her to deny it."

Lucinda said nothing. Gallagher did not look at her. The world about them was losing the last of its light. In the far distance, pinpricks of starlight had appeared on the dark blanket of the land as man-made lighting took over from the fleeing day.

"I think the point has been made," Dalgleish said. *"Don't!"* he barked suddenly, and the big automatic roared once.

Lucinda gave a high-pitched, sharp cry and fell heavily. Something dropped next to Dalgleish.

"Lucinda!" Gallagher shouted, anguished, and turned to reach for her.

"Leave her alone!" Dalgleish ordered. "Leave her, or it will be the same for you."

Lucinda was making a whimpering noise.

"For God's sake, Uffa! She's badly hurt!"

"Leave her, I said!"

There was just enough light for Gallagher to see the big gun pointing at him. Dalgleish reached down, never once losing concentration, and picked up whatever had dropped near him. Another pistol.

Dalgleish said as he straightened, "Take a look. That should dispel any further doubts. What's a nice country girl doing with a weapon like this on her person?" He threw the pistol far away from him. The gun sailed away in the darkness, over the edge of the Table.

Gallagher did not hear it land.

Dalgleish said, "Her bag. Get it! Come on! Hurry!"

Gallagher went down cautiously on one knee and groped around. He found the little bag within which Lucinda had brought the sandwiches. The empty orange juice cans clattered dully from inside it. She was breathing shallowly. No other sound came from her. He wanted to do something to help.

"Hurry it up, Gordon!" Dalgleish said impatiently. "And please don't do anything stupid. I'm not taking any chances with you. Throw the bag towards me. Try to hit me with it and I shall shoot. Stay down. I can still see well enough, even in this."

Gallagher did as he was told. The bag landed at Dalgleish's feet with a tinny thump. Dalgleish reached down guardedly and opened it. He shook it empty. Something heavy dropped out with the cans and the ghostly white flutter of the used napkins which the wind promptly took with it. They disappeared swiftly, weak fairy lights darting into oblivion.

Dalgleish said, "She came well prepared. A second pistol. Nothing if not thorough, our erstwhile Lucinda, now Major Alieva, native of Azerbaijan."

The new gun followed its predecessor over the edge. Gallagher, feeling helpless, didn't like it at all. Dalgleish was no pushover, as he had shown on several occasions. It looked as if, Gallagher thought grimly, both he and Lucinda were going to spend the night in the Quiraing, after all; except that they would know nothing about it.

Dalgleish was still looking for something, but didn't find it.

"Damn!" he said. "I should not have expected such a bonus, I suppose," he went on. "The thorough Major would not have been so careless as to bring it with her. Still, it was worth a try. I'll just have to go to Duncarron."

Gallagher wondered what he was looking for.

Dalgleish straightened again, said, "You must be so thoroughly confused by now, Gordon. First, let me tell you about those people you killed last night at Kincarron Lodge. They were British, and American."

"What? Rubbish! They were Russian. You gave me the location yourself!" He said nothing about the man he had seen.

"Of course I did. And I wanted the pictures. I wanted proof of armed men, military men, in a supposedly non-military area. The KGB hit it on the head when they decided that Scotland is where they should be directing their energies with regard to the siting of the new missiles. The place you went to last night is one of the new joint British-American communication centers, with more American control. You've got me the proof of its existence."

Gallagher wanted to vomit. *Jesus, Jesus.* But he had *seen* that Russian. A double? It was anybody's bloody guess.

"The Department is *not* going to love you,

and as for the Americans. . . ." Dalgleish stopped to let the words sink in.

Jesus, Gallagher thought numbly. *Jesus.*

"If you're wondering about the man who killed Jamie Cameron," Dalgleish was saying, "and whom you subsequently took out. He was from the same crowd. He was after my 'cousin' the Major, not you."

Gallagher listened with mounting horror to Dalgleish. The Department had been right all along. Dalgleish had been turned.

"You're probably wondering why I shot her. Trust . . . or rather, the lack of it. I don't trust the KGB, and I don't trust bloody Fowler and that lot, just as I didn't trust Kingston-Wyatt. The Major kept a watch on me. She was my contact, but also my intended executioner. Just as you were."

Gallagher said, "How many bloody times do I have to *say it? You* sent for *me.* I was abroad for several months. I didn't know you were still alive. And I don't work for the bloody Department any more!"

"You conveniently returned to this country just after I did."

"Bloody coincidence. Ever heard of it?"

"In our line of work, coincidences don't exist."

"Your line of work," Gallagher corrected.

"Have it your own way," Dalgleish said reasonably. "When Kingston-Wyatt left me to rot in Russia, I was made an offer which—as the saying goes—I was unable to refuse. I was offered a choice of holidays in friendly neighborhood psychiatric hospitals: Leningrad, Kazan,

Chernyakhovsk.... Choice of drugs too, to keep me happy." A harsh bitterness had crept into Dalgleish's voice. "Aminazin to give me skin cancer, destroy my memory or make me spastic. Sulfazin to make my body so excruciatingly painful I would lie motionless for fear of moving. Or how about our friend Reserpine to destroy my braincells? A wonderful, varied choice. They never tried anything out on me. They didn't have to. Then they brought me beautifully faked pictures of Kingston-Wyatt screwing Delphine Arundel. God only knows how they managed it.

"There were more pictures. Kingston-Wyatt meeting for coffee with a KGB brass-hat whom everyone knows has not been outside of Moscow for years; Kingston-Wyatt in a men's lavatory. . . ."

"Jesus Christ! Oh, come on, Uffa. The Department wouldn't believe that."

"Oh, no? How would Kingston-Wyatt be able to disprove it? In the present climate of panic, all it needed was my threat to reveal all to the newspapers. Whatever . . . it was enough to put the shits up the bastard. Have my revenge, they said, and do something for us at the same time."

Gallagher said, *"You* were responsible for Kingston-Wyatt blowing himself away?"

"Don't sound so shocked. You should be grateful. After all, he did nothing to save the woman you loved. You wanted to kill him yourself."

"Christ!" Gallagher said again, softly.

"Then they told me about the missile sites,

and about the bluff they were playing with the West. They told me they had put it about that there was a dissident intelligence group inside the KGB *and* the GRU. I was to make great play of this when I got back. You see, they had *wanted* us to feed someone in to check on the story. Someone they could then make use of. They also wanted Kingston-Wyatt removed."

"But the secret aircraft—what about it?"

"Just as there is no Windshear Group, there is no secret aircraft."

Gallagher did not know what to believe. He remained silent as the fingers of the wind grew more insistent. It was going to blow one hell of a storm, and here he was, stuck in this place with a nut who had once been a friend, and a badly wounded—possibly mortally so— Lucinda. He would always think of her as Lucinda. She was strangely quiet. Had she already died? He dared not look.

"Of course," Dalgleish continued into the wind, raising his voice a little, "the KGB could not let me live, once I'd done their work for them. You see, my 'cousin' the Major is a sleeper. She has been here for eight years. Not even the Rezident knows who she is. I could hardly be left alive with the knowledge."

"So how did the people who sent the man in Duncarron wood know about her?"

"Who knows?" Dalgleish said unhelpfully. "There was a Lucinda MacAusland, you know. No relation of mine, naturally. Never even knew the people. But they had been picked. You see, the old man last saw his real daughter as a baby. Wife divorced him, married again, as he eventually did, went to live in the south. Her new man took her on holidays to Switzerland. As Lucinda grew up, she and the mother took to going by themselves. The man flitted around after trying unsuccessfully to get into the young Lucinda's knickers. Her mother stayed married, screwed every penny she could out of him. One day, when Lucinda was in her twentieth year, they had an accident on a steep alpine road. According to the story the world knows, mother died, but Lucinda survived with a few scratches. The truth is, Lucinda died too.

"But presto. Enter a new Lucinda, nee Irina Alieva, groomed and battery-schooled for two years for her role, and made to endure several months of painful remodelling of her features. She was furnished with the real Lucinda's total history. She could even tell you everything about the expensive school she attended in Gloucester. As for the old man himself, he was more than happy to see again the daughter he thought he'd lost for ever. Funny, isn't it, how the mother always gets the child? The real Lucinda would probably be still alive today if things had been different. As it was, the gymslip-fancying husband was not all that sorry to see both mother and daughter go, so there was no trouble with the new Lucinda becoming the heir to Duncarron. Funny how things turn out. I believe the Major actually grew to love the old man as her real father. We'll never know whether the accident which killed both the real Lucinda and her mother was staged or not."

As Dalgleish paused, Gallagher felt something touch his hand.

A gun!

Gallagher kept absolutely still. She was alive! But where had the gun come from?

The weapon prodded him urgently. He did not react, not wanting to give Dalgleish warning. The gun prodded again, butt first. He would have to be very, very quick and, in the gloom, deadly accurate. Dalgleish would not allow him more than one chance; and even that was dicey.

He took the gun slowly, making quite sure there was no movement from the rest of his body. He didn't know how well Dalgleish could see, whether Dalgleish could detect small movements so deep in shadow. He fixed a point on Dalgleish's chest in his mind.

He had a good grip on the gun now. Another automatic. It felt light. He hoped it had good stopping power.

Now!

He brought the gun up in a sudden sweep, halting dead on target.

Dalgleish was fractionally slow, caught out by the totally unexpected development. "What . . ." he began.

Gallagher fired rapidly, three times. The weapon snarled waspishly, but it had stopping power all right. Dalgleish was hit three times. He staggered backwards, arms outflung as if to regain his balance. He tripped over Lucinda's discarded bag and seemed to be propelled even faster on his way.

He continued pedaling backwards. Gallagher watched, fascinated, as the moving shape staggered closer and closer to the edge. Then suddenly, Dalgleish's automatic began to roar, spitting its anger into the ominous, dark sky. Then the shape abruptly disappeared.

"Your guardian angel!" Gallagher heard in a rising scream. It was a scream of anger, of frustration but oddly, not of fear.

The scream died thinly, suddenly, as if it had been switched off. Gallagher stood up slowly, threw the lightweight automatic into the darkness with all his strength, then he lowered himself again to take hold of Lucinda.

"Ah!" she said with a sharp gasp. "Careful!"

He stopped. "Where are you hit?"

"Don't move me yet. I've been lying here conserving my strength." Her voice came strongly.

Gallagher felt better. He waited.

"Are you sad about your friend?" she asked him presently.

"Yes."

"You're thinking of university days." She still sounded like Lucinda.

"Yes," he said again. "Where did that gun come from?"

"My lower leg. I had it strapped just above my boot. That's why I wore these trousers with the bottoms tucked in. I knew if I failed with the first gun, he would look in my bag. The one in there was deliberately placed for his benefit. He'd never expect a third one. I was right. Ah!" She gasped again.

"Look. Don't talk. Save your strength. I've got to get you to the car. This wind's getting worse. It's going to be hell getting back as it is. It will be torture if the storm catches us here."

"We can find shelter."

"And you could be dead by morning. No. We're leaving."

"In that case, move me only when I'm ready."

"All right," he agreed reluctantly. He wished he could see where she was hit. At least it would give him an idea of her condition.

She said, "Most . . . most of what Uffa told you was. . . ."

"Lucinda. Don't talk. Please. Save your strength."

"You're still calling me by that name?"

"Of course. That's what I know you by."

Her hand stroked his arm. "How sweet."

"Now rest. Don't talk." The wind began to tug at him, still petulantly, and not yet strong enough to cause a serious problem. But it would eventually, if they did not get a move on soon.

"I'll talk if I want to," she said defiantly, the old Lucinda MacAusland was back. "She was quite a strong person, you know, the real Lucinda. I had tapes of her voice. Most of what Uffa told you was true," she began again, "but there were also plenty of half-truths, lies and wrong information he'd been given. First let me put you out of your misery. The people you fought last night were not American, *or* British."

"Then why—"

"Send you there? I wanted you to go there, and I gave him the story about the communications center. He was told he'd get final instructions from me. It was known, of course, that he would be unable to do it himself."

"Are there communications centers?"

"You know there are, but not at Kincarron Lodge."

"So you gave him the Windshear story?"

"Yes, and he also got it in Russia. Throughout, he believed it to be a KGB arabesque."

"And it isn't?"

"No. Windshear does exist. The secret aircraft does exist."

"Am I to believe that?"

"Yes."

"Why?"

"Because you're talking to one of the Group. Because I have the film of the aircraft. That's what Uffa was looking for, to give back to the KGB as proof of his good faith. I think he might have tried to bargain with them. He might have tried to have a copy made. They'd have killed him anyway."

"You are Windshear?" Gallagher said slowly.

"Yes." She sounded as if she wanted to laugh. "And the film is in your car, under my seat. That was just in case I hadn't made it. That was why I asked about whether you thought the car was safe."

Jesus.

"And the shots I took? Are they worthwhile?"

"Oh, they are. They are."

"My God," Gallagher said, almost to himself. He didn't tell her about the man he had recognized. She could sort it out later, with Fowler.

"The man in the wood was coming to kill me. Uffa was right about that." She coughed suddenly.

"Lucinda!"

"I'm all right. Don't fuss. You'll get me worried."

"Are you ready to move?"

"No."

"Don't be so stubborn. Majors are not supposed to be."

"Not true. Some majors can be very stubborn. They're notorious for it. Worst rank to be. Too high to get away with it, but too low to have real power. Colonel's the best. By the time you get to General, you're in trouble."

He wondered if she were becoming delirious. A crazy conversation.

But she said, quite calmly, "They wanted you to kill him, you know."

"Who?"

"The Department. They wanted you to kill Uffa. He was right about that too."

"I didn't want to kill him."

"But you did."

Gallagher said nothing to that. There was no way of denying it. Dalgleish was dead, lying mangled somewhere at the bottom, and he had shot him.

"They planned it well," Lucinda was saying. "They no longer trusted him and wanted him out of the way. They knew it would be difficult to get close. How to do it therefore? What would make him vulnerable? Isolation.

Isolation would create a desire for help, but from a totally trustworthy quarter."

"Me?"

"You. They read Uffa accurately. Read you too. You'd help Uffa, but not the Department. They knew that if Uffa had truly been turned, or even if he was only unstable, sooner or later it would come to what happened just now. They banked on your skills. If they were wrong about Uffa, they would still have benefited."

Gallagher said, "If you hadn't given me that gun, *we* would have been lying at the bottom."

"The Department was prepared to take that risk."

"With my bloody life?"

"But of course."

"The bastards used me," Gallagher said softly. "Bloody Kingston-Wyatt."

"He must have been a clever man."

"I would prefer low cunning."

"A vital asset in a senior Intelligence man."

The wind gusted fitfully about them.

Gallagher said, "How are you feeling?"

"A little longer and I'll be ready to move. I'm not in shock, so I'm fine. I believe," Lucinda went on, "the KGB must have used something on Uffa. He just didn't remember it. I've had long talks with him. There were times when he would just drift out of the conversation. At others, he'd be perfectly all right." She gave a sigh, as if all the talking had made her suddenly weary.

Gallagher moved so that he could use his body to shelter her from the increasing wind.

"Careful!" she said.

"I'll be careful," he said gently. "But I really do wish you wouldn't talk. It can wait."

"I want to talk. I want to tell you. You're debriefing me." She gave a weak chuckle.

"The Department can do that."

She made no comment, and Gallagher misunderstood her silence.

"Lucinda!"

"Don't shout. I'm all right."

"I thought perhaps. . . ."

"That I'd died on you? Don't worry. The MacAuslands are a tough breed. I grew to love him, you know," she went on after a pause. "Like my own father. He was a kind man in his own way. When he died, I felt a great loss."

"When you told me about the music . . . the Brandenburg . . . which father were you thinking of?"

"The real one. He died when I was twelve."

"Was he KGB?"

"No. Army." She would not say more about him.

"Who was the man who killed Jamie?" If she wanted to talk, keep her talking. That way she wouldn't fall asleep . . . for good.

"KGB."

"But why?"

"Perhaps they have found out I am with Windshear. Although I am here as a KGB Major, I am actually GRU. Uffa did not know that. As you heard, he believed I was to eventually kill him."

Gallagher listened to all that she was saying to him, marveling at the way she had fooled him so completely. She was a consummate actress.

"When you came with me to Kincarron, were you really as frightened as you looked?"

"Only when you told me about Jamie. I knew then that someone had come for me. I was frightened for Windshear. Time will tell whether anyone has been caught."

"What about when I came back and saw you outside the car? What had you been doing?"

"Waiting to see if you needed help."

"You were *armed?*"

"Yes. But I couldn't tell you. There was a time when I thought—briefly, I'll admit—that *you* were after me."

"Oh, come on."

"Anything was possible."

They fell silent as the wind came at them firmly. Gallagher decided he would still be able to walk quite safely in it, carrying her on his back. He could remember the route back.

He said, "The trip back to the car may get a little hairy."

"We'll make it," she said.

I'm glad you think so, he didn't say.

"Why don't you ask me about last night in the room?" she demanded.

"There's nothing to ask about that."

"You must be wondering whether I was just doing my job."

He said nothing, not trusting himself to speak.

"I wasn't," she said, so quietly, he nearly

missed it. Then she was speaking more loudly, too briskly. "Uffa once said to me there was no real difference between East and West. People were simply controlled in different ways. He gave the car as an example. In the Soviet Union, very few people have cars, but here in the West most people do. But you pay savagely for the privilege. Although the motor industry depends for its life on the customer, and the nation benefits greatly from the industry, you make it almost impossible to get pleasure out of it.

"You are taxed in all sorts of ways, fuel is expensive, and you are not allowed to park it; for which, of course, there are more penalties. Uffa said motor cars are not for pleasure but for the simple purpose of collecting revenue. He found the spectacle of a vast industry creating goods that no one was supposed to enjoy quite amusing. The age of the Philistines, he called it."

"And you? What do you think?"

"There are times when I wonder whether our group is doing the right thing in trusting the West; but if we are to save both sides from destruction, we do not really have a choice. I think I'm ready to move now, Gordon."

"Right. I'll just get my bag and the camera, and we'll be on our way."

He found the camera where Dalgleish had left it, returned it to the bag and went back to where Lucinda lay.

"I'm going to carry you in a fireman's lift. Tell me if I'm hurting you when I pick you up."

"All right."

He went down on one knee, began to pick her up.

"Aaah!" she gasped. "No, no. Don't stop now. I'll . . . I'll . . . I'll be . . . all . . . right. Aaaah!" Her words turned into a strangled scream.

"Lucinda. . . ."

"It's better if you continue. I couldn't bear to go back down."

"All right . . . if you're sure."

"I'm sure. Believe . . . me."

"Right. I'm going to stand now." He took a firm grip on the bag and rose as smoothly as he could.

Lucinda gave a whimpering moan, then: "I'm all right. All right."

"Right then. We're off." He began walking across the Table. The wind tugged playfully at him, not yet giving him any trouble. Though she was not a small woman, he found she was surprisingly easy to carry.

"Are you comfortable?" he asked.

"I'm . . . I'm fine."

"Head not too low?"

"No, no. I'm OK. Stop fussing."

He smiled. "Yes, ma'am."

The easy part, he knew, was the walk across the Table. After that, the fun would really begin. Despite the ominous approach of the storm, he found he could see reasonably well in the gloom, now and then lit up by distant flashes of lightning which heralded what was to come.

She said, "I didn't tell them about you."

"Who?"

"Moscow."

"Thank Heaven for small mercies. Now shut up."

"Yes, sir."

He smiled again.

Ulvanov entered the room, looking shaken. Skoryatin was already there. He looked quite calm.

Ulvanov sat down, beginning almost at once, "The Scotland operation is totally compromised, Vladimir."

"Yes, Comrade General," Skoryatin said, deliberately retaining the formal.

Ulvanov jerked his head back slightly, as if stung. This was an ominous beginning. This dandy before him would try to discredit him. Well, he would have a fight on his hands. No one tried to flatten Ulvanov with impunity.

He said, "You are remarkably undisturbed, if I may say so, *Comrade,* for a man who has had several of his field men killed, and others facing imminent arrest."

Skoryatin said, "Dalgleish was your problem, Comrade."

"My problem!" Ulvanov exploded furiously. *"You* were meant to have him killed!"

"I have no doubt he is now dead," Skoryatin said smoothly. "The British will have got him. But he was in *your* custody before he . . . er . . . escaped." Skoryatin's eyes were suddenly as dead as slabs of stone. "Had he not escaped, Comrade General-Major Ulvanov, my operation, *our* operation would now be intact. As it is. . . ." He shrugged eloquently.

Ulvanov looked at him, hating every bone

in his body. Ulvanov said, "Perhaps the Tu-22P should be recalled." He sounded apologetic, he thought, and now hated himself for it.

"You know we do not contact the aircraft once it is airborne, Comrade," Skoryatin said coldly.

Ulvanov could feel the chill of Siberian winds coming out of those eyes.

The Tu-22P described a beautiful curve high above Iceland and headed for the north-western reaches of Scotland.

Kakunin's left forearm lay on the integral armrest of his seat. His hand was curved round the shaped side-stick controller that protruded no more than about three centimeters above his fist. The stick did not move. Control of the aircraft was secured by pressure. Computers gauging the force of the pressure exerted, moved the aircraft about its axes accordingly.

He eased back on the pressure as the Tu-22P completed the turn. It settled on to its new heading.

"Beautiful," he murmured. "Beautiful!"

Narenko said, "You sound as if you are making love to it, Colonel."

"She's a thoroughbred, Alexei. A thoroughbred. How are we doing?"

"Still invisible to the world."

"Does this wonderful piece of Soviet machinery not gladden your heart, Yuri?"

Valensky said, "It is nothing more than I would expect, Comrade Colonel."

Kakunin sighed, "Oh, Yuri. The Party must be proud of you."

Valensky reached into the panel by his side and pulled out the gun. He pointed it at Kakunin.

"Colonel Kakunin, this flight will not go on!"

Kakunin turned his head sharply at the tone of Velensky's voice. His eyes stared, then narrowed beneath the raised visor of his helmet.

"Have you gone mad, Major?" He did nothing stupid. His control hand was hidden from Velensky, but the co-pilot had a similar side-stick. To put the aircraft under full control of the computers would require movement that would warn Velensky. Kakunin awaited his chance.

"And you, Narenko!" Velensky went on. "Remain perfectly still! I shall keep my eyes on the monitors at my station. If anything deviates, I shall shoot the Colonel."

Narenko believed it. He did nothing.

"And now?" Kakunin said.

"I shall destroy the aircraft." It was said calmly.

"What! You *are* mad!" Then the strangeness of what the little shrimp Velensky was saying sank in. "You really do mean it."

"Of course." Velensky seemed to have acquired a sudden presence. His eyes were not mad, but philosophical, and at peace with himself.

"Why, Velensky? *Why?* You of all people!"

"Ah, yes. Me." Velensky's voice betrayed that he was smiling in his mask. "You two thought I was put in here to spy on you. Don't try denying it. It was very obvious." The gun did not waver. "I won't kill you if you two do as I say. Colonel, you will take the aircraft lower. At a height that I shall give you, you will both eject. I shall stay with the aircraft. I shall send out a mayday with the co-ordinates of your exit. The NATO forces will be only too glad to rescue you. Your immersion suits will protect you for long enough."

"Do you really expect me to turn my aircraft over to you, Velensky?" Kakunin's eyes glanced unwaveringly at his co-pilot.

"You do not have a choice, Colonel. I respect you as a pilot; as a man too. But if you do not do as I say, I *will* shoot. Inside this aircraft and at our present height, the result would be quite devastating."

Velensky glanced at his monitors to satisfy himself that Narenko was behaving. Nothing had changed. He looked at the windshields. There was nothing to see through them. The blast shields were up. The aircraft was in full avionics mode.

Kakunin said, "You have not answered my question. Why?"

Velensky answered readily enough. "Because this aircraft will mean the end of *both* East and West. We cannot win, whatever those geriatrics think. I am not delivering this to the West. They would make use of it and are therefore no better. The only choice is to destroy it. Now, Colonel, take her into a shallow dive. Keep her invisible, Narenko. She will die unseen."

Kakunin obeyed. He was still waiting. A chance would come.

"Are there many more who think like you, Velensky?" Kakunin asked conversationally. "Only someone very familiar with our routine could have placed that weapon on board. Someone who knew how to get past the security checks."

"You do not really expect an answer to that, Colonel."

"No. I suppose not."

Surreptitiously, Kakunin had released his main straps, but his ankles were still shackled to the retaining straps that would pull his feet towards the seat during ejection, keeping them from flailing. Nevertheless, he lunged at Velensky. It was a serious mistake. It is possible he never thought Velensky would shoot when the time came.

Velensky had time to fire just once, but the bullet tore through Kakunin's suit to slam into his chest. Kakunin grunted and fell back against the side-stick, as the bullet, deflected by a rib, turned downwards to lodge against his spine, creating havoc as it traveled.

The Tu-22P tipped its nose and plunged earthwards at speed. Velensky put reverse pressure on his own side-stick in an attempt to counteract Kakunin's weight. The aircraft continued to plunge. Pressure on the left-hand stick was obviously greater.

"Get out, Narenko!" Velensky shouted into his mike. "Get out before it becomes unsafe!"

But, unbelievably, Kakunin was *moving*. He was trying to get at Velensky, but the force of the dive was preventing him. His movements, however, eased pressure on the stick. The aircraft now responded viciously to the sudden transfer from forward pressure to reverse before Velensky, seeing Kakunin move, could correct it.

It tried admirably to cope. It had pulled its nose up and was rocketing into a climb when Kakunin, not quite in control of his body, was thrown back against his seat by the sudden transfer of gravity. He again fell against the side-stick, this time applying sideways pressure. The aircraft kicked itself over into a high-speed stall. Kakunin died against the stick. Velensky could not apply corrective control. No one had thought to incorporate a control isolation system into the design. That would have given Velensky pilot command of the Tu-22P.

The aircraft fell to earth once more.

Narenko knew he was not going to make it. With tears of rage and despair, he switched off all the immune systems. Instantly, every monitoring system in the GIUK air defense net registered their falling presence. The net quivered like a spider's web that had sensed the first beats of an approaching fly's wing. The resulting vibrations shot through the system like an electric shock. Fighters began to scream skywards like demented beasts slavering after prey.

Narenko began to broadcast in English: "Mayday! Mayday! Mayday! This is a Soviet aircraft and we are falling! We have a weapon on board! I repeat. We have a weapon on board! Mayday. . . ."

The fighters held off as if someone had screamed plague. Communications links hummed with traffic. Surface and submarine fleets of both power blocs headed for the predicted point of impact. Alert warnings were sounded. The world braced itself.

The Tu-22P plunged into the freezing waters, taking its crew and its weapon with it. The weapon did not explode.

Gallagher heard aircraft roar overhead in the angry night as he approached the car. He identified them as Tornadoes. The sound of their Turbo-Unions on afterburners was unmistakable. He wondered idly if they were F.2s, the new interceptor variant.

It had been a nightmarish journey. Several times, he had stumbled but fortunately, he had not dropped Lucinda. A few times, he had slammed himself against unforgiving rock. His body ached. After each stumble, he had asked her anxiously if she was all right. Her answer had been the same. "I'm all right. Stop fussing." God. She was amazing.

He put her down gently. "We made it, Lucinda! We made it! Just hang on a little longer while I open the car."

She said nothing as he hurried to do so. He paused. For once, he was not going to check it. She couldn't wait. If there was anything wrong, so be it. He inserted the key and turned it. Nothing happened. He breathed a sigh of relief.

The rain had been holding off. Now, it began to warn him with swollen droplets that spattered loudly on the car. The wind came at him frustratedly, as if resenting their safe passage out of its domain.

He opened the passenger door, ran back to where he'd left Lucinda, picked up his bag with the camera still in it, dropped that behind the seats and went back for her.

"All right, my brave Major," he said gently. "Your turn."

He began to pick her up. She made no sound.

"What's this?" he said jokingly. "Finally got accustomed to my rough handling?"

There was still no reply. He paused, suddenly aware of a terrible sogginess about her. It was not the rain, he knew.

"Lucinda?" Quietly. The limpness of her body told him all he wanted to know. "O dear God," he said in the same quiet voice. "O dear God."

For how long had she been like this? For how long had he carried her dead body upon his back? He raised his face to the rain that came down out of the dark sky.

"You bastards! he yelled. *"You bloody bastards! Damn you all to hell!"*

He was thinking of the Department, and the Russians, and the Americans; but most of all, of Dalgleish.

After a while, he was not sure how long, he put her very gently into the car, reclined the seat so that she could lie with dignity. Then he got in and put the Brandenburg cassette into the stereo. He fast-wound it until he got the Fourth Concerto. He wound some more, to the second movement.

He started the *quattro* as the haunting *Andante* began flooding out of the four speakers. It had been her favorite, she'd said.

The storm finally broke in all its fury as he took her down the mountain.

Thursday

"And that's the lot?"

"Yes," Gallagher said. He had told as much as he wanted to.

They were in Fowler's office. Gallagher had caught the ferry from Skye, driven Lucinda's body all the way to Duncarron from where he'd called the Department. Fowler had flown straight up from Northolt in an RAF aircraft which had landed him at Plockton. A chopper had been waiting to take him to Duncarron. From then on, everything had been taken out of Gallagher's hands.

Gallagher had given only the briefest of answers to Fowler's questions. He had not wanted to speak to anyone. Pausing only long enough to sponge Lucinda's blood off the back of his jacket, he had promised to visit Fowler in a day or so. Sympathetically, Fowler had agreed. Winemaster had somehow turned up too, grinning at Gallagher and saying "no hard feelings." Gallagher had turned away from him. Winemaster's clouding face had shown the American would not forget that in a hurry.

Gallagher had driven all night back to London. The following day, he had taken the *quattro* back to Central Garage to have it thoroughly cleaned. Lucinda's blood had been on the seats too. The garage people had been shocked, but Gallagher had not enlightened them.

"A very brave young woman," Fowler was saying.

"Yes. I'll never understand how she lasted so long, with her side shot away like that. The trip back to the car must have been sheer hell for her, but all she would say to me is, 'Don't fuss.' "

"Very brave," Fowler repeated. "She wanted to last long enough to tell you as much as she could. By the way, the film you shot has enabled us to identify a few people who have been posing as attachés. And you were right about the one you recognized. We've been after him. There'll no doubt be a few expulsions, and they'll send back some of ours. The usual tit for tat. As for the other film, the one she left under the seat . . . amazing stuff. Everything about the aircraft, even within the cockpit. May have been taken by a pilot. Whoever it was knew exactly what would be of most interest. A pilot would know."

"And now you know your Windshear group does exist."

Fowler nodded slowly. "We'll just have to wait for the next piece in the puzzle. I don't suppose she gave you names."

"In her place, would you?"

"Don't suppose I would," Fowler admitted

honestly. He sighed. "Hell of a tussle going on out there in the GIUK gap. Every blasted ship in the world seems to be searching for the aircraft that went in. The Russians insist that, as it's their aircraft, it is up to them to salvage it. Of course, as we want to know what the hell it was carrying, we're insisting it's in NATO waters and therefore we should salvage it. There's the precedent of the Korean airliner. We've got them by the short and curlies with that. The world is in for a few tense weeks."

"She said," Gallagher began, eyes staring levelly at Fowler, "that the Department, that's you *or* Kingston-Wyatt, intended me to kill Dalgleish all along."

Fowler did not blink. "This is certainly news to me."

"You would say that, wouldn't you? And Kingston-Wyatt isn't here for me to ask him."

Whatever Fowler had been about to say was interrupted by Winterbourne's entrance.

"Ah, Gallagher!" Winterbourne said brightly. "Heard you were in. An extremely good show! Really quite outstanding. I do think you should be back on Department staff."

Gallagher stood up. He stared at Winterbourne. "They give anyone a knighthood these days. All you've got to do is fart in the right direction."

He nodded at Fowler and went out.

Winterbourne could scarcely contain his anger as he glared at the closing door.

"Fowler! You . . . you heard that! You heard—"

"No, Sir John," Fowler said. "I did not."

* * *

Moscow.

Skoryatin looked out on the snow on this the first day of December.

He smiled. There was satisfaction in the smile, but a touch of grimness too. He had just heard that Ulvanov had been removed from his post, and all privileges withdrawn. Poor Ulvanov.

Skoryatin looked down at the glass in his hand with the generous helping of neat vodka in it. He moved closer to the window, staring at the snow. He raised the glass to his lips and drank a toast.

You will not be forgotten, Yuri Velensky, he said in his mind. *Nor you, Irina Alieva.*

An aide entered the room. "The Secretary will see you now, Comrade Colonel-General, to discuss your ideas for the salvage."

Skoryatin put down his glass. Patted his new uniform.

"Thank you, Comrade."

The aide stood aside to let him pass.

Epilogue

Gallagher wondered why he had come, but knew the answer to that almost before the thought had come into his head. The invitation to this cocktail evening had been from the chairman of one of the client firms that paid exceptionally well for his photo assignments. Never bite the hand that feeds. He grimaced. It was all bondage.

He glanced uninterestedly about him, barely seeing the dinner jackets and the expensive dresses of the assembled company, each trying to out-talk the other. His mind was on other things; on the most advanced bomber in the world lying somewhere at the bottom of a cold sea; on Dalgleish and Lucinda—never would he think of her as Irina—dying in the Quiraing, adding more ghosts to that ghostly place; on the men he had killed; on Winterbourne's idiocy; on Kingston-Wyatt; on his lonely neighbor who had got in the way, and again on Dalgleish. . . .

"Gordon, dear boy!" The host. "Having

fun? So glad you could come." He had a woman in tow; eager eyes, thirtyish.

Gallagher's mind continued to run its private video: Karen, Celia, Lauren, Lucinda—all women who had come close to him and whom he had lost; to other men, or they'd been shot. Some option. But there was one. . . .

"Heather," the host was saying, "this is Gordon, my ace photographer—when he chooses to work for me, that is. God knows who else takes up his time. Partner's wife, dear boy, so do be careful." He winked and moved on to his other guests.

Gallagher talked with Heather Danser—with an "s" she'd told him, eyes predatory—and wished he were somewhere else.

Eventually, she said, "You do speak English marvelously well."

"I do, don't I," he said as if surprised, "considering I was born here."

She didn't know how to take it. The host came back at that moment, rescuing him.

"Sorry, dear boy." A low whisper. "I thought such stupidity was beyond even that one. Couldn't help overhearing."

Gallagher smiled at him, but left as soon as he decently could. Back at his home, he picked up the phone and on impulse, punched in a long number. The evening was still young over there, even allowing for the time difference. But it was several months now. There was no reason why she. . . .

The phone rang at the other end, and was picked up. *"Ja?"*

"This is Gordon. . . ."

A shriek, then a squeal. "Gordon! Oh, Gordon! Such a surprise! So many months—almost a year, I think—and I thought you had forgotten me!" The words had almost run into each other. Now she paused. "How did you know I would be here? I was just thinking about you."

"I didn't. . . ."

"Please," Sigga von Kregelmann interrupted. "Can I come to England to see you? I will catch a plane tomorrow. . . ."

"I have an even better idea. I'll come to St. Goar."

"Oh, yes! You still have your car?"

"It is even faster now."

"Oh, wonderful! We have no speed limits on our autobahns."

"Just what I was thinking."

"When will you come?"

"Tomorrow."

"It will be so nice to see you."

When he eventually hung up, he was feeling much better. The *quattro* could do with a nice fast run.

It was what they both needed.

Born in Dominica, Julian Jay Savarin was educated in Britain and took a degree in History before serving in the Royal Air Force. Mr. Savarin lives in England and is the author of LYNX, HAMMERHEAD, WARHAWK, TARGET DOWN!, TROPHY, and WOLF RUN.

CAMPBELL ARMSTRONG

Agents of Darkness

Suspended from the LAPD, Charlie Galloway decides his life has no meaning. But when his Filipino housekeeper is murdered, Charlie finds a new purpose in tracking the killer. He never expects, though, to be drawn into a conspiracy that reaches from the Filipino jungles to the White House.

Mazurka

For Frank Pagan of Scotland Yard, it begins with the murder of a Russian at crowded Waverly Station, Edinburgh. From that moment on, Pagan's life becomes an ever-darkening nightmare as he finds himself trapped in a complex web of intrigue, treachery, and murder.

Mambo

Super-terrorist Gunther Ruhr has been captured. Scotland Yard's Frank Pagan must escort him to a maximum security prison, but with blinding swiftness and brutality, Ruhr escapes. Once again, Pagan must stalk Ruhr, this time into an earth-shattering secret conspiracy.

Brainfire

American John Rayner is a man on fire with grief and anger over the death of his powerful brother. Some say it was suicide, but Rayner suspects something more sinister. His suspicions prove correct as he becomes trapped in a Soviet-made maze of betrayal and terror.

Asterisk Destiny

Asterisk is America's most fragile and chilling secret. It waits somewhere in the Arizona desert to pave the way to world domination...or damnation. Two men, White House aide John Thorne and CIA agent Ted Hollander, race to crack the wall of silence surrounding Asterisk and tell the world of their terrifying discovery.

If you would like to receive a HarperPaperbacks catalog, please send your name and address plus $1.00 postage/handling to:

HarperPaperbacks Catalog Request
10 East 53rd St.
New York, NY 10022